RECKONING
The Regonia Chronicles: Book Four

By Elexis Bell

I

This is a work of fiction. Resemblance to actual persons, living or dead, is purely coincidental.

Copyright 2021

ISBN: 978-1-951335-36-6

All rights reserved.

No part of this book may be reproduced in any way without express permission from the author.

Eager to stay up to date on the latest dark fiction from Elexis Bell?

Sign up for her newsletter on her website.

www.elexisbell.com

Chapter One
Regonia

Tenna

Heavy rain falls, mingling with the blood on Sevlah's battered flesh. Torchlight sparkles on jagged bone, catching on the bits of stone caught within his flesh.

I keep a careful grip on his slick, shattered leg as we move over the bridge to Taron Tribe's mountaintop settlement. Krona holds the other mangled limb, and Sailahti's arms are hooked under Sevlah's, bracing the bulk of his weight.

Darkness reaches up over stone rails, ready to pull us down. The gaping maw of the ravine yawns, hungry and waiting, and the wet black stone beneath us promises to topple us at any moment. Sailahti slips. My heart leaps into my throat, and Sevlah moans painfully as his legs jostle in our grip.

Trailing in our wake, Olivia gasps, but we right ourselves quickly. Ricardo's gentle voice whispers beneath the storm as he comforts her.

Up ahead, Dresde turns with a hand over his heart. He holds the torch aloft and asks, "Did anyone fall?"

I shake my head and say, "No," all the while hoping that Olivia and Ricardo have their translators on. Or that they've learned enough Regonian to know he still means us no harm.

He turns, leading us forward. Massive guard towers loom over us with lights blazing in the upper rooms. Guards stare down at us, but the night hides their expressions. My heel catches, striking a stone that sticks up higher than the rest, and Sevlah groans once more with the adjustment to my gait. Guilt writhes within me.

The sky splits open with flashes of light, and my heart rattles in my chest. Fear grips me, and panic digs sharp claws into my heart. But I don't run for cover. I keep my steps even, careful. For Sevlah's sake.

Running won't help.

If the lightning comes for us, that's it.

We keep moving, passing the guard towers and the open gate. It creaks shut behind us, moved by massive pulleys and ropes. The stone path smooths out beneath our feet as we move into their settlement, and I silently thank all the Taron ancestors who worked to carve peace from the jagged mountainside, saying a special thank you to those who worked Ameeka into every rooftop.

Sevlah hangs limp in our arms, but we no longer jostle him with each step. I listen carefully, straining to hear his breath. Nothing greets my ears but the steady patter of rain on stone. A glance finds his dark eyes closed, his mouth slack. His head lolls against Sailahti's shoulder.

My heart sinks.

Dresde calls out, urging his people to stay inside, promising an explanation when the storm passes. Relnoc moves forward, pale blue braid whipping in the wind. She carries a torch like his, guarded from the rain by a solid plate of Vaikala and its Ameeka coating.

But behind her, a young man runs, pushing a cart toward us. "Settle him here!"

We do as he bids us, carefully setting Sevlah's broken body atop the cart, then follow as he pushes it to the nearest building. My heart thuds in my chest, desperate to move faster, to get out of the storm, to keep Sevlah alive. His blood pools around him, diluted by rain and spreading over the entire surface of the cart.

Olivia gags but holds her gorge.

Before us, two massive stone doors open into a nearby home, sliding seamlessly to admit us as one of the home's occupants waves us in. A young woman bursts in behind us, carrying a large healer's bag, settling it on the floor for the man who brought the cart.

As Dresde and Relnoc move furnishings aside, aided by the family whose home we've just invaded, the young healer assesses Sevlah's wounds. His expression turns grim, confirming my fears.

Ushered in by people I've never met, clamoring to aid us despite clearly being dressed for bed, we all move out of the healer's way. The man sets to work, chewing at his lip determinedly, hands moving deftly.

But we step into the family's dining room.

They bring us towels and basins of water. They stoke the fire in the hearth that borders this room and the room where Sevlah bleeds. With provisions laid upon the table, they take their leave.

"Come," Krona whispers, "let us clean up."

His voice comes out gentle, tender. It pulls the tears free from my eyes. Swallowing back the lump in my throat, I join him at the basin, scrubbing vigorously to clean the blood from my hands, my arms.

Dresde and Relnoc enter, steps heavy but voices soft.

"Hestoon is a gifted healer," Dresde says. "Our Tribe boasts no better. If your warrior can be saved, he's the one for the task."

Rage and fear churn within me, boiling, moving closer to the surface. I grit my teeth, count my heartbeats. I try to still myself, to hold my tongue.

"We will do all we can to see him unbroken," Relnoc begins, "but he lost much of his spirit."

Because you left us out there.

I ball my hands into fists, listening to the trickle of water and blood dripping from the rag in my hand as it splashes into the basin. Settling the towel carefully on the side of the basin, I turn to face them.

"Why now?" I ask, nerves frayed and hands trembling. "Why leave us out there for days only to bring us in now?"

Acid drips from my words, and they take a step back as if struck.

Krona turns, putting a gentle hand on my back.

But I need answers.

I step forward, and they glance at each other. I can see it on their faces, see that they know I could best them both in battle.

They know.

"There were… disagreements," Dresde offers. "Some of our advisors thought your return an ill omen."

Their stupid omens kept us out in the storm? Their omens may have cost Sevlah his life?

I flex my hands, staring hard at them. They flinch before my gaze, and I raise an eyebrow in challenge.

"Their disapproval spread. Some of our people rallied to their cause," Relnoc explains, midnight eyes gleaming. "You have no idea the disquiet in our Tribe these last days."

"And you have no idea the *disquiet* in my heart while carrying the shattered leg of my warrior, my *friend*, through a lightning storm," I hiss. "You are their chieftains. Why should you not remind them of duties and honor? Why should you let your alliances fall?"

Krona steps before me, forcing my gaze to land upon him. I stare into cool green eyes, and he puts his hands on my arms.

"Tenna, you know we would have done the same in their position. They don't know the truth of star-sickness yet. Their duty is to their Tribe first, just as ours is to our Tribe."

"I know," I concede. "But we cannot afford to lose any more of our warriors. And it's Sevlah…"

He nods, whispers, "I know." Moving closer, he leans his forehead against mine. "I know."

I pull in a deep breath, forcing myself to slow, to center on this moment.

To draw on his strength.

"What losses have you suffered?" Relnoc asks, but her voice comes out haunted. "How many did the stars steal from you?"

Krona touches my cheeks, warm hands soothing and gentle against my skin. I nod, brushing my nose against his. Drawing in a deep breath, I pull back. "Thank you," I say to him.

He inclines his head and grabs a clean rag. Dipping it into clean water, he wipes the rest of Sevlah's blood from my hands. He touches my neck, meets my gaze.

A question lingers in his pale green eyes, and I nod in answer. Turning to face Dresde and Relnoc, I say, "We have a great deal to tell you."

Settling into an elaborately carved chair near the hearth, I drop my head into my hands, shoving fingers into wet hair. Pulling them free, I sit up in time to see everyone else take their seats at the table.

Together with Krona, Olivia, and Ricardo, aided by videos on Olivia's various devices, we explain everything. We tell them that the Drennar are alive, that the stars hold no sickness aside from the corrupted hearts of individuals. We explain the technology that exists in place of star-sickness, likening it to the pulley systems we use for the ramps and our simple machines for refining vaikala.

We tell them of the experiments done on us, of the Awakening and the loss of a third of our Tribe, eliciting gasps and horrified expressions. We tell them of the tribunal that followed.

They gasp at the sight of Rone, of Lustran. The ancestors, the species, we thought dead. We tell them of the devices spread across Regonia, watching us, listening to us.

"What do they want with us?" Dresde asks, horrified.

"We don't know yet. Rone wasn't part of the team watching us, and she's been removed from all tests ever since her latest modification."

The Taron chieftains stare at one another, confused, appalled.

Afraid.

"We take war to them," Olivia says in perfect Regonian.

Relnoc and Dresde stare at her, still unable to fathom the small person before them. Their eyes roam over dewy brown skin and eyes with flecks of brown, green, and blue. They look at each other, then back at her.

"You? *You* plan to take war to them?"

"Only in the most literal sense," Olivia says. "I fly the…"

She looks to me and in her Human tongue, asks, "What's the word for our ship? Is there one?"

"It's an old word. A Drennar word," I say, using Regonian so Relnoc and Dresde know why she switched languages. "The word is, 'Soot Insenmeruna.'"

Olivia speaks it, free of accent, and Relnoc's brows raise. She nods, looking Olivia up and down. The chieftain's dusky skin gleams in the firelight, almost matching mine. Admiration glitters in her coal black eyes as she appraises Olivia, but something else, maybe fear, lingers there too.

"I'm also making a… surprise for the Drennar," Olivia continues, still in our language. "A very special form of technology. We have plans to keep them from taking any more of us, plans to keep them from taking any of you."

Relnoc and Dresde glance at each other, faces falling beneath the weight of potential abductions.

"And that's why we've come here," Krona says. "We're waiting to find out from Rone whether or not they broke through Olivia's defenses on Termana, but even if they do, they shouldn't know we plan to strike. So, for now, we have the element of surprise."

Squeezing his hand beneath the table, I say, "The Drennar have every other advantage though. Advanced forms of technology, even compared to Humans. And numbers. We have no figures for their total population. Rone couldn't get those for us. They're spread over multiple planets with new generations maturing in containers constantly."

I shake my head at the thought of it, brows rising in disbelief at the very concept I speak of.

"But on the nearest planet, Novay, their home planet, they number in the hundreds of thousands since most live on other planets. We have one chance to get this right," I say, glancing at Krona.

Pulling in a deep breath, I look back at the Taron chieftains. Voice grave, I continue, "Our odds aren't great. But if we had more warriors, they might be better."

Realization dawns, and I watch the color drain from their faces.

"You want us to send our people into the Realm of Stars?"

"We ask for aid," I hurry to say. "In whatever form you're willing to lend it. Warriors to fight in the stars to secure our futures, supplies, or even warriors to help protect our village in our absence… That would free up more of our own warriors to fight."

They relax in their chairs, nodding.

"We'll have to speak with our advisors. This is…" Dresde trails off, staring into the hearth.

"It's a lot to take in," I say. "We've had time to understand, and we know you need that. We can wait for your answer. But depending on how things went on the Human world, our time may be cut short."

I hate the words I speak, hate the doubt I carry for the Humans and the strength of Atlantis.

My stomach lurches at the thought of them taking Maria, stealing away the family she and Matteo were so excited about.

But the Drennar do things we never even considered possible, things the Humans have yet to figure out.

"We'll consider your request," Relnoc says. "For tonight, we'll bed down here. We're not going out in the storm again, and that will keep you close to your warrior in case Hestoon needs you."

Chapter Two
Regonia

Krona

In the larder of the Taron family's home, Tenna nestles against me, head resting on my chest. We pull blankets and furs up over us, settling in on the floor. Through the small hatch to the root cellar below us, Olivia's soft cries tug at my heartstrings.

Her introduction to gore hasn't exactly been subtle, and her current condition can't be helping.

Sighing, I say, "Do you think–"

But Tenna says, "Thank you," at the same time.

So, I ask, "For what?"

"For calming me down earlier. We can't afford to risk losing allies, especially not because of my temper."

With a soft chuckle, I wrap my arms tighter around her. "If you hadn't said something I would have. That's how we work. One of us says the harsh things, and the other stays calm. We trade off. It's what we do."

It's why we work.

Smiling, I kiss the top of her head, savoring the smell of her, the feel of her pressed to my side. I trail my fingertips over her back, delighting in the shiver that runs through her.

Will I ever take a moment like this for granted again?

A shadow of my time locked away on Ulysses Station slithers through me, and I tighten my hold on her. Days felt like weeks which dragged into months there, laboring beneath the weight of fear and grief and rage. I can still feel the edge in my voice from screaming and singing myself raw so many days running.

But we're back together now. No experiments separate us.

We're in our element. Leading, fighting, loving. This is us.

And I never want to go another day without her.

I breathe her in, closing my eyes.

"What were you going to say? Before I interrupted," Tenna says, voice drowsy with the warmth of encroaching sleep.

Hope and fear come crashing down on me. I draw in a deep breath and begin, "If we survive all of this, if we make it back home after dealing with the Drennar, if we have a home to come back to..." My voice trails off, burdened by the weight of everything to come.

Tenna kisses my chest, soft lips pressing delicately against my skin.

It gives me the strength to continue. "Do you think we should retire from battle for a few years? Let Kala go and fight?"

Tenna props herself up on her elbow, mossy green eyes shadowed. "I... I'm still strong enough for battle. I know I was shaken earlier, but—"

I shake my head and sit up, pressing a soft kiss to her neck. "That isn't what I meant," I assure her. "I know you're strong enough. I know that, even with tears in your eyes, you'd still break seven Vaerkin on your own in a few heartbeats."

She chuckles. "Maybe not seven."

"I wouldn't doubt it for a second," I say, lips brushing over her neck. "I just meant... Maybe it's time for us to start our family?"

She draws back, meeting my gaze. A slow smile tugs at the corners of her lips. "Really?"

I nod, tucking dark strands of hair behind her ear.

In an instant, she's straddling me, kissing me. The force knocks me onto my back, and I throw my arms around her, chuckling against her lips.

She moves against me, stealing the breath from my lungs, and suddenly, laughter seems a waste of air. I crush my lips to hers, one hand tangling in her hair, pulling her tighter to me.

We gasp, and she breathes out, "I'll go see the Memory Markers and the Healers as soon as we're done in the Realm of Stars."

Slowly, I trace my fingers down her abdomen, trailing them over the delicate skin they'll mark. Two lines, one starting beneath each breast, moving slowly downward, traversing ribs and stomach, swooping at a diagonal to converge beneath her belly button.

She shivers against me, and the movement sends heat shooting through me. A guttural moan escapes me, and she kisses my neck, drawing it out.

I touch her chin, pulling her up to meet my gaze, and my thumb traces her bottom lip. I trail my fingers over her neck, tracing the path the fertility tonic will flow down her throat, between her breasts, and down to her stomach.

She sits up, letting my hands roam over her bare skin, letting my eyes trace the shape of her. Heat builds within me, and every muscle in my body tenses. I run my hands up her muscular thighs, grasp her firm buttocks.

She settles down over me, taking me in, and the universe seems to crash down around me. She breathes out a soft moan, slowly rocking her hips. I grip her thighs, digging nails into tender flesh.

Her hands splay out over my chest, and she moves faster. My heart pounds in my chest, and blood roars behind my ears.

But I need more.

I push myself up to sitting, grasping her hip, cupping her breast. Our mouths meet, hot and desperate, and her hands tangle in my hair, pulling me closer. Wrapping an arm around her waist, I drive myself deeper, desperate to soothe the ache building within.

She pulls one hand from my hair, trailing it down over my neck, my chest, my stomach. Between us, her fingers dance, and her head tips back.

Her hair slides from her shoulder, and I kiss her neck, her collarbone. I bite the soft flesh at the base of her neck, and she gasps. Spasms grip her, and she cries out. Her fingers stop their rhythmic motions, and she grasps my back, nails digging in deep.

"Krona…" she breathes.

And my world implodes.

Stars burst over the backs of my eyelids, and shivers rock my body. A soft growl eases past my lips, and I bite down harder, gripping her buttocks and pulling her down over myself.

My breath comes in staccato bursts, ragged and rough. Slowly, I release her neck, kissing the spot I know will bear my mark in the morning.

Tenna touches my chin, lifting my face for a kiss, delicate and sweet. "Hoo kai voo mai," she says, lips brushing mine with every syllable.

"Hoo kai voo mai," I say.

You are my sound.

She kisses my jaw, my neck. Smiling against my skin, she says, "I can't wait to do this for real."

Chuckling, I say, "I thought this was real? Is this another experiment?"

She laughs, filling my ears with sweet music. "I certainly hope not. You know what I meant."

A gentle nip at my shoulder sends a shiver through me, and I let out a breath, savoring every sensation. "I can't wait either."

Chapter Three
Novay

Rone

At our table, Sentrah bows her head, mumbling beneath her breath. The lights behind her skull plate move in slow, steady rhythms, pulsing gently through her neurons.

I tip my head to the side, watching her carefully. Beside me, Lustran does too.

Our meal sits before us, nothing more than capsules of concentrated nutrients, but one of the recruits expressed a desire to eat together. I smile, recalling the squeal of delight that Curata emitted when the topic was first broached a day ago, the flick of her hand that brought a table and chairs free of the alonarium at our feet.

But she wasn't the only one drawn to this Human custom. Sentrah had shared a secret smile with another recruit, and now, they sit with hands joined, muttering soft words over their capsules.

My mind shoots back to the first day I met Sentrah, to how she jumped at the potential of me falling away from logic and descending into religion, then to the day Lustran and I thought we found her praying in her room. I replay the memories within my mind, looking at them anew.

Was she hoping I had found religion too?

When I said no, was she defensive? Disappointed? Is that why she hid it later?

Now, I watch her, pull her words closer. Human words, beseeching a god's blessing on their food.

Shock rolls through me, and I glance at Lustran. He meets my gaze with furrowed brows and parted lips.

"What now?" I mouth.

But he only shrugs and shakes his head, eyes wide.

After one last glance at the prayer pair, I mouth, "I'll talk to Reginald."

Lustran nods. He looks away from them just in time to escape their notice as they draw their prayer to a close.

Curata glides through the door, securing his attention, and suddenly, I'm the only one at risk of upsetting Sentrah and her friend. I busy myself composing a silent message and send it off to Reginald.

But the response comes too quickly, and it isn't one I'd expected.

My heart falters, and I draw in a sharp breath.

"They breached Odyssey station," I whisper.

Sentrah and her friend fall silent. Lustran and Curata stop mid-sentence. Toorasten stands in the doorway, hand resting over the heart in his humanoid chest rather than the one in his scaled-horse body.

"Atlantis stood, but they..." I trail off, shaking my head. Swallowing a lump in my throat, I say, "They made an alonarium airlock and cut through the station wall. They took everyone they needed for this experiment. They looked for Olivia."

Turning to face Lustran, I say, "They know she kept them out. They know where she is."

"Do they know about us?" Curata asks, high voice suddenly hollow.

My eyelids flutter as I say, "I don't know."

She apparently runs a surreptitious sweep of their files, a quick study in the hidden channels we've been using, for she says, "Not yet."

"Do they know the Humans mean to... That we mean to..." I can't speak the words.

She shakes her head. "We're safe for now. But they'll probably be more careful. Especially since Atlantis 2 is spreading over Regonia as we speak."

"Maybe they'll hesitate to bring her here?" Lustran asks.

"Maybe," I say. "But we can't count on it. We need to warn Olivia. Quickly."

My meaning doesn't go unnoticed.

I watch their faces, see each one calculate the risks of sending a message routed through transmitters on Regonia rather than bounced off a distant planet. I see them weigh the risks of having our allies captured and brought here, throwing away all our careful plans and calculations, if we don't warn them.

"They're on the mountain now, yes?" Sentrah asks. "It wouldn't need so many routing points."

"Can we get the message to them without tipping our hand?" Lustran asks.

Worried glances move around the table. Whispers shudder through the hall as this new revelation moves through our people in waves.

"I don't know," I whisper.

"Would you mind if *I* try?" Curata offers.

Again, her high ranking comes back to me. The Expressionless Drennar may well be on high alert after finding out that thousands of bodies disappeared from one place and appeared in another, right under their noses.

But if anyone can warn Olivia without getting caught, it's Curata.

Chapter Four

Regonia

Ricardo

Through the night, Olivia tosses and turns in my arms. I wake early, stroking her back, trying to soothe her, but she wakes with a start, gasping as she sits bolt upright. She stares at her hands, turning them over, inspecting them.

"What is it?" I ask, hoping whatever nightmare she tells me about this time will be less bloody than its predecessors.

She runs her hands through her hair, drawing her knees up and resting her elbows on them. "More of Sevlah's blood. I can still hear him, still hear the sound of the rocks. All I see is his blood."

Sitting up, I rub her back, moving my hand in slow circles. I kiss her shoulder, desperate to comfort her, but at a loss for words.

"Do you think he'll be okay?" she asks in a whisper.

Sighing, I wrap my arms around her. "I don't know. Regonians are pretty resilient. And he's here with people who know how to treat his injuries, people who know how a Regonian would need to be treated." The words sound hollow. "I don't know. But I hope he makes it."

She nods.

After a moment of silence, she glances at her Link. "We'd better get up there."

I kiss her shoulder one more time, and we dress. After packing our clothes and gear away, we ascend the ladder out of the root cellar only to find Krona and Tenna already gone from the larder. My nerves coil tightly in my gut, and I reach for the taser at my hip, reminding myself that I can defend us, if need be.

When still among Daen Tribe, I recoiled at the thought of carrying it. But now, I'm thankful Tenna insisted, thankful she was wary enough of their long-lost allies and the change of heart they may have had.

With a steadying breath and a last look at Olivia, I push the door open, moving into the home. My eyes rake over the room, scanning for any threats.

But no Regonians wait for us.

Cutlery shines on the table, laid out with handmade dishes and fresh foods the likes of which I've never seen. Tangy scents rise to meet me, making my mouth water.

But voices murmur in the next room, drawing my notice.

I don't recognize the voices, don't hear Tenna or Krona, or even Sailahti, among them. My pulse quickens.

Where are they?

"Stay here," I whisper.

Though I want to, I don't look at Olivia, don't take my eyes away from the doorway. Slow, quiet steps lead me closer, and I unsnap the holster of my taser.

Please, don't let me need this…

My mind races with the nightmare of trying to get out of here if Taron Tribe turned on us, if they took Krona and Tenna. Kind and honorable as they seemed, Relnoc and Dresde mentioned that their advisors opposed interacting with us at all, let alone bringing us into their settlement.

What if there was a coup? What if the advisors overthrew them and took Krona and Tenna hostage? What if they killed them?

A million grisly scenarios play out in my mind, each one bloodier than the last. And with every one, our odds of survival diminish.

How many are in this village?

What would we even do? The taser won't work on more than one at a time.

Inching along the wall, I draw in a deep breath, ready to peer around the corner. But Tenna's voice stops me in my tracks.

"Voo mai isveneisahs hoo," she says.

It takes only a moment to recall the meaning of the phrase. *My sound honors you.* Their way of saying, "Thank you."

I breathe a sigh of relief, closing my eyes and dropping my head back against the wall.

Krona speaks, easing my mind further. "Hoo walraklar nahn, Hestoon. Daet tae taesei coomlar naki vensen sur hoo. Joo elo."

I pick out bits and pieces, but I need to know the context, need the meaning quickly so I can make sure we're safe. I have my Link translate the words I don't know.

"You did all, Hestoon. The future will come without more change from you. We wait," the translator voice speaks into my mind.

Another sigh crosses my lips, and I snap the strap back into place over my taser. Stepping away from the wall, I approach Olivia. She still stands motionless, shoulders inching upwards, hands worrying at the edge of the stone table.

She must not have heard them.

Only then do I wonder why they're whispering.

Chapter Five

Regonia

Olivia

Tenna leans over Sevlah, dark braid dangling above his chest. She touches his shoulder and whispers in her native tongue, "May the strength of your sound pull you through."

Krona puts a hand to her back. With his other, he reaches for Sevlah's pale hand. Grasping it, he says, "If the fight is too much, we'll find your sound and carry it with us."

But I can't look at Sevlah, can't face the shape of his legs, afraid of what I might see. My eyes roam over the room, desperate for anything to look at that isn't bloody or broken.

Hestoon curls into a ball on the floor by the wall, burying himself in a mound of furs and blankets. He leaves only his hand sticking out.

Did he sleep at all last night?

Guilt twists my gut.

He was up all night with Sevlah, someone he may never have met, someone I just spent days with and yet can't even look at. We just climbed a mountain with Sevlah, and I can't even glance in his direction, all because of a little blood.

But it wasn't just a little blood.

A wave of nausea rolls through me at the thought, and I close my eyes, going still. When it eases, I remind myself to go easy, to let myself off the hook.

Nausea isn't exactly surprising right now.

I open my eyes, and this time, I don't try to make myself feel guilty for avoiding Sevlah's broken, battered legs.

Instead, I look to Relnoc. She hovers in the corner of the room, black leathers shining in the light of the nearby hearth and hands clasped before her. Tears glisten in her charcoal eyes, shining against skin like dusk. She tucks strands of pale blue hair behind her ear, hand shaking slightly.

And when she sees us, she surprises me with a gentle smile.

Only then do Tenna and Krona look up from their unconscious warrior. The strain on their faces eases slightly.

"We were going to wake you soon," Tenna says. "We wanted to let you rest as much as we could."

"Dresde should be back soon," Krona says. "Then, we'll go meet with the Taron Tribe Council of Advisors."

Much to my delight, they speak Regonian. Luxuriating in the chance to really put my new language to the test, I launch myself into the conversation, asking how Taron Tribe works, how the power is distributed.

Relnoc stares at me uneasily, but Krona reassures her. "She is family."

The words reverberate through me, bouncing around in their language and ours. I test my own response.

They are family. Loo kai ahrn.

We're family.

I'm *family, part of a family.*

A good one.

I smile, moving forward and tugging Ricardo along with me. Tenna and Krona bracket us, settling their arms on our shoulders.

Relnoc tips her head to the side, gaze raking over us both in turn. "You have the marks of Daen?"

I nod, extending my arm and turning it over and back again, letting her see the marks on my wrist. But her eyes drift up my arm to the mark on my bicep.

"You fight a difficult battle," she says.

The blood drains from my face, and shame rushes in to take its place. But Krona's words from long ago echo through my mind.

"Joo kai isvane coom Isvens," I whisper. *We are strong with Allies.*

Relnoc draws in a deep breath, nodding her agreement. She takes a few steps forward, reaching for my hand. "May I see the rest of your marks?"

I hold my arm out in answer.

She glances at the mark for my mother's traitorous death, then at Krona and Tenna who still hold tight to Ricardo and I, to Sevlah. "Your new allies are not like this one," Relnoc says, thumb tracing the black circle. "Honor and strength guide them."

My throat grows tight, so I merely nod.

Relnoc turns my arm over, looking for any others. On finding the underside of my arm bare, she releases my hand. Suddenly, I wish there were more, wish I were more connected, wish she could know me better with such a simple gesture.

But there is one more.

Turning, I pull the back of my shirt up. "Ricardo?"

His golden eyes meet mine, and I smile.

"Will you hold the front of my shirt down?"

In halting, accented Regonian, he answers, "I could show her mine, if you'd like."

Pursing my lips, I nod. "That might be better."

I turn to face him, eyes tracing his abdomen as he lifts his shirt up over his head, removing it entirely.

Again, Relnoc eyes us curiously. "Why him?" she asks.

I glance to Tenna and Krona, at a loss.

With a smile, Tenna says, "You'd find no judgment here if you abandoned your shirt altogether. We don't have those things you call 'bras,' and women may go without a top if they please. We dress primarily for warmth and comfort or protection in our tasks."

"Oh…"

"Your women must always wear shirts?" Relnoc asks. "What if you're hot?"

I shrug. "We just…" I search for better words, but settle on, "We wear them anyway. Unless our baby needs fed, we leave our shirts on in public."

Relnoc's brows come together, and she purses her lips. Finally, she says, "I do not know your world."

She analyzes the mark of The Awakening on Ricardo's back, mumbling, "I do not know this mark." Her eyes trace the line down his spine, the horizontal lines reaching out over his ribs. "What is this one?"

"The mark of the Awakening," Tenna answers. Her voice cracks as she says, "The night Efsi's partner was killed. The night a third of our Tribe perished at the hands of Olivia's mother and Ricardo's brother. The night the rest of the Human race learned of our existence and the crimes committed against us, just out of sight. The night we learned of the treachery the Drennar have perpetrated. Those nights are the Awakening."

"We all bear that mark now," Krona adds.

Relnoc rises to her full height, dark eyes haunted. She swallows, nodding. Her mouth opens as if to speak, but she closes it again.

Ricardo pulls his shirt back on, then takes my hand. The door at the front of the house opens and closes, and moments later, Dresde strolls in, black skin glistening with tiny water droplets.

Light seems to play within the depths of his jewel green eyes, reminding me of the mountain peaks.

"Another storm?" Relnoc asks.

"No," he answers. "Just soft rain. The Advisors are gathering. We should go to them."

***

On all sides, foreign words fly around me. I drink them in, savoring the feel of them on my tongue.

But their meanings give me pause.

The Taron Advisors make no move to conceal their reluctance, hemming and hawing at every turn.

A shockingly pale man with eyes black as pitch wags a finger at us, lamenting the star-sickness we've undoubtedly brought down upon them, chiding Relnoc and Dresde for bringing us into their midst.

Relnoc stands, hands planted upon the intricately carved stone table. She looms over him, eyes hard. "Would you leave one of our own on the mountain to bleed, Skahsven?" she hisses. "My father made an alliance with Tenna's parents before you were even born. Tenna and Krona gave us designs for ramps to keep the Vaerkin from scaling our peaks. The peace we've enjoyed since? We owe it to them. Yet you would have us abandon them for superstition?"

"Star-sickness is hardly superstition," he sputters.

"Except that it is," Dresde says, voice calm. "And even if we'd left them out there, if star-sickness is real, their return to Regonia would have led it to us eventually."

"You took a risk," Skahsven says.

"We upheld our honor," Relnoc says.

"And now, we have choices to make," says a woman with pale blue hair shot through with silver. She turns to Tenna and Krona. "Can you really expect us to send our warriors to the stars? To leave ourselves open for attack?"

"Attack from whom?" Tenna asks. "Krona and I saw to it years ago that the Vaerkin would never trouble you again."

Her words are ice, and I marvel at her, at the woman who leads a nation, the woman who designed fortifications for a freaking mountain. The same woman I took dancing in the bar on Odyssey. She's so much more than I ever could have imagined.

They both are.

Beside her, Krona says, "We are not so rigid as to accept only aid in battle. If you cannot bring yourselves to send warriors to prevent a fight that will someday be on our doorsteps, we ask that you station warriors at our village to help protect those among us who can't fight. Then, more of our warriors can go to battle."

I watch the exchange, gripping Ricardo's hand beneath the table.

"If what you say is true, if there really is war to be had in the Realm of Stars, how are you to stand a chance against the Drennar? If they're so powerful, how could you ever fight them?" the pale man asks. "And why should we believe a word you say about this? It sounds... It sounds... impossible."

Tenna and Krona glare at the Advisor.

Through gritted teeth, Tenna says, "I wouldn't send my people into a doomed battle. The Drennar are indeed a powerful enemy, but we have… plans." She looks to me, features softening. "Olivia, why don't you show them what you showed Relnoc and Dresde?"

And finally, it's time for me to play my role.

Swallowing, I prepare myself for a million questions, a million things I need to explain. Few people understand me when I talk about tech, and the Taron Advisors and Chieftains have had no interaction with it until our arrival shoved this stuff in their face.

But maybe I don't have to get super technical.

Deciding to take a slightly different route, I skip the preamble. Setting my Link to interface with the Comms device on a rudimentary level, I say, "We have things called cameras that record what's happening so we can watch it later. Up until recently, when I fixed them, the Drennar were using them to spy on us. When they left you all here on Regonia, they hid cameras all over the planet. They've been spying on you, as well."

I project a video onto the black stone wall of the Taron council room, showing them sweeping views from the tops of their guard towers, the sun shining green through the crystalline peaks.

The Advisors gasp in unison. Even having seen this last night, Relnoc and Dresde still reach for each other, jaws falling open.

"They watch your bridge."

I switch the video to the feed from a random camera, showing them the Bellona gardens they've cultivated on stepped portions of the mountain. Members of Taron Tribe, including the man whose home we slept in last night, move among the small white flowers.

"They watch your fields."

Another change reveals a bedchamber, shocking me. A man sits on the edge of his bed, oiling his armor.

Before I can flip to the next camera in the rotation, suddenly wishing I'd chosen specific cameras and thoroughly disgusted at myself for accidentally showing this man's bedroom to people who might be strangers, Skahsven says, "Vlakti…"

Impossibly, he grows paler before me. His voice grows thin as he stands, approaching the wall and tracing the figure depicted upon it. "They watch our beds?"

"They do. Just as they once watched ours. They still think I'm back on our planet…"

This change shows them the view of my room before I removed the cameras. I sleep soundly, and for a moment, I find myself searching for the bottle that must have knocked me out.

"I changed their devices, made them show what I want them to show. What you see now happened years ago. Like a memory, it's still there, held within the device for them to look at whenever they want."

A chill skitters over my spine, and I feel it reverberate through the room.

"Have they no honor?" Dresde whispers, horrified.

"They don't understand the concept," I tell them. "They don't understand emotions or loyalty. They want only information, no matter the cost." Pausing, I let them absorb all I've told them before I add, "Or at least, most of them."

"They change themselves. What you call star-sickness is merely them changing their bodies, implanting things within themselves, altering the fibers of their being."

Skahsven steps closer to the wall, staring at my room back on Odyssey, looking at the things within it. But he steps in front of the projector, and his silhouette slants across the wall.

A few Advisors jump.

"It's fine," I assure them. "You've just blocked the projector's view of the wall." I tap the little comms device. "It uses light to put that image there. If you step between it and the wall, your shadow will block it out."

Stepping toward the comms device, Skahsven bends to stare at it. "What is this?"

Sitting down, I say, "This is what they told you was star-sickness. It's something we call technology. It's a tool, absolutely harmless on its own. The danger comes when people use it poorly, as the Drennar have done."

As my mother did.

But we don't need to get into that just yet.

I pick the device up and show Skahsven the button to turn the projector off. He presses it, and the beam of light disappears.

"The ramps and pulleys that Tenna and Krona designed to get up here, that's a form of technology. They're not as complex as this, don't have as many parts or functions, but they're tools, just like this," I say.

"And the Drennar have been using things like this to watch us sleep, watch us fight, watch us live and die and bring new generations into the world..." he whispers.

I nod, swallowing. "But I've manipulated the cameras, the tools they watch you with, to show them something else. Just as I did on my home planet. And now, I've made a new tool, a new form of technology, to tip the scales in our favor. And we have people on the inside to help us."

"You have people there already?"

"They've been abducting Humans for hundreds of years, my father included. We never heard from any of them again. Until one Drennar changed herself, altering her brain and body so that she might feel the emotions we feel. She fell in love with my dad and let him contact me with another tool, similar to this one."

A smile spreads over my lips. "And she's changing other Drennar to feel, too."

Turning the projector back on, I show them the messages Rone sent with my dad, then the messages with Lustran after she and dad were separated.

Beyond the window, the sun glides toward its highest point, but still there is so much more to show them.

And then, a new message arrives.

A direct message, not bounced through transmitters on other planets, not sent to the comms device.

It comes straight to my Link.

The blood drains from my face.

What happened?

I turn to Ricardo, meeting his eyes as I say, "Someone sent a message to my Link."

His brows furrow.

I glance at Krona and Tenna before opening it, containing it to the screen of my Link and the translator in my ear. Beside Rone, the Drennar that looks like a fairy, Curata, sits, wings beating frantically and sending rainbows over the walls behind her.

Speaking hurriedly, Rone says, "Atlantis held, but they made a new airlock and cut straight through the shell. They got in. They know where you are, and they're coming for you, Olivia. It'll only take them a week to get to Novay. Please… prepare yourselves."

Curata waves, but only half-heartedly. Her shimmering skin seems to reflect only shadows. The video feed cuts out.

"They're coming," I whisper, staring at the blank screen of my Link.

Silence falls over the room, taut and heavy.

"How long?" Tenna whispers.

I check the timestamp of the video, find that it was sent yesterday, and say, "Six days."

Without missing a beat, Tenna and Krona rise to their feet. "We have to get back to our village. We have to warn them. Can we trust you to look after Sevlah?"

Relnoc and Dresde nod. Dresde opens his mouth to address the Advisors, but Krona stops him.

As Tenna stows my devices into my pack, Krona says, "We have a battle coming to us now. If you are still our allies, send warriors to help. If not, don't. You have six days to decide."

With that, he and Tenna sweep us out of the room, gathering Sailahti on the way. Krona scoops Ricardo up, and Tenna gathers me into her arms. They take off at full sprint, and the Taron village blurs past.

We reach the Vyrto stables before I can even catch a breath, and without bothering to gather the rest of our gear, they shove Ricardo and me onto the back of the Vyrtons we rode up here.

Who went and got them from the overhang last night?

Before I can ask, Tenna leaps onto the Vyrto's back, sliding in behind me, and Krona jumps up behind Ricardo. Sailahti mounts her Vyrto, and Relnoc runs out of the council house, blowing on a great horn. It bellows into the air, low and thrumming, and my ears ring.

But the guards open the gates.

Tenna issues a command to the Vyrto, and it turns in place. The massive beast rears back, and I slide backward against Tenna's chest.

"Hold on," she says.

I grasp the beast's mane and clench my thighs.

What am I in for?

The Vyrto launches out of the corral, leaping over the fence and into the stone street. It bursts through the town, rocketing through the gate and over the bridge.

My stomach lurches, but I swallow it back, trying not to watch the pebbles fall over the edge of the bridge. But in an instant, we're across, leaping over the remnants of the rock slide and hurtling toward the first cliff.

Chapter Six

Novay

Reginald

"She's… religious?" I whisper, stunned.

My eyes trace the shape of Rone's face, peering out at me from the wall. She nods, dark hair swaying with the motion. Her wings flutter behind her, brushing the wall, and she pulls her legs up underneath her on the bed.

Beside her, Curata paces.

"Is that a good thing?" she asks. "Or should we be worried?"

"I don't know," I answer honestly. "It might strengthen her morals. It might make her a pacifist. It could turn her into a bigot or a violent terrorist."

I shake my head.

"Would it help if I found out which religion she's practicing?" Rone asks.

"I don't think so. They all had extremists."

Guilt slithers through me at the thought of using this, using her religion, even unintentionally, to get her on our side. And it seems that we're already using it. She's clearly sympathizing with the Human race in some way or another, or she wouldn't be praying to our old gods.

Rone and Curata go on talking, debating the merits of each religion and the statistics of violence and corruption within each one. They analyze the whole history of Human religion in the form of numbers and wars, adding philosophical debates that normal Drennar would never take into account.

But my mind drifts. Ice flows through me, and a shiver rolls down my spine.

Am I... Am I doing the same thing Eva did?

Am I just as bad as her for getting them to change themselves to have emotion?

Is it better that they're doing the experiment instead of me wielding the scalpel?

I remind myself of their ready consent, of the fact that Rone got the experiment before I ever spoke a word to her, that she convinced the room full of Drennar that they needed this in order to understand us and they jumped at the chance. Yet, I can't escape the fear that they might not have chosen this if they knew exactly what was in store for them.

"Rone? Curata?" I ask.

They turn to face me once more, and a slow smile spreads over Rone's lips, melting my heart. But a lance of pain follows quickly on its heels.

"Knowing what you know now, if you could go back, would you still want to go through with this? Would you still want emotions? Would you get the experiment again if you knew what it would lead to?"

I try to keep the worry from my tone, but it must slip through. Rone puts a hand out, and I reach forward, touching the part of the wall that bears her image.

"Of course," she says.

Behind her, Curata nods, eyes half awe and half remorse. "I understand so much more now than I ever did before."

Nodding, I shove my guilt away for now, but I know it'll be back later. "Okay," I say, then refocus my attention on what to do about Sentrah finding some sort of god.

Chapter Seven
Regonia

Krona

Our Vyrtons carry us swiftly down the mountain. Rocks skitter over the edge as their hooves beat the stone path. At every cliff, we let them rest, grazing on mosses as Tenna and I lower the ramps.

As their hooves clear the edge of the final ramps with Sailahti leading Olivia and Ricardo, we heft the ropes as quickly as we can, muscles straining in the name of speed. The stone thuds into place atop the cliff, and I sling myself up behind Ricardo.

As soon as Tenna scales her Vyrto, settling in with Olivia, I call out, "Rein!"

Our Vyrtons rush forward, hurtling down the path. The sun dips in the sky, preparing to tuck itself in for the night. Rays of light cascade through the crystalline peaks, casting a teal hue over us, but darkness will soon follow.

My heart beats frantically as if trying to outpace the speeding animals, and my head fills with thoughts of the Drennar catching our people unaware. Waves of ice water wash through me as I imagine the carnage they might wreak before our warriors can even take up arms.

Charging forward, the Vyrtons carry us downward at an alarming rate. Ricardo's fists tighten in the wild wisps of mane whipping about us, and I almost pity him. He and Olivia aren't used to this sort of riding.

We have no other choice.

He never complains, nor does Olivia. We keep a manic pace, desperate to reach the next of our camps before night falls. Somehow, the idea of sleeping beneath the stars seems more dangerous than ever.

My eyes drift slowly upward, glancing at the horizon and the darkness consuming it. Shivering, I refocus my attention, thankful that my Vyrto knows the path so well.

Six days.

Shy of an ambush, have we ever faced such little warning of a battle?

I shake my head. Before now, we've always seen our enemies coming. We've always known, or at least guessed at, what they would do, always experienced the slow build to battle. But the Drennar are not Roon Tribe or Vaerkin. They're not guided by emotion or a desire for honor.

They're a foe wholly unlike anything we've yet seen. And I can't help but wonder, despite all we told Relnoc, Dresde, and the Taron Advisors…

Are we equal to this fight?

Now that our plans have been thwarted, now that we're not sneaking onto their planet, cloaked by Rone and her Tribe… Can we best them without the element of surprise on our side?

The clearing which hosted us several nights ago comes into view, and I breathe a sigh of relief, hoping the tasks of setting up camp and the promise of conversation will busy my mind.

But rage and indignation quickly follow, sweeping through me with violent heat.

They dare to come for us.

We will make them sorry.

Chapter Eight
Novay

Rone

Reginald sits on his bed, facing me. Well, facing the image of me on his wall. I watch him, thrilled to see his face. My heart gallops as my eyes trace his features, lingering over full lips and warm brown eyes shot through with streaks of blue.

I send a quick message to Curata, thanking her for setting up an enhanced version of my private channel and an improved loop for us.

I reach for the wall before me, tracing the image of him, tracing his shoulders, his cheek. My heart pounds in my chest, and an acute agony rips through me. I want to hold him, want to feel his arms around me. I want to kiss him, want to lay with him.

Heat swells within me.

He smiles, but he seems weary. Dark circles hover beneath his eyes.

Stuffing down the desire building within me, I ask, "How are you holding up?"

He shakes his head, one brow rising. "I don't even know anymore." His words ring hollow, and his eyes slip out of focus. They find their way back to me slowly.

He runs a hand over his face and says, "I just… I wish there was something more I could do. I hate knowing that I can't help her."

I meet his gaze, whispering, "You've done more than you think. A lot of our ideas have been yours, or at least, informed by what you told us. We're still learning about these emotions and their implications. We're still learning about Humans. You happen to have some experience with the subject."

My comment earns me a smile.

"I suppose I do," he says. Grasping the lighter subject, he chuckles and adds, "I just hope the Drennar they sent know what they're in for. Pregnancy wreaks havoc on the body. It has some… effects. Mood swings and cravings, gestational diabetes, all kinds of stuff."

"When Eva was pregnant with Olivia," he says, eyes going wide for an instant. "She was a handful. Cranky from not sleeping, not that she'd admit it. Hungry all the time."

My heart skips a beat hearing him talk of Eva without a tinge of hatred for what she became. My stomach turns uneasily.

"She didn't get any morning sickness, but she was really sensitive to temperature changes and smells," he goes on. "They're going to haul in a few pregnant women who'll give them a little more than they bargained for."

My gaze falls to my legs, crossed beneath me. I fidget, one thumb worrying at the nail of the other. Reginald keeps talking, explaining the various problems with Eva's pregnancy, but the words wash over me, slipping by without my notice.

"Are you okay?" he asks.

I snap back to attention, hating my lapse. Nodding, I say, "Yeah, it's just... weird to hear you talk about her so... casually. I guess I've just gotten used to you saying how much you don't like her. It's weird to hear you talk about the good times with her, the good memories."

"I'm not sure I'd call those particular memories good. She got a bit mean," he says with a laugh. "But I understand."

"Are all pregnant women mean?" I ask, shifting the topic ever so slightly.

"No," Reginald says. "But when you come across one who is, it's hard to forget."

I laugh, but he stops, jaw falling open. A smile tugs at his lips. "Mood swings… We can use this…" he whispers. "If they bring them here, we can make *sure* they regret it."

"And *this* is why I said you're still helping, even if you don't feel like you are," I say.

He blushes, dropping his gaze for an instant. "Thank you." His eyes meet mine, darkened and sultry.

Heat pools within me again, and I say, "You should tell me what you had in mind. But first…"

I slide my hands up my waist, over my breasts, and behind my neck. Reginald draws in a deep breath as I untie my top, letting it fall away from me.

***

Eager to go over our plans, I move through the halls in search of Curata. My stomach turns at the thought of Olivia being brought here, at the thought of what they might do to her and her baby, but I must prepare myself. Whatever opposition Daen Tribe and the Human soldiers may intend to offer, I see no likelihood of success.

Even now, my mind fills with all the scenarios that could play out, all the ways they may fight. All the ways they'll lose.

I swallow thickly at the desperation, the hopelessness, burrowing deep within my heart.

But I will not sit idle.

Reginald's sacrifice in coming here all those years ago, his hopes of saving his daughter, will not be in vain. And with our latest conversation of the logistics of collecting and caring for so many pregnant women fresh in my mind, a plan stirs. But I need to consult Curata and Lustran first, and if my suspicions serve me correctly, I'll probably find them together.

I turn the last corner of the hall to find the door open, admitting a clear view of the two of them sitting on her bed, speaking softly, smiling shyly. Their eyes meet often, but only for an instant each time. They laugh together, and Lustran rubs the back of his finger against her wrist.

But when they notice me, he pulls away, blushing furiously.

I tip my head, considering him and wondering why my presence should make him shy. But I have more important things to worry about right now.

Turning my attention to Curata, I ask, "When the Drennar land on Regonia…" I pull in a deep breath, hating the situation we've found ourselves in. "Is there a chance they could fail?"

She sits up straighter, shifting from whatever scene I interrupted to business in half a heartbeat. "Of course. There's always a chance of failure," she says. Her brows furrow as she adds, "But as you know, every possible step will be taken to minimize it. Drennar are nothing if not careful."

My heart drops, and all the little tendrils of hope that I'd been clinging to slip further from my grasp.

Curata's focus turns inward for a moment, and the little circuits in her irises pulse and shift, casting pale light onto the strands of baby blue hair that hang about her face. When she returns to us, she tells us the exact odds down to a thousandth of a percent, accounting for many variables.

The blood drains from my face, and I close my eyes.

How can I ever tell Reginald this?

Despair runs through me like ice in my veins.

No. We knew their odds were bad. We knew that.

We have a plan.

"Well…" I begin, "it sounds like we need a contingency plan. Reginald and I came up with an idea."

Chapter Nine
Regonia

Olivia

Another full day passes before the Vyrtons carry us, headlong, into the village. Tenna leaps down, but I can only slide to the ground, entire body aching. My legs give way briefly, and the long grasses try to swallow me up.

Krona, Ricardo, and Sailahti dismount, feet hitting the ground as Kala and Melnara sprint toward us.

"What happened? Where's Sevlah?" Kala asks, dark, grey eyes scanning the horizon behind us as if searching for him.

Fear tightens Melnara's sage eyes, even as her hands go to the club and dagger hanging at her hips. Yet again, I marvel at their strength, their willingness to fight even when terrified.

"The battle is not here yet," Tenna tells them. "We have a few days, still. And it isn't Taron Tribe."

Instantly, Kala turns to face upriver. The wind whips at her dark braids, tossing them over her shoulders, and the setting sun frames her with streaks of purple.

But even now, she's too accustomed to this world, the world they've always known, to expect the real enemy.

"It isn't Roon or Vaerkin that threaten us either," Krona says. "The Drennar are coming. They want Olivia and a couple other human soldiers. We don't know if Taron will aid us in the fight, but they care for Sevlah, even now. He was injured in a rockslide near the bridge."

Staring at me, Melnara asks, "They come for her?"

A shiver rolls through me.

Does she want to offer me up?

I swallow, nerves pulling my hands together in front of me. My eyes fall to the ground, and guilt turns my stomach at the thought of what I've brought upon them.

"They do. They didn't breach Atlantis, but found a different way in. They know she's here," Tenna answers.

"Where will we hide her when they come?" Melnara asks without a bit of hesitation.

My eyes snap to her, shocked.

Catching my expression, she asks, "What?"

"I… You could save yourselves some trouble and hand me over…" The words come out a whisper, spoken with my eyes glued to the ground once more, spoken with everything in me hating that I say it, just in case they decide to do it now that the thought has been put out there.

Shaking her head, she gently touches the Mark on my arm, the one for my mother's betrayal. Releasing me, she says, "Hoo kai ahrn. Joo walrak rahn vemirn ahrn."

Her words pass over me, distracted as I am, and I let my Link translate them.

You are family. We do not betray family.

My heart stutters, and tears prick at the corners of my eyes. I glory in the sound of those words, letting them repeat in my mind in both languages.

But they don't seem real.

They don't seem like words meant for me. Rather, they simply seem like the words she's expected to say as an honorable woman born of an honorable Tribe.

Ricardo's hand finds mine, lacing our fingers together. Tenna and Krona glance at each other, leaning their heads together. Tenna touches his neck, soft and sweet. Then, she turns to us.

"We have many plans to make. Ricardo, we'll need you there," she says. "Olivia, use whatever time we have left to finish your latest project. You likely won't have access to your devices if we fail, but do not think for a second that we'll let you go willingly."

I nod, throat too tight to speak.

***

The evening passes in a blur of coding, set to a soundtrack of battle plans. Only when yawns threaten to outnumber words do they dismiss the meeting.

I rise from my perch in the corner with creaking joints, setting the comms device aside to crack my fingers. As Kala and Melnara leave, Ricardo approaches, eyelids drooping heavily over golden eyes.

"Would you like to stay here again, or would you rather see your new home?" Krona asks.

I glance at Ricardo, at the slump in his shoulders, then ask, "Can we stay here one last night?"

Smiles greet my request, and I lead Ricardo up the stairs to our room. As we climb, I sync to the comms device, transferring everything I have to my Link, just in case.

Even if they take me, I'll keep working.

Chapter Ten

Regonia

Ricardo

Sinking into bed with Olivia, I pull her close. The path ahead promises to be difficult, even if tonight's strategy session with Krona and Tenna and all their most trusted warriors did go rather well.

We have plans. We have battle formations.

We have a system.

I pull in a deep breath, let it out slowly.

We have a system, and I'm not leading it.

But even with that little bit of relief, the stakes are too high. Despite all our work and all our plans, fear flows through my veins. I kiss the back of Olivia's head, pulling her tighter against me.

Can we do this?

Drowsily, I reflect on all we've overcome thus far. The experiments on Odyssey and Ulysses followed by what was basically a full-scale rebellion. The tribunal. Olivia's depression and alcohol abuse.

My thoughts stutter at the memory of her suicide attempt.

But she's here.

And she seems happy. Worried, yes, but happy to be alive.

She nestles in, scooting back and getting closer. She wraps her arms around herself, grasping my bicep, my forearm, pulling my arms tighter.

We can handle difficult. We can handle long odds. Right? We've done it before.

I breathe in the scent of her, wanting to linger, to commit every bit of this to memory. The feel of her hands on my skin, the press of her backside against me, the sound of her breathing. All of it.

But exhaustion overwhelms me, and I fall asleep quickly.

***

Morning finds us too soon, and I sit on the edge of the bed, stiff from two days riding at breakneck speed. I drop my head into my hands, rubbing my face to try to wake up. My mind drifts through the remnants of my thoughts last night. I'd meant to come up with something, anything, to offer up at this morning's meeting.

But worry and sleep robbed me of my mind.

There's too much at stake here. I can't afford not to put everything into this.

Olivia turns over, reaching an arm around my waist and pulling me back. "It isn't time to get up yet," she says, voice warm. "Come back to bed."

Sitting up, she brushes my hair aside and kisses the back of my neck. Heat trickles through me, sending pinprick shivers from my head to my toes.

But there's so much to be done.

My mind fills with all the arrangements we have yet to make, all the contingency plans that we have yet to think of. What if Taron doesn't send aid? What if they do? What if there are only a handful of Drennar? What if there's an entire army of them?

I have to protect Olivia.

I have to protect our child.

As a member of modern society, she has basic self-defense training. As a pilot, her training was elevated.

But what good will that do against an army of Drennar?

Her hand slides up my chest, then back down again, trailing slowly to my waist and down to grasp my hip. Desire pools within me.

But can I afford the distraction? Will a few stolen moments cost me our future?

Will I regret not taking these moments if they take her?

Olivia loosens her grip, pulling back. "What is it?"

Only then do I realize the rigidity of my posture, the stiffness of my hands on my knees. Swallowing, I turn to face her. "I just…"

I take a deep breath, letting my eyes roam over her soft, tawny skin, her long dark hair. The predawn light gleams in hazel eyes, and that glow tugs at the corners of my lips.

Hating myself as I say it, I tell her, "I need to get out there. I need to be with Krona and Tenna. I need to…" I swallow, closing my eyes. My voice breaks as I add, "I need to keep you safe. I can't let them take you."

Olivia leans her head against mine, hands coming to rest on my neck. Her thumbs trace my jaw, and I suck in a breath.

"Enjoying the time we have before they come doesn't mean letting them take me," she says. "You can go down there and stare at their maps, but no one else is awake yet. You'll just be down there, stewing, alone."

"Maybe I should," I say. "I need to do something to make sure you're okay."

"Do you remember those old instructional videos about airplane safety?" she asks.

I scrunch my brows, pulling back to stare at her. A small laugh escapes me. "What are you talking about?"

"Apparently not. I thought everyone saw them after they were discovered in the archives." She scoots back, leaning against the carved wooden headboard. Patting the bed beside her, she says, "Come here. I need to tell you this."

I shake my head, chuckling under my breath. "You need to talk to me about old airplane safety videos?"

Pulling a blanket up over herself, she casts me a sidelong glance. "Humor me?"

I climb up beside her, tucking into my portion of the blanket. She laces our fingers together, tracing her thumb over the back of my hand.

"So, back when planes were a thing, if something went wrong, oxygen masks would drop from the overhead bins."

"Okay…" I say, still not quite seeing where she's going with this.

"They always told people to put the mask on themselves and then on their children or loved ones. Do you know why?"

I look at her, brows furrowed.

"Because if you pass out while struggling to get someone else to put a mask on, then neither one of you get a mask, and you both pass out."

"Okay…"

"You need to take care of yourself. You need to go into this with a clear head. Krona and Tenna do too, but I can't persuade *them* to stay in bed and relax for a few minutes before launching into battle plans. They might persuade each other, but I don't want to get involved in that."

Despite everything, I laugh.

"I've never had much of an affinity for war or fighting," she says. "But I know a thing or two about pushing too hard. I don't want to see you go down that road."

My chest swells, and I raise her hand to my lips, kiss her palm. Releasing her hand, I wrap an arm around her and pull her close. She curls up against my side, one hand on my chest.

Planting a tender kiss on the top of her head, I say, "Francis was wrong. You are good for me."

She swallows, and when she speaks, her voice is thick. "I hope so."

Her lips press softly against my collarbone, and she leans against me once more. My fingers trail over the bare skin of her arms, and we sit, watching the sun peek out at us, reaching over the horizon.

Chapter Eleven
Regonia

Tenna

The early rays of dawn pry at my eyelids. I stir in Krona's arms, but he sleeps peacefully. Tendrils of dark hair sweep over his forehead, just touching his lashes. I brush them away and kiss his soft skin.

Slipping from bed as smoothly as I can, I watch him, hoping not to wake him. He needs rest.

My feet touch the cool floor, and I pad over to the window. Light reaches toward me, welcoming me home. I close my eyes, feeling its caress on my skin, warm and gentle.

With a sigh, I gaze upon our lands, see the smoke rising from chimneys throughout our village. A few people work in their gardens, in the fields, making steady progress to rebuild our home. My heart glows with pride at their tenacity, their resilience.

And then, my eyes turn to the mountains. I search them for the peak Taron Tribe occupies. I trace the route down, willing them to come to our aid.

But no campfires dot the path.

Drawing in a deep breath, I try to believe that they'll send help, that they'll honor the old alliance.

Footsteps sound behind me, light and agile, but I know the sound of him. Krona slips his arms around my waist and kisses the nape of my neck. He rises to his full height, and his breath rushes out over my hair.

"Will they come?" I ask, voice quiet, burdened by the uncertainty pricking at my heart.

"Relnoc and Dresde are honorable. And we didn't part on uncertain terms last year."

I sigh. "But how much has changed in our absence?"

Krona tightens his arms around me but remains silent. For a long moment, we stand, staring at the mountains.

"All we can do is hope," he says. "Hope and prepare for the worst."

***

I stand before Kala, our Ullavekyns, and Ullavesans, as well as all the Specialists among the Humans. Shoulders back and chin lifted, I say, "Kala, Melnara, you'll have to stay behind, though not with Olivia and the other women the Drennar seek."

They both nod, resigned to their fate beyond battle.

Addressing the rest, I reinforce our previous discussions of rearranged hierarchy. With it all settled, Krona wraps his hand around mine, and a smile creeps onto his face.

And then, I move onto some good news.

"Provided all goes well," I say, heart heavy with all that could go wrong and yet light with the future I hope for. "Krona and I will step back from battle on our return in the name of providing Daen Tribe with heirs."

Smiles shine before us, and warm words flow forth. They beam at us, Kala and Melnara most of all.

And suddenly, I see why Krona wanted to tell them today. We could have waited, but they needed this. They needed a bright spot in the clouds of our current circumstances. They needed something to hope for beyond survival.

I grasp his hand tighter, smiling back at them.

I just hope we live long enough to follow through.

***

After speeding through our midday meal, Krona and I fetch our weapons and armor. With great care, we oil and sharpen each piece accordingly, hoping to spare our trade workers a little effort.

They'll certainly have their time occupied in the coming days.

We hang our battle wear on racks and head out to meet our Ullavesans. They should have stock of everything that was lost in the Descent of Man and all that has been reclaimed by the earth, as well as what was volunteered for our use from personal armories.

We walk the old stone paths. Grasses and wild bushes climb the fences, clog the paths, but already, they begin their return to the earth, trodden under foot.

Krona comes up short, hand pulling at mine, and I turn to look at him. Lips wide in a magnificent smile, he stares at the mountains. I follow his gaze, not daring to hope, and see a plume of smoke rising from the first camp on the path.

Relief washes through me, and tears spring to my eyes, showing me the true depths of the fears that played in my heart.

"They come..." I whisper, voice light.

And though we can't know the numbers they send us or the weaponry they bring, my heart soars.

Chapter Twelve
Novay

Reginald

She was coming here anyway.

The thought sours quickly, but it's the only comfort I have. I pull in a deep breath, trying to ease my mind, but it does nothing.

Olivia was coming here anyway. She'll just be here faster.

Without her allies to defend her, stuck in what amounts to a cell.

And they'll be experimenting on her.

I close my eyes and grit my teeth.

Stop.

Find a bright side.

Maybe she has her new program done already. Maybe her experiment will be more pleasant than mine. Maybe they'll be gentle since she's pregnant.

But maybes bring no relief. They float around in my head, hollow and fragile.

She'll just be here faster.

But that disruption in our carefully laid plans, that potential to end all of this sooner, is a double-edged sword. It slices my heart in two, fracturing every shred of hope I dare to hold.

Maybe.

Maybe.

Maybe.

I pace my room, waiting. I know they're coming for me soon, but what more could they do to me? What more can they put me through?

Maybe.

Maybe.

Maybe.

She'll just be here faster.

My heart clenches.

The wall slides open, and one of the Expressionless stares at me. Twin fans of blue light shine from its cold eyes, sweeping over me. I try not to flinch, but it plucks at nerves already wound tight.

The beast before me doesn't speak, doesn't gesture. The lights stop, and it merely turns, expecting me to follow.

And I do.

Morbid curiosity tugs me along in its wake, aided by the knowledge that if I don't go willingly, they'll only force me.

The same foreboding hall, the same cold room with the same arrangement of statuesque creatures staring at me. The same chair in the middle of the room.

I take my seat with my heart in my throat. My head fills with all the things they might show me.

What they did on Odyssey when they cut their way inside. What they're doing to the people they took.

A natural disaster taking Olivia's life on Regonia.

My hands curl into fists, and I close my eyes. Hoping to drive the thought away before it takes shape, before my mind shows me my daughter mangled by weather we haven't experienced in centuries, I focus on what Rone said.

We'll see what happens, and then we'll use it to our advantage.

Her eyes practically glowed with determination when she said it. But my head is still full of Maybes, tearing through my heart with reckless abandon.

"Open your eyes," a dull, monotone voice says.

I do.

On the wall before me, numbers appear.

03:16:30:00

They shine, unchanged, and for a moment, I wonder what they might mean.

But then, the numbers change, and my heart sinks. They tick away with each passing second.

03:16:29:59

No...

Eyes falling from the numbers before me, I count the days since they showed me the video of the Odyssey breach, head full of Rone's predicted time for their arrival on Regonia.

A shudder rolls through me.

Three days, sixteen hours, twenty nine minutes, and fifty two seconds.

I look back up, mouth gaping in horror. "Why…?" I breathe, desperate for an answer I know they'll never give me. My mind fixates on the last number, counting down in glaring red.

Forty seven.

Forty six.

Forty five.

No! Stop this!

I drop my gaze, watching my hands and hoping they leave me in peace for a while rather than forcing me to stare at the countdown, but it doesn't help. I can practically hear the seconds ticking away, even in this silent room, even with no motor or gears to click or whir.

Maybe she'll have her program done.

Maybe they'll fend off the attack.

Maybe.

Maybe.

Maybe.

Each thought, each heartbeat...

Another second closer to them going after my daughter.

A pedestal rises seamlessly from the floor before me, spreading wide to form a desk. I know they expect calculations, expect me to take their tests.

I sit up to do so, grateful for the distraction.

But the countdown glares in my periphery.

Chapter Thirteen
Regonia

Krona

We prepare ourselves for war, eyes ever watchful of Taron Tribe's progress down the mountain. Warriors and Human Soldiers train side by side, adapting to each other's skills and weapons.

Every Soldier has a taser, the lightning rods whose bite I first felt on Odyssey. Every warrior has a spear or an axe, carved of Malakar bone and sharpened to split hairs.

Taron Tribe moves closer, eking out slow progress on the mountainside, but it gives me hope. Large numbers would slow their journey.

Yet, every glance at the sky, every time I mark the light, my nerves wind a little tighter. Adrenaline flows through me as morning becomes afternoon becomes evening. When we retire for the night, I lay awake, fingers itching to crack skulls, to get justice for the wrongs the Drennar have done and still plan to do.

To free our people of their watchful eyes and the ever-present threat that they may one day come for us. To keep them from stealing away more people from Termana.

Tenna rolls over, turning to face me. Her hand slides up my chest and her leg eases over mine. She murmurs softly, nuzzling against me.

I breathe in the scent of her, sweet and earthy. My hand curls around hers, and I bring it up to kiss her palm.

She stirs, gazing up at me. "Sleep, my sound. We still have a few days." She smiles and kisses my chest. She moves in closer, pressing bare breasts to my ribs. Her hand moves low, gliding over my abdomen. "Do I need to exhaust you?"

I chuckle, craning my head to kiss her. "You might…"

***

Another day passes with our eyes darting to the mountain pass. We tap Juno trees, treating our armor anew and sharpening our weapons. I move as I always used to, delighting in the familiar motions. We run drills, and I savor the feeling of my muscles stretching, pushing, pulling.

My body awakens after so long spent in the Realm of Stars doing so little. I breathe the air of my home, feel the grasses I've run in all my life. Tenna's eyes glow as we spar in the same field in which she claimed her position as Queen, and the life we've built warms my soul.

All my life, I've trained for this, jumping into the role of a Warrior to lend honor to the death I craved, the death the battle within pushed me toward. But all those years shaped me, led me here, prepared me for the coming battle.

Though so many things could go wrong, the blood roaring through my veins sings promises of success. Such a deceitful song, one that could undo me, make me too certain. But I've heard its voice before, know to let it strengthen me with hope, not lull me into false confidence.

Staring at the sky, peering past the moons, I try to pinpoint the place where we'll see the Drennar.

Which direction will they approach from?

With their planet, something we thought to be one of our moons, barely visible on the edge of the horizon, they could make any number of choices. But the most logical is to come straight for us.

No hiding behind mountain ranges. No surprising us from the opposite side of the planet.

Straightforward and clear cut.

And why would they need the pretense of an ambush anyway?

Shouldn't this be an easy task for such *advanced* people?

I tear my eyes from the sky, scowling. Then, I throw myself into a sparring match with Melnara and Sailahti, pushing myself harder.

***

As the light falls below the horizon, a plume of smoke rises from the camp in the foothills. My heart soars, knowing they'll reach us in the morning.

Tenna and I walk through the village, passing Olivia and Ricardo's new home on the way to our own. A smile spreads over my features at the light burning beyond their windows. Slow, sultry music seeps out, and their shadows move on the wall, shifting in time with the song.

Did they struggle to light a fire in the hearth? Do they like their new home?

A quiet hope fills me, quickly followed by determination.

We have to make sure they get to live out long lives here.

***

Long strands of teal whip around my legs, and Tenna touches the small of my back. My eyes lock on hers. She smiles, and I know she must be thinking it too.

Taron Tribe is here.

We aren't alone.

Pulling in a deep breath, I nod, and we turn to face the party slipping free of the foothills. My breath catches in my throat at the sight of them, relief giving way to trepidation. Massive numbers of Taron Warriors stream over the path with Relnoc and Dresde at their lead.

But the chieftains sit astride two Malakarns.

The massive beasts' black hides shine in the mid-morning light. Long grasses tickle the membrane wings stretching from their bony forelegs to their thin back legs.

My heart races, remembering the times I've faced these wild beasts in the mountains. I can still see my reflection in seven beady eyes, can still feel the pointed tip of the beast's head digging into my shoulder.

But these beasts walk along, *carrying* Relnoc and Dresde.

They don't rip them limb from limb. They don't wield those razor-sharp talons on the warriors behind them.

And yet, the rest of the Tribe still gives them space.

Kala and Melnara approach, joining us in the field. Slowly, more and more footsteps slither through the grass as the rest of our warriors and many of our people filter in, doubtless gaping at the tamed beasts of the sky.

The light moves higher, chasing our shadows beneath us, and the Taron warriors get closer. The Malakarns shriek, slashing at the grasses beneath them, but Relnoc and Dresde keep the beasts on the ground.

They stop a careful distance from us, and my heart skips a beat.

How tame are those things?

Relnoc slides from hers, grabbing a rope attached to a harness on its head to hold it steady. Dresde does the same, smiling at me.

"You've been busy, old friend," I say, letting my admiration and wariness come through in my tone.

He chuckles, "I always had a knack for these creatures."

That he has.

"They're the only tame ones so far, and they don't like anyone but us, but their nest could prove useful." Pride echoes through his words, but this isn't the pride of the foolhardy, attention-starved warrior he was in his youth. This pride has stood trials. It has seen its own flaws and grown from them.

"If they're anything like Vyrtons, the young should be easier to break," Tenna says, admiring their new mounts.

Does she wish for her own?

Relnoc nods, affirming that this is their hope.

But there are bigger things to address than even these beasts.

"Thank you for honoring the old alliance," Tenna says, and though I doubt anyone else can hear it, relief rushes through her words.

Relnoc and Dresde incline their heads and smile.

Barely audible over the gentle susurrations of the grasses swaying in the breeze, Relnoc whispers, "We don't abandon family."

Light trails over her dusky skin, reflecting off the track of a single tear.

Chapter Fourteen
Regonia

Olivia

Regonia sprawls before me, but the window of the ship separates me from her. I stare out during one of my breaks from working on my present for the Drennar, but all I can do is wish to be out there. For the first time, the cockpit makes me feel disconnected from the stars, from the universe, instead of connected to it.

Because I could be *on* this planet.

I could be a part of it, part of something bigger, without metal or glass or a spacesuit between me and the stars. I could breathe the universe in, feel it on my skin.

Realization dawns on me, and my jaw falls open. Drawing in a deep breath, I wonder if I'll ever look forward to flying again.

My heart gives a painful little twinge, and I shake my head, trying to clear it. Stuffing down painful revelations, I dive back into my programming, piecing together mass destruction. Guilt trickles in, but I stuff it down.

We'll warn them.

We'll give them a chance.

Hours go by, filled with layers of encryption. Symbols and numbers flash over the screens around me, scrolling as I think through them.

The light moves through the sky, warming the cockpit. I lean forward, letting it hit my skin. My eyes close, but my mind speeds along, sending data scrolling madly over the screens.

My skin warms in the midday light, and I sigh contentedly. Drawing in a breath, I open my eyes to the rolling plains, the sweeping grasses.

And the army approaching from the foothills.

They're here! Holy shit, they're actually here!

I smile, quickly transferring everything to my Link, and rush from the ship. Hope buzzes through me as I sprint through swaying strands of teal and aquamarine. The sun shines bright overhead, warm and pleasant on my skin. My legs pump harder, propelling me faster toward the point on the horizon where Daen Tribe and all our Soldiers gather.

The village blurs around me as I push myself, passing stone keeps and paddocks full of recently rounded-up livestock. My feet slap the stone pavers, battering the weeds into submission.

I burst into the open field, breathing heavily. A sharp pain lances my side at the exertion, so I slow. Stumbling to a jog, then a walk, I move through the crowd, shocked that they part to let me pass.

I guess they expect the Human Ambassador to need to be near the front?

In my periphery, I see another ripple in the crowd where Regonians move aside, and I know Ricardo must be moving through them as well. My smile widens at the thought of seeing him so soon. I hadn't expected to see him again until dinner time.

I catch a glimpse of curly black hair pulled back, a peek at golden eyes, the outline of his strong figure.

Excitement bubbles up within me as I turn my gaze forward, catching sight of Relnoc and Dresde. They stand beside massive, winged beasts with wide, pointed heads. Their black skin gleams in the bright light, and awe pulls my jaw low.

What are those?

My steps slow further, and I amble forward, barely registering an exchange of thanks from Tenna to Relnoc. That phrase I love so much falls from the latter's lips.

"We don't abandon family," she says, and my heart warms at the prospect of being part of that family, even just being adjacent to the family she references. Something about this place just feels connected in a way that Termana and the stations never could.

I slow to a stop beside Tenna, eyes fixed on the creatures before me. Ricardo's footsteps come closer, halting between me and Krona. His hand finds the small of my back, but my gaze never strays from the animals that Relnoc and Dresde apparently rode here.

Dresde's mount turns seven shining black eyes on me, tipping its head to the side. My lungs expand, lifting my chest. Warmth flows through my veins as my eyes rake over its sleek body, the thin membranes of its wings with veins showing through just a bit darker than the surrounding skin.

Massive talons encrust its feet, each one easily the size of my forearm. It could kill me with a single swipe, could impale me with the razor-sharp tip of its beak.

But it's beautiful.

I take a step forward, drawing even with Tenna and Krona.

And the animal moves, too. It takes a single, long stride and drops its head to consider me carefully. Each eye takes me in, analyzing me closely.

I ache to move closer, but something tells me to wait.

Only two meters away, the animal's head looms as large as me. It inhales, and I feel the air rushing past me, lifting my hair and sending it forward as the beast exhales.

Shadows play over its skin as it dips its head once, then rises to its full height, turning and arching to lift its wings slowly. They expand, engulfing us all in shadow before fluttering at its side once more. Ridges of dark bone jut out from its hips, tracing the curves and lines of its hindquarters, then sweeping down the sides of a scaly tail.

And all I can do is marvel at it, breath caught in my chest.

Turning to face me once more, it dips its head again. Then, it takes a step back, shaking the earth beneath its mighty frame as it moves behind Dresde.

Only then do I notice the expression on the Taron chieftains' faces, on the faces of the Taron warriors behind them. They stare at me, eyes occasionally darting to the dark, winged thing before us.

"He's never taken to someone so easily," Dresde says, voice hushed and full of awe. "It took a full planting season for him to regard me with such respect."

"That was terrifying," Ricardo says behind me.

"It was magnificent," I say.

Silently, I wonder if someday I may be able to fly here, and tears of joy prick at the corners of my eyes.

Chapter Fifteen
Novay

Rone

The timer ticks away on the wall behind Reginald. He looks anywhere but at it, staring at the floor when he turns to tap the table for a bubble of water. His fingers tap anxiously on his knees after he drinks it down, and his leg bounces.

I've never seen him like this before.

But then, he's never had a countdown to his daughter's kidnapping glare at him for days on end.

I keep myself from glancing at it for his sake, trying not to draw his attention to it, but I figure the time left. Nineteen and a half hours. The ships will descend into Regonian atmosphere tomorrow morning.

I sigh and try to make conversation with Reginald to distract him. He glances over his shoulder, sees the glowing red numbers counting down. His shoulders slump, and his face falls.

When he turns to face me again, his brows reach for each other, and a deep breath puffs out his chest.

"What do you think they're doing right now?" he whispers.

"Will it help you to talk about it?" I ask.

"I don't know." He shrugs and looks back at the timer, slowly ticking Olivia's freedom away. "Trying to ignore it isn't helping. It's worth a shot."

"Well," I begin, crossing my legs beneath myself and popping a bubble of water into my mouth. "I'd say they're probably preparing their weapons and armor, coming up with battle plans, that sort of thing. Olivia is probably hard at work on her programming."

Reginald leans back against the wall, head resting against the timer above his bed. He crosses his legs, sticking them straight out across his bed. His eyes fall to his hands, fidgeting on his lap. "Do you think they convinced Taron Tribe to help them?"

My stomach clenches. "I don't know. I hope so."

"Would it make a difference?" His eyes rise, meeting mine from across the room, from across the compound, from across the world.

My mouth falls open, moving without sound for a moment as I remember Curata's calculations. Tomorrow's outcome will doubtless be shown to him, but for now, I can give him a bit of hope.

Maybe he'll actually sleep tonight.

Tracing the dark circles beneath his eyes, black smudges on tawny skin, I say, "It would. Aid from Taron Tribe would just over double their chances of success. And not just because of their numbers. They've fought together before, so the familiarity helps too."

He nods, breathing in slowly.

But I don't tell him just how low their odds are, even with help. He must know, but I can't bring myself to hurt him.

We talk as long as we can, saying goodbye only when we can no longer expect our looped footage to be believable to any Drennar watching.

An approaching signature in the hall draws my attention, and I force myself to rise. I slide my wall open before Lustran even knocks, catching him with his fist raised and ready. He laughs awkwardly, dropping his arm to his side.

As we walk to meet with Curata, Lustran fidgets, asking about Reginald. I confirm the toll this is taking on him, heart twisting in my chest as I speak of the impending attack.

"How are *you* handling it?" he asks. "Not well, I suppose." He reaches out, touching my forearm lightly.

I drop my gaze to my hands, just now noticing that my fingers worry at each other. My wings flutter restlessly, another little thing I hadn't noticed.

A self-deprecating chuckle escapes me. "I guess not." I shake my head. "I just… want it to go well. I want…"

I want her to be safe. I want him to be happy.

But neither seems possible.

Lustran wraps an arm around me, pulling me against his side as we walk. It surprises me, but the contact feels nice. I lean against him, wrapping my arms around my stomach and chest. Warmth flows through me, teasing out the tension within me.

Sighing, I say, "Thank you. I didn't realize I needed a hug quite so badly."

It's been so long since I was with Reginald. I haven't touched anyone, or been touched by anyone, since.

Is that another thing emotions make necessary?

The dark circles under Reginald's eyes pop back into my mind, and I wonder how much a hug might help him.

"Do you think Curata could help me with something?" I ask Lustran.

He doesn't answer as we meander into the common room of our little compound. Sentrah and another woman sit on the floor, hands joined and eyes closed. We walk silently, respecting their prayers, nonsensical as they may be.

Let them find comfort where they may.

Once we move into another hall, branching out and winding our way toward Curata's room, Lustran answers me. "Probably. I'm not sure there's anything she can't do." His tone takes on a reverent quality, soft and low.

I pull back, staring up into his face. Realization dawns on me, spreading a smile over my face.

He slows to a stop, blushing and looking down. "What?" he asks, refusing to meet my gaze.

"Do you… Have you fallen in love with her?" I ask, casting a glance down the hall.

He shushes me, eyes darting this way and that. Voice dropping, he asks, "How do you even know if you're in love?"

"You remember that thing she mentioned a while back? Intuition, the sense of what is… You just know."

"That isn't exactly helpful," Lustran says, finally resuming his walk down the hall.

"I know," I say with a laugh. "Love sneaks up on you. You don't even realize you're in it until…"

"Until it's too late?"

"Something like that."

"So, what did you want Curata to help you with?" Lustran asks, not so subtly changing the subject. He nudges me as we walk.

***

I bide my time through our strategy session, well-aware that my request pales next to the other things we need to sort out. My nerves have me tapping my fingers, just as Reginald tapped his fingers and feet to the brutal beat of the timer.

If only I were the one doctoring the footage and scans… Our time to plan wouldn't be so long simply because I wouldn't be able to maintain them as long.

I could ask her sooner.

I chide myself silently for my selfishness, reminding myself just how important these coordinated efforts are.

But still my heart aches. Still my fingers drum away on the tabletop in Curata's room, a recent addition carved from alonarium to match the round table she read about in old Human myths.

When our time finally draws to a close, I say, "Before you drop us back into the footage, could I ask you for a favor?"

Curata smiles. Her iridescent skin shines, showing off shimmering pastel highlights. The odd light she's created, some flickering blue version of the fire other species use for heat, sends shadows rolling and jumping over her.

I outline my request, doing my best to stay objective, but my heart jumps into my throat, choking off the words. She pauses for a few seconds, gaze unfocused, drawn into a million calculations. My heart gallops, and my nerves wind tight.

But when she speaks, she surprises me.

"Easy," Curata says. "Can you wait until tonight? It won't be as risky then."

"Of course," I say, readily agreeing to any terms she might put forth. My face threatens to split wide open as my smile grows. "Can you really do it?"

She giggles, nodding. "I should hope so. I'll have to do a lot more later, but this will be good practice."

I almost feel bad for doubting her. Almost.

Relief washes through me, and I jump up, rushing around the table to throw my arms around her. She laughs into my hair, arms wrapping around my waist.

"Thank you…" I breathe out, sending soft hair fluttering every which way.

"It's no problem. And anyway, there's something that I was thinking about, something that needs done. If you have the stomach to do it yourself, that is." Pulling back from me, she says, "If not, I'll go along. I'll have to make a pit stop on the way, so you'll have some privacy, at first."

My skin warms, but curiosity moves through me.

Curata lays her hand on the table, and the alonarium seems to ripple up from the floor, shifting through the table and sending the excess pooling beneath her palm. It moves as if a liquid, defying gravity according to her will, and the table reforms in its wake.

When she pulls her hand away, a tiny sphere rests upon the table. I narrow my eyes, leaning closer to get a better look. Carefully, I retrieve the tiny sphere she offers, cradling it carefully in the crook between two of my fingers.

At a loss, I shake my head. "What is it?"

"A breath of fresh air," she says.

I furrow my brows, wondering at her meaning and awaiting her explanation.

But she doesn't offer one.

"Can you stow that in a safe place? I'll explain later. For now, I need to put us back into their reality."

Her phrasing catches me off guard, but I know she only means our time is up. I shift the alonarium of my shirt, forming a small pocket at my belly button, using it for cover, then stow the little ball inside and seal it away.

Lustran turns to Curata, a smile ready on his lips and a blush crawling over his dark skin as he puts a hand to the small of her back. Her pale skin turns a delicate, shimmering pink at her cheeks, and I smile.

I watch, trying to see the shift in her features as she manipulates the footage she's been fabricating this whole time, blending it to show us as we are.

But I only see her slow blink when she finishes.

****

Anticipation races through my veins. My wings flutter behind me, ready to be off, ready to see Reginald again. My heart races, and I focus outward to keep from analyzing each beat.

Beside me, Curata gives a nervous giggle, wings beating the air in time with my own. Their currents feel weird. I'm not used to being around another person who has them, even if hers are so different from mine. Their wind stirs my feathers, and I wonder what effect mine might have on hers.

But she cuts off my thoughts.

"I've never... broken a rule before," she says. "I mean, I know we don't have rules, not really, but this feels like it's breaking one. It's breaking his experiment. I'm nervous but... It's exciting."

I laugh, happy to put an end to Reginald's suffering, even if only temporarily. But I have to burst her bubble.

"We've broken other 'rules,'" I say, watching the exhilaration fade from her eyes, morphing into confusion. "We haven't exactly been reporting accurate data here lately."

"I guess you're right," she says. "But that was different somehow. Why was that different?"

I shrug. For some reason, I don't want to know, and the realization surprises me.

Shouldn't I care?

Knowledge and data are the entire point of our species. It's why we do what we do. It's why we've put people through so much.

To learn.

To gather information.

But I'm not that person anymore, not quite that species. At least, not in any way that matters.

Briefly, I wonder if my trust in Curata's ability to puzzle it out faster than I could is what keeps me from assessing it myself. But I know how I was before.

I would have analyzed the situation myself, then compared my findings with hers to determine accuracy. She would've been a whetstone to sharpen my own intellect.

Memories of my own unfeeling stares, the sweep of my analysis beams over living people, wash through me, and I shudder. Their expressions, mixtures of horror, fear, and rage, paint themselves across my mind, flooding me with guilt.

But we're fixing it.

We're making it better.

I tap the little ball still carefully concealed within my pocket in a protective gesture not unlike an expectant mother touching her stomach. The likeness sends a jolt of longing through me.

We're fixing this.

And it starts now.

I glance at Curata and find her thoughtful, doubtless contemplating exactly what I don't even care to know. Maybe her curiosity has been increased by the new understanding emotion has granted her.

Either way, I wait, not-so-patiently, for her to finish her deliberations and for the clock to fall into place. I try to be still so as not to disturb her, but I find myself shifting from one foot to another, begging time to move just a little faster.

And though it doesn't listen to my requests for speed, time eventually drags itself forward.

Curata snaps to attention, and a smile sparkles on her face. "Ready?" she asks.

I nod, and my body tenses, nerves winding tight.

I'm finally going to get to see him again.

Sure, we have to...

I blanch at the thought of what we have to do, then remind myself that Curata will be the one to do it. But I can't think about it, can't bring myself to imagine the blood, to imagine his flesh cut open, good as the intentions may be, *necessary* as it may be.

Curata moves her fingers. The floor opens before us, moving and undulating, forming into a perfect staircase of alonarium, tailored to carry us away beneath the compound. Behind us, the excess alonarium pools within her room, shaping itself into a tiny mountain range, and I wonder at her decision to sculpt such a thing at a time like this. I take a step forward, placing a foot on the first stair.

But footsteps in the hall stop me short.

Lustran peeks in at us, cheeks red. He mumbles, "Be careful." He meets Curata's eyes, but only for a second. Then, he vanishes back down the hall.

I glance at her only to find a delicate smile playing on her features.

At long last, we move forward, descending into a pale, blue-grey tunnel. She pulses soft blue light through the walls, illuminating us from both sides and casting conflicting shadows. Curata wiggles her fingers, playing with the dark shapes on the walls, and for a moment, it even appears as though she's rippling the alonarium her shadow falls upon.

Awed by her, by all she's managing simultaneously, I push myself faster to ease the strain on her. And to reach Reginald that much faster. Clad in soft slippers, my steps barely make a sound. I trail my hand along the wall, heart pounding in my chest.

My smile widens, and I track our progress, analyzing the distance between our compounds. Each time we pass beneath a transmitter station, my breath catches at the thought of potential capture.

But we pass undiscovered.

The tunnel stretches out into the distance, a seemingly never-ending grey hellscape. About halfway through, we come to an offshoot. Fear slithers through me. My brows furrow, and I stare at Curata.

"This is… yours, right?" I ask. "Please, tell me you made this tunnel too."

She giggles. "Of course, I made it. No one else makes tunnels. These are just our alonarium reserves. I thought you knew that?"

"Yeah, I just… I'm nervous."

She smiles. "Well, this is where we split up, so hopefully that doesn't make you even more nervous."

I draw in a deep breath.

"I'll be there soon. Whatever you want to do without me there…" Curata winks. "Well, do it fast."

She turns and meanders down the little branch, casting a single glance back at me.

I blush, then take off at a jog, aching to see Reginald again. The hall blurs around me, and I send a message to Curata as I near the end. She works her magic, and a staircase takes shape before me.

I skid to a stop at the base, staring up at the dark room above.

Is he already asleep?

My heart sinks. I climb the steps, slow and steady. I take deep breaths and send a message to Reginald asking if he's awake. Instantly, I receive a response, and my heart soars.

Stepping into his room, I whisper, "I have a surprise for you."

He rolls over in his bed to stare at me, eyes wide and jaw hanging open. He shakes his head. Voice hushed, he says, "How?"

And then, he springs to his feet and crosses the room in two steps. His arms wrap around me, and I crush him against me. Our lips meet in a fevered, desperate kiss. My body burns, aching to have him closer.

A tear slides down my cheek, and I clasp the back of his neck. Pulling back just enough to breathe, I whisper, "I missed you."

"I missed you too," he says, voice cracking beneath the weight of his emotions.

Our lips meet once more, and his hands tangle in my hair. My hands slide over his chest, down and around, slipping beneath his shirt to glide up his back. He caresses my neck, traces my jaw with his thumb. Fire trails along in the wake of his touch, and I crave more.

But he pulls back, staring at me, eyes tracing my edges, hands coming to rest on my cheeks. "Are you really here? Is this actually happening?" he asks, incredulous.

I laugh, sputtering through tears. "I'm really here. Have you been hallucinating or something?"

I remember the head wound he suffered not long ago, and a sudden jolt of fear slithers through me. Concern slices my heart open, and I ask, "You haven't, have you?"

He laughs, shaking his head. "No. Just daydreaming. A lot." His chest rises with a breath, and he adds, "I think it's the only thing that's kept me sane."

I chuckle softly, leaning my head against his. "Good. You scared me there."

I touch his neck, breathing him in. Pulling him close, I savor the feel of him pressed against me, the softness of his skin beneath my kisses. But tear tracks decorate his cheeks, leaving salt on my lips.

Cupping his cheeks, I stare into his rich, hazel eyes, shining in the light of the tunnel. I search his gaze.

His mouth opens, but no sounds form. Slowly, he closes it, then tries again.

"They'll be there tomorrow…" he croaks. "They're going to attack. They're going to take her. After everything she's been through…" His voice breaks, and he trails off.

His thumb traces my lips, sending delicate shivers skittering over my skin. His Adam's apple bobs as he swallows. "What are we going to do?" he asks.

"Whatever it takes," I say.

Sighing, I close my eyes. "That reminds me… I don't have much time. Curata will be here soon, and… her task in coming here isn't exactly pleasant. There are things we're going to have to do in the future that…"

I fall silent, hating the thought of his blood seeping out at the end of her knife. I shake my head.

There's no way I could do it.

Thank god she offered.

"Rone?" Reginald begins. "What is it? What does Curata need to do?"

"There's a mod you'll need in the future. Since we're already practicing getting around unnoticed, she wanted to go ahead and do it tonight. But… that means surgery."

Reginald gulps, but nods. His chest rises against mine, and he says, "Okay."

"You don't have questions? Don't you want to know what it is?"

"Of course, I do," he says with a laugh. "But I trust you. If you say I need it, then I'm sure I need it."

My cheeks warm. "Well, you do seem rather fond of breathing," I say. "And the air beyond your compound would kill you."

"Surgery it is, then," he says with a laugh. One of his hands traces my spine, grasps my hip, as if trying to memorize the shape of me. "Will they be able to tell though?"

I shake my head, but Curata answers behind me.

"Nope. I've taken care of that."

Our heads jerk toward her, and my heart falls.

I'm not ready to see him cut open. I'm not ready for our time to come to an end.

Why couldn't you take longer to find what you needed?

I turn to Reginald, brows furrowed and lips turned downward. I sigh, knowing I'll have to say goodbye soon, not knowing the next time I'll see him.

One corner of his mouth lifts in an attempt at a smile, but when his hand rests on my cheek, the touch is bittersweet.

"I love you," he whispers.

My breath catches, but I manage, "I love you too."

Drawing in a fortifying breath, I take a step back, letting my hand slide all the way down his arm to grasp his hand. Our fingers lace together, and we face Curata.

Her wings seem to shine with a light of their own, glittering with the traces of blue light glowing in the tunnel behind her. She smiles, and says, "It's nice to finally meet you, Reginald. You'll want to lay down for this."

Chapter Sixteen
Regonia

Tenna

My Vyrto shifts beneath me, taking a wide stance. In my periphery, I see Krona's mount do the same. I turn to watch the Malakarns that Relnoc and Dresde sit atop, still and unperturbed. Their massive, outstretched wings flutter softly, black membranes filling with a gentle breeze I don't even feel.

I breathe deeply, waiting for Drennar ships to descend from the Realm of Stars, to land upon our planet for the first time in many generations. My chin rises as I reflect on the change we've wrought in their absence, the growth of our Tribe.

Gazing out at our lands, at the rolling plains of aquamarine and teal, the jagged black mountains with their emerald tops, the river sparkling perfect midnight blue in the distance, my heart leaps.

I'm home, finally, and I'll do whatever I must to protect my it, to protect my family.

I almost pity the Drennar I'll meet on the battlefield. Almost.

My hands go to my axes hanging at my waist. I trace their edges, lovingly, reverently. It's been too long since I felt their weight, too long since I wore this armor. The dark leather fits perfectly, bends with me. Tanned and treated with Juno sap, it's stopped every blade I've faced. The new Ameeka backing promises to protect me further.

I turn, taking in row after row of warriors and soldiers, all ready for battle. Black leathers adorn our warriors. Taron warriors sport the same black leathers with sleek Malakar bones inlaid for strength. Human soldiers wear sturdy fabrics and metal plates. They seem so bulky, but they're used to them.

Pride swells within my chest, sending warmth coursing through me.

Atop the roof of our keep, a horn blows. Bone swords and axes thud against shields behind me. I look upon our enemy, not in the fields where we so often fought in the past, but in the sky.

Three sleek black ships descend, dropping beneath the clouds, but the smooth crafts never land. They hover at the same height as our first camp on the mountain path.

My heart sinks.

How will we fight them in the air?

Squaring my shoulders, I watch them, waiting to see what they'll do.

We'll find a way.

In the distance, more warriors approach. The stark white armor of Roon Tribe, dented, scratched, and bloodied, stands out in aquamarine fields. They approach, on foot and on Vyrtons, in a show of solidarity I never expected.

Tears prick at the corners of my eyes, and I wonder if Olivia sent them a message somehow, if Relnoc or Dresde sent a messenger. Or if they simply want to stop the invaders from the stars.

I glance at Krona, only to find his eyes glued to the ships hovering above the battlefield.

"Cowards," he mutters. "Dishonorable." The venom in his words sends a trickle of adrenaline through me.

"Krona," I say.

When he tears his eyes from the sky, I direct his gaze to Roon Tribe. The anger melts from his face, and awe shines in those beautiful, pale green eyes. A quick laugh bursts from him, and he shakes his head.

Be it self-preservation or honor that brings them to the battlegrounds with their eyes and spears turned upward, I can't say. But I'll take it.

Another ally, another pool of strength to draw from. Another barrier broken.

I swallow thickly.

Movement above draws my gaze. A panel on the ship slides away, revealing Drennar soldiers standing in the opening. Cold and unmoving, they stare down at us, their black-clad forms silhouetted by the lights within the ship.

One steps forward, breaking from the line. Massive wings unfurl from its back, and a collective gasp breaks free of the armies behind and before me. It flaps those great feathered wings, hovering.

Waiting.

Another steps forward, and wings like those of the Malakarns spread behind it, membranes so thick as to block out all light behind it.

My heart races as one after another fly free of the ship, gathering before the opening. A mass of winged creatures flaps above us, blocking out the sun and casting shifting shadows over us all. I try to estimate their numbers, but it's no use.

Fans of blue light sweep over us, and though I knew to expect it, I flinch. A few screams erupt from the fields.

But only a few.

I eye Roon Tribe carefully, and they react no more poorly than we do. Someone must have warned them. Someone must have sent for them.

Good.

They know what we're in for.

Relief washes through me, despite everything.

Fans of blue light move over us, seeking their prey, but they won't find Olivia or the other two pregnant women among our ranks.

I smile.

Chapter Seventeen

Regonia

Ricardo

Our ranks stretch all the way to the village, and I rake my gaze over rows of Regonians and Humans. To my left and three rows ahead, Krona and Tenna perch atop Vyrtons, guarded by massive antlers. Relnoc and Dresde sit astride winged creatures, and now I wish they had more of those beasts tamed.

Drennar fill the sky, wings beating the air as they search for Olivia. And though dread creeps through me, though fear slithers through my veins like ice water, I smile.

I don't let my gaze stray to the stone building beside me, the one that holds Olivia and the other pregnant women. Its sturdy walls would normally act as an armory, located on the outer edge of the village, between homes and fields.

But today, it protects the woman I love and the child she bears.

Careful not to glance at it, not to even lean toward it, I watch the creatures in the sky. My heart thuds as we wait for them to land, wait for them to make a move, to attack.

On the front lines, the Malakarns stare up, faces contorted, eyes narrowed. They toss their heads back, and violent shrieks erupt from their razor-sharp beaks. My blood curdles at the sound, and the hairs stand up on the back of my neck.

On the mountain peaks, shrill cries of fury answer them, piercing the air with a desperate ache for bloodshed. My heart freezes.

But only half of the Drennar pause their search. They turn cold blue gazes upon the mountains, upon the Malakarns which Relnoc and Dresde struggle to keep on the ground.

Fans of light sweep over them, giving the Malakarns pause for just a moment. More fans of light glide over our ranks as the rest of the Drennar seek Olivia.

But the Malakarns launch themselves into the air, ascending to throw themselves upon the invaders. Unused to sharing the sky, they attack the Drennar in a flurry of sharp beaks and talons. Relnoc and Dresde cling to their mounts, swinging axes when they dare move their hands from their harnesses.

My breath catches in my throat as hordes of Malakarns descend from the mountains to join the fray, ganging up on a particularly unlucky Drennar. One of her four arms flies up, firing a beam of some sort from a sleek white weapon. It catches the front leg of one of her assailants, blowing it clean off and raining blood over the swaying grasses below.

But the beast doesn't stop.

And neither do its companions.

In a heartbeat, they tear her limb from limb, flinging one arm down, then another. Dark red blood pours over the field, a strange juxtaposition of the chaos and gore above and the serene grasses below. More gore flows as a Malakar tears her wings off, and they let her fall. She plummets, landing with a sick thud.

One down.

Too many to go.

But already, the Malakarns move to new targets.

Tension hangs around us, heavy and thick in the air. Nerves drawn tight, I wait for the Drennar to descend, forced to ground by the beasts that rule these skies.

Beside me, a Soldier whispers under her breath, "It looks like demons and angels..." She swallows, then falls silent.

"I never thought I'd root for the ones that look like demons," I say back, hardly aware that I've spoken.

Three more dismembered Drennar plummet, landing in a series of grisly thumps. They don't move. No light shines from their eyes.

My gaze returns to the sky in time to see Relnoc's Malakar drive its razor-sharp beak into the chest of a Drennar, piercing flesh and bone with ease. Leaning forward, Relnoc swings her axe, cracking the Drennar's skull wide open.

With a kick, her mount pushes the body off its beak and sends it careening downward in a flutter of wings and blood. Four more fall behind that one, then a few more.

My heart hammers wildly in my chest, and for a moment, I think we may be safe. They may never reach us.

But a panel slides open on the second ship.

More Drennar pour from its gaping black maw, rocketing straight to the ground. I barely have time to register a couple Malakarns barreling inside the ship to wreak havoc. A deep sickness churns in my stomach as one, then another, Malakar drops, slashed membranes of their wings flapping behind them.

The first Drennar sets foot on the battlefield, stepping over its fallen brethren without a glance, without so much as a wince. He scans his surroundings, turning his head from side to side, eyeing us coolly. And all the while, fans of light emanate from his eyes, taking us in.

Two more land behind him, all near-exact clones. Four arms and black wings, the same grey skin, the same shaved heads. They move together, synchronized in every step, and a chill trickles over my spine.

Are they the same person?

Four more land, falling into perfect step with their brethren. Up above, a hundred copies of the woman that was torn apart go to battle with the Malakarns. Below, more and more copies of this man alight in swaying grasses.

Blood speckles their faces, their wings, their clothes, as they walk toward us, gradually moving clear of the aerial battle. And they never flinch.

Ice water runs through my veins as fear grips my heart.

What are we up against?

My lungs spasm, and my heart lurches. Panic sinks its claws into me, but thoughts of Olivia huddled in the armory shake me out of it.

I have to protect her.

We can't let them take her.

I square my shoulders and pull out my gun. My free hand rests on my taser as I stare at the advancing enemy. The clones land, masses of Drennar walking forward in sync. Each step they take as one sends a shudder through the earth.

My heart skips a beat.

Tenna calls out, "Sve!"

And we charge.

Krona and Tenna ride forward, Vyrtons carrying them at breakneck speeds. I run, full tilt, but the riders leave me in the dust.

A handful of Drennar land before me, before the Human Soldiers whose feet pound the earth behind me. I raise my gun, firing away, but the Drennar closest to me barely flinches.

The aerial battle expands, spreading to block out the sun and drenching us in shadow. Blood rains down in trickles and mists. Feathers drift to the ground, and a pale grey arm plummets, landing with a thud in front of me.

I jump over it, sprinting forward. Pulling out my taser, I aim, hoping it works. All Rone's assurances flit through my mind, but as I pull the trigger and watch the probes fly through the air, doubt fills me.

Will they pierce the Drennar's skin?

Will it actually have an effect?

Even with the needles they used to draw blood from the Regonians, the needles we've since learned were made of their bones, I wonder if it'll work.

Maybe this thing has special armor beneath its skin.

But the prongs find their mark.

Electricity courses through the Drennar, and its body convulses. Vivid eyes roll back, and limbs flail. Bright blue and white electricity arcs from one fingertip to another, pulses through it, ripples over its skin.

Holy shit...

More descend. Still more step forward, but we meet them with tasers and spears, with guns and axes. A clamor rings through the air as weapons crash down on hardened Drennar suits and skin. Shouts of pain pierce my ears, but the strength of our battle cries buoy my spirits.

Another Drennar falls to my taser, disappearing into the swaying grasses as his knees buckle beneath him. The sun blazes above, and my heart swells.

All around, electricity and Regonian weapons, tailor made to break toughened skin and flesh and bone, cut our enemy down. Above, Malakarns fight a gruesome battle, raining gore down upon us. But the strange alien equivalent of Valkyrie fight them tooth and nail, and feathers fall as frequently as fingers. Dark scales and flashes of grey skin flutter in the breeze.

Sneaking through the grasses, I slam the taser home, pushing it against the spine of a Drennar and bringing it down without a second thought. Another stands over a Regonian with one foot on her neck, and I slink through the swaying lengths of turquoise.

Coming up behind him, I push my gun against his spine and pull the trigger, unwilling to sacrifice the woman beneath his feet with the use of the taser. So close, the bullet pierces even the sturdy frame of a Drennar.

But it doesn't come out.

Briefly, I wonder if it ricochets within, the way some of the smaller caliber bullets of old would within a skull. Regardless, the unfeeling being turns on me, taking his foot from the neck of the Regonian woman.

She springs to her feet, barely taking a second to recover, and thrusts her spear up into his neck. The sharpened tip drives up, exploding out of his mouth and spattering me with dark blood. He falls with a sickening thud, plunging her spear deeper and turning himself into a pike. My stomach lurches, and my chest heaves.

But this battle is far from over.

Hands shaking, I nod when the Regonian warrior meets my gaze. She inclines her head, rises to her feet, and flings herself back into the fray. Vaulting over a pair locked in combat, dark braids flying wild in the wind, she swings her axe low, decapitating the Drennar and landing in a roll.

I turn, analyzing the scene around me. And what I find surprises me.

Only a few of our people lie dead in the sweeping aquamarine grasses. I look closer, watching the Drennar, and see that they use only non-lethal tactics, incapacitating us whenever they can spare our lives.

But why?

I grind my teeth when the answer comes to me.

They can't experiment on us if we're dead.

Rage boils within me, curling my fingers into talons. My hands tighten on my taser, my pistol. I glance around, looking for another Drennar to bring low, another vile creature to erase. Another crime to avenge.

Raising my gun, I fire a few shots at a Drennar nearby, luring him toward me. He comes, and I sprint to meet him. Dropping into a slide, gliding on blood-slick grass to slip under him, I press the taser to his ankle as his leg passes over me, and he goes down with a swishing, thrashing thud as convulsions echo through him.

He would have taken Olivia. He would have taken our baby.

He might have experimented on her dad.

I tense with fury.

A man with eyes as cold as every other Drennar here breaks into a run. For all his speed, his breathing barely accelerates, perfectly controlled, even and measured. His placid face chills me to my core as he comes for me, sprinting far too quickly.

I barely get my arms up before he's on me. My taser grazes his arm as he shoves me, sending me flying. I watch him convulse, falling into a twitching heap, as wind whips past my ears.

My back slams into a wall of stone, and all the air rushes from me. Something inside snaps, maybe a rib, and pain lances through my torso.

Behind me, tiny stones fall to the ground. I push myself to my feet, turn my gaze upward, staring at the crack I've left in the wall. I cough, wincing at the pain that writhes through me. A fleck of warm liquid sputters onto my chin, and I wipe it away. Fear spikes through me when my hand comes away bloody.

Is that… my blood?

I step forward, intending to reenter the battle, but the world sways beneath my feet. A trickle of something warm slides down the back of my neck, but I don't reach for it, afraid of what I'll find.

A screech rings out, and I jerk my head up. The world tips, but time slows as I watch. A Malakar and a Drennar swirl in the sky, locked in a death grip and pouring blood over the world as they plummet.

Wings beat furiously, desperate to slow their fall, but a talon-encrusted grip wrenches the Drennar's wing free of her back. She doesn't flinch, doesn't scream.

She falls further, coming closer, and I see her blink once.

Reaching forward, she pulls the Malakar's head forward, piercing her own chest with its beak and locking her arms around its head to hold it in place. Her legs wrap around it as blood pours from the wound on her chest, and it beats its wings frantically, desperate to escape the death spiral.

But they crash into the roof of the building at my back.

Shrieks ring out as I tumble to the ground, pushed forward by the crumbling wall. Olivia's voice carries from inside the armory, and panic surges through me. The ground tips and tilts beneath me, but I try to push myself up, try to go to her.

But I'm not the only one who heard.

A Drennar separates from the battle, sprinting toward me, leaping over me. I lift a weak arm to press the taser to his foot, his thigh, to anything, any part of him, but my head spins.

And I fall.

He sifts through rubble, tossing the Malakar and the fallen Drennar aside with ease. Four arms shift the wreckage quickly, and he finds her, taking refuge in a sturdy doorframe.

My heart falters, and I choke as I scream, "Olivia!"

I cough, and blood spatters the ground before me. My lungs spasm, and pain riots within me. Terror and agony twist my gut into knots.

Adrenaline courses through me, pushes me to my feet. My body screams for relief, but I move into the wreckage, one weary step after another. Rubble trips me, bringing my knees crashing down onto jagged stone.

But my eyes never leave Olivia.

Pale and staring up in horror, she screams as he grabs her. She kicks and punches, but he merely spins her within his multi-armed grasp, turning her away before massive wings unfurl.

He launches himself into the air, soaring over my head, just above the battle on the ground, just below the massacre in the air.

I reach for him, but my spinning head rebels, tipping me backward. Blood seeps from the wound on the back of my head. Every breath comes out a gurgle.

But the darkness doesn't come for me, doesn't spare me the sight of him flying away with her in his arms. A sob tears through me, and agony twists like a knife in my chest.

In the distance, Tenna calls commands, but her words drift over me, just one more piece of noise in a cacophony of useless bloodshed.

They took her.

We failed her. I *failed her.*

Another sob racks my body, and a lance of pain shreds my insides. Darkness creeps in at the edges of my vision.

But the Warriors of Daen Tribe begin assembling themselves into something reminiscent of a staircase. I chide myself, convinced that I've lost it, that I've lost too much blood to think clearly.

Why would they stand like that?

Why would they need to be stairs?

But Krona and Tenna sprint toward them, launching themselves up into waiting hands and running upward. My jaw falls open when their Warriors fling them up into the air.

Their grasping hands find their mark, jerking the Drennar and Olivia downward as they swing from his ankles.

I gasp, and the pain that rockets through my body tips me over the edge. Darkness claims me, but I whisper, "Olivia…"

Chapter Eighteen

Regonia

Krona

My heart drops into my boots when Ricardo screams, "Olivia!"

His voice breaks, and my mouth goes dry.

I put my opponent down with a well-placed blow of my axe, and my head jerks toward Ricardo. A cold wave of horror washes over me, and my skin prickles.

Squirming, fighting, Olivia swings fists and feet at the Drennar who holds her to his chest, pinning her with four strong arms. His dark wings beat the air viciously. His blood drips from a wound on one of his arms where her knife is lodged, surprising me.

But he holds her tight.

And though Ricardo is near her, there's no way he can help her now. The blood soaking the back of his armor, matting his hair to the back of his head, fills my veins with ice.

No…

The Drennar launches himself into the air, and I track his progress, track the path he's following toward the ships. My gaze meets Tenna's. Face pale, mouth open in horror, she whispers a plan.

I nod, then run.

She falls into step beside me, easily keeping pace as we calculate the path of the Drennar. Turning slightly, we pick up speed, moving through the battle with a slash of our axes here, a roll to dodge a blow there.

But the ears of every Drennar blink three times, and they unfurl massive wings. Shooting up into the air, they escape the battle, soaring toward their ships. Malakarns still patrol the air, having dispatched or chased away every Drennar above, and now, they have new targets.

But I keep my eyes on Olivia's squirming frame, on the vile beast that would kidnap a pregnant woman for experiments. My insides twist at the thought.

But the battlefield has opened.

A path appears through bloodied, flattened grasses. We leap over bodies, passing Warriors with terrible wounds and blood splattered over their features. Tenna calls out the order, commanding our wall breach formation.

A stairway of hands appears before me as every nearby Warrior complies, guarded by Taron Warriors. We sprint, launching ourselves into their hands with practiced ease.

Their hands dip with each step, but only slightly, braced up by strong frames, by muscles honed for maneuvers just like this. I don't even watch my steps, don't need to.

My eyes trace the path of the Drennar carrying Olivia. My heart pounds, blood rushing in my ears. Our Warriors lift us higher, hands held above their heads, but they don't have to reach further.

The Drennar approaches, and they launch us into the air, fling us at him. My heart leaps into my throat for a breathtaking moment as my hands reach, grasping open air.

But we calculated properly. And Olivia's squirming kept his focus from us, kept him from diverting.

My hands wrap around one ankle. Tenna's hands wrap around his other. My shoulders jerk as we fall, pulling him down with us in one sharp move. His wings beat harder, desperate to rise, to fly higher, but we're too heavy.

I climb up, arm over arm, and wrap myself around this vile thing's leg like a child. My eyes meet Tenna's as she does the same.

As I tighten my grip, she calls another command for the Warriors below us. They shift, a writhing mass of anger and sorrow and burning determination.

They toss each other up, wrapping arms around our waists, hanging from our legs. Every added weight pulls on my joints, puts pressure on my bones.

But it's working.

The Drennar fights harder to stay aloft, flapping like a frightened animal despite his expressionless face. But our Warriors grasp each other, and despite all his efforts, they pull us down.

His ears blink three times in what Rone calls a transmission. A message.

We crumble into a mass of bodies on the ground. Tenna twists his neck in one smooth move, and I wrest Olivia from his dead arms. Her hazel eyes are wide, desperate. Blood trickles from her forehead, decorates the sleeve of her shirt. Pulling her to me, I look to Tenna.

"We have to get her to safety," I say, knowing they'll descend once more.

They were only retreating because they had their prize, but now…

Already, wings batter the air, and fans of cold blue light sweep over us. Before we even get a chance to move, a dome of cold grey descends over us, cutting through bodies and limbs as it slices into the earth.

Screams echo in the horrendous sphere as we rise into the air, and blood pools upon the earth they scooped up with us. A Warrior near the edge presses a torn-off shred of her shirt to the stump that remains of her arm, gritting her teeth and biting back sobs.

My palms sweat, and I look around at the broken and battered Warriors huddled at my feet, at the body parts lying at Tenna's and Olivia's feet. Reaching out a hand, I lace my fingers with Tenna's.

She swallows, stepping forward with brows furrowed. Pulling Olivia in, she hugs us tight, then kneels to see to the wounded. I do the same, making tourniquets to staunch the bleeding of severed limbs wherever I can.

"Olivia," I begin, remembering her reaction to blood on the mountain. "Close your eyes."

She doesn't speak, and I can only assume she complies. My hands busy themselves with tearing off the bottom of my shirt, and I hurriedly fashion a bandage.

But a quiet hiss draws my attention, and my head jerks up. A small hole in the top of the sphere emits a sweet gas.

Far subtler than the gas Ricardo and his fellow guards used on Ulysses all those months ago, more like the smell of the tea Tenna's mother would brew on sleepless nights.

Bellona flowers.

My shoulders fall, and I turn to Tenna. I shake my head, mouth opening and closing without sound.

She reaches out, touches my cheek, and we settle in as the darkness reaches for us. My head lolls, falling against Tenna's. Her shoulders go slack, and she droops against me.

Chapter Nineteen
Regonia

Olivia

A strange, sickly-sweet smell fills my nose, and Krona and Tenna share a look of dread. Eyes drawn tight, brows kissing, they each nod and settle in on bloody grass. They slump against each other with heads lolling.

My mouth goes dry.

"What is that?" I ask.

But I'm not sure I want to know, not sure I can handle the answer.

The woman with the severed arm near the edge of our torn earth pod begins hyperventilating. "Kai Bellona?" she asks, voice rising with every syllable, contorting the Regonian words. *Is Bellona?*

My heart falls.

If that's Bellona, they'll be out soon.

I glance at the wounded, stomach writhing at the sight of the blood, the gore. Disembodied limbs lie tangled with the bodies of those who are… mostly intact. It seeps under me, slick and far too warm. Sickness creeps up my throat, but I swallow it back.

Be still, little baby.

Please.

Krona nods, movement slow and clumsy, but it draws my gaze from the too-clean cuts through flesh and bone all around me, from the pale skin and suddenly-slowed breathing of the woman with no arm.

"Vane…" he says. *Potent.*

Already, his eyelids fall.

Tenna reaches for me, but her arm falls before it rises more than a few centimeters off her lap. She mutters something, but the words escape me. Jumbled and quiet, they tangle in the air.

Just like the disembodied legs bent at unnatural angles behind me.

I gag, forcing myself to be calm. Or at least, trying to. My heart convulses in my chest.

Why didn't I try to convince them to give me up?

I was so caught up in them wanting to save me, in them thinking of me as family... I didn't even think about how many we'd lose.

Tears roll over my cheeks, hot and angry and filled with the familiar ache of guilt, my oldest friend come back for a visit. For half a breath, I try to tell myself that I wanted them to save me because I'm one of our two pilots, because without me, they can't fly anywhere.

But my heart knows better.

I wanted them to want me around.

Is that so bad?

I lift my hands, intending to jam my fists into my eyes, but they come up wet with dark blood. The thick liquid runs in rivulets down my wrists, showing me the true cost of my selfishness.

I can't bear to look at the bodies, the unconscious, the dead and dying. My stomach churns, and a sob rattles through me, shaking my entire body.

"Tenna," I begin, intending to apologize.

But when I look at her, I find her jaw hanging open, her eyes mostly closed, and her body slumped against Krona. His sturdy frame leans heavily to one side, propped against the broken pieces of his tribemates.

Swallowing, I force myself to move, to try to save the woman they were helping. I crawl past them, hands sinking too far into blood-soaked earth. I ache to close my eyes, to stop breathing the tang on the air.

But I can't.

It coats my mouth with every breath.

Getting closer, I take the ends of the strip of fabric in hand, pulling it tight around the stub of this woman's arm. A horrendous squelching sound fills the air, and I squeeze my eyes shut against the sight of her flesh peeking out at the end of her arm.

Sickness rises once more.

And panic follows on its heels.

As I tie off the fabric, desperate to ignore the give of her flesh, I wonder when they'll inject something to put me out. I stare up at the ceiling, grateful for an excuse to look away from the broken bodies.

But the little hole in the top of our sphere is gone. Only smooth grey remains.

With the tourniquet tied, I wipe my hands on my pants just above the knee, staining the only clean section of fabric. Tears fall freely, and I slump against the outer wall, half hoping they'll mess up and drop us.

Guilt sweeps through me at the thought of taking Krona, Tenna, and this unnamed woman out with me.

Maybe the wall could just open up and spit me out, let me splatter.

But the baby…

I sob harder, shoulders shaking with the effort. My thoughts weigh me down, pulling at the tattered strings of my sanity.

What life will this child have?

Abducted before birth, experimented on from day one. What kind of life is that?

I shudder. But even that life, that miserable existence, isn't enough to make me wish the child away. I rest a hand on my belly, finally starting to form a little bump.

I cry, body quaking. The sphere shifts, lifts. I put out a hand to steady myself, cringing as I slip in the dark blood of people who tried so hard to save me. The dark feathers of the Drennar who tried to carry me away lie everywhere, torn from his wings in their furious onslaught.

But only half of him is in this little bubble.

Split by the sphere's completion, he lies broken. His head, an arm, one wing, and the upper half of his torso rest within, but I can't stand to look at him. I slam my eyes shut, but even then, all I see is his frigid eyes, his expressionless face. The dark blood seeping from him.

He isn't human, obviously. Not even in the way that matters. He felt nothing, cared about nothing more than his experiment, his task. Even as I pummeled him and stabbed him midair, not even a hint of frustration showed on his face. When Tenna and Krona grabbed him, pulled him down, there was no fear.

A sob rises to claim me even just thinking of the sacrifice they may have made for me. Opening my eyes, I scoot across the slick grass toward their slumped forms. I want to lay them down, but blood glistens on the ground.

So, I let them lean against each other in unconsciousness as they do in their waking moments. I take their hands in my own, clutching tight.

"Thank you…" I whisper, but the words come out rough, choked by tears. "I'm sorry."

I'm sorry I failed you.

I'm sorry you're in so much danger.

I'm sorry I can't help you.

I smooth strands of dark hair back behind their ears. My fingers leave smears of blood on their cheeks and temples, and I shudder.

But I don't get time to explore the rest of my emotions, don't get time to apologize for my mother starting all of this or for the insidious motives of the Drennar. A loud clatter sounds as the sphere seems to drop onto something, some surface. I jolt with the impact, teeth slamming together on my tongue and filling my mouth with the taste of copper.

As if the smell wasn't enough.

My heart hammers in my chest, and I wait. The little hole at the top of the sphere reopens, and I brace for some sort of gas, some weapon or other.

But nothing comes.

The hole widens, and I wonder for half a breath if I can get out, if I can figure out a way to take Tenna, Krona, and the unnamed woman with no arm with me.

But the hole widens further.

And horrors wait beyond, staring down at me.

Two sets of cold green eyes shot through with whirring gears of electric blue peer in as the walls slide further and further down. Sleek grey skin stretches tight over their foreheads, their scalps. Masks of the same color protrude from their faces, covering their noses and mouths, but…

They aren't masks.

These beasts have no mouths, no noses. Only the filters, only the massive masks that pull air in. Their skin reaches over the masks, over the small honeycomb openings.

My breathing hitches, pulling in more of the sweet smell of Bellona gas. I shake my head, backing away as they reach for me.

But I hit the wall of the dome quickly.

One lowers a small, blue-grey tank into the dome, then grasps my shoulders. I squirm, try to get away, but it holds fast.

"Tenna! Krona!" I shout, heart racing.

I kick and scratch at the Drennar that holds me, but the Bellona gas continues to pour in, swirling in the air around us in visible clouds. My friends don't even stir.

Despair claws at my insides, ripping holes within me. My mind careens from one desperate plan to another, and my chest grows tight. The world narrows to a dark tunnel, and all I see are the two creatures standing over me.

My scalp prickles, and I break out in a sweat, suddenly boiling. Struggling to breathe, I try to calm myself, try to stave off the worst of the anxiety attack that creeps over me, suffocating me.

But the second Drennar reaches in, affixing a hose to the little tank. Its ears flash once, then smaller hands break free of its wrists, taking the hose in their grasp.

A scream rips through me as those extra hands come closer. I thrash, breath ragged as I try to escape, but the large hands, the normal ones, pin my head to the wall.

"Tenna! Krona!" I scream. "Please!"

But they slumber on.

Its small hands press a mask over my face, and I'm gripped by the fear that it'll melt into my flesh, that I'll look like they do with a honeycomb for a mouth. I try to scream, try to twist away, but it holds me in place, fingers digging into my scalp.

My palms sweat, and my eyes dart around the partially dismantled sphere. Blood and broken bodies. Dark feathers on the ground and monsters up above. Tenna and Krona unconscious, unable to defend themselves.

Unable to help me.

Hyperventilation sweeps in, and I gasp, over and again. My lungs fill with the faint sweet smell of whatever pumps into my mask. Every breath pulls more in, and at first, it only serves to intensify my terror.

But slowly, warmth seeps through me. With every choking, strangled breath, more of the sedative makes its way into my system.

The agonized horror that filled me mere moments ago… fades. I try to hold onto it, not sure why I do it, but it slips through my grasp. My head lolls. My eyelids flutter closed. The pressure on my shoulders, on my head, disappears as those horrible hands release me, and I slump against the wall.

But who… was holding me?

Why'd they let me go?

My thoughts slip, growing disjointed and foggy. Vague feelings and meanings float through my mind, imbued with more meaning than they should hold.

The warm darkness of my closed eyes calls to me, begging me to never look upon the world again. Gentle heat swells within me, easing my descent into sleep.

And I forget the worlds, forget the blood.

I forget myself.

And drift away.

Chapter Twenty

Regonia

Ricardo

Three days later

I wake to soft whispers and a too-bright light. I groan, slamming my eyes shut as I force myself to sit up. Pain courses through me when I try to move, try to breathe, but rage pushes it aside. Pulling in short, shallow breaths fill my chest with agony, I open my eyes.

But I don't find the sun above me, don't find the rubble of the broken armory beneath.

The medbay of the ship wraps around me, instead. Dr. Sullivan rushes toward me, begging me to lie back down, but I swing my legs over the side of my bed. My eyes dart around the room, looking for Olivia.

But she isn't here.

She'd be here if she could, I know she would. And I don't see Krona or Tenna.

My heart sinks, torn by rage and sorrow. It twists within my chest, breaking me into pieces.

They can't.

They can't take her.

My hands ball into fists, grasping the smooth white sheets.

They are not taking her. They're not going to hurt her. Not if I have anything to say about it.

I grind my teeth together and rip the IV from my arm. I don't bother with my clothes, don't care about this stupid medbay gown. My bare feet slap the floor as I take off.

Dr. Sullivan calls after me, voice hollowed by shock, "Ricardo! What are you doing?"

"I'm getting her back," I spit through clenched teeth, but I know he can't hear me.

I storm off through the ship, scowling and picking up speed. Pain lances through me with every breath, and every movement jars my ribs, pulls at the bandage wrapped around my chest.

But I don't care.

I dig my nails into my palms and move faster, sending a clipped message to Hugo on the way.

Footsteps close in behind me, so I push harder, panting with the effort. A tear slides over my cheek as the rest of my life spreads out before me, bleak without Olivia, without our child, without Krona and Tenna. I shove the thought away, replacing it with thoughts of what I'll do to any Drennar that stands in my way when I get to her.

And I *will* get to her.

"Mr. Bordeaux!" a woman calls behind me, but I don't know her, don't care what she might have to say.

She catches me easily, stopping my hobbling gait with a gentle hand on my arm, drawing my attention to just how fast I wasn't moving. I fight the urge to shake her off, to keep moving, but I don't keep myself from glowering at her.

Dr. Sullivan's deep voice booms through the hall, just a few meters away, "Ricardo, please!

You have a pneumothorax! You need to rest and let it heal!"

"What the fuck does that even mean?" I scream. "Why would it even matter? They took her! Who gives a fuck about pneumo-bullshit?"

"Pneumothorax means your lung collapsed," Dr. Sullivan says.

Shit...

A breath rushes from me, sending a spike of pain through my chest.

No wonder breathing hurts.

Hugo bursts into the hall, wincing as my voice echoes through the enclosed metal tube. I don't spare another word for Dr. Sullivan or the nurse.

"Get me up there," I growl.

Hugo stares at me, open-mouthed. His face falls as he says, "I... I can't. We need another pilot for take-off."

"Teach me. Tell me how to fly this thing. I'm not as smart as Olivia, but I'm not stupid. Tell me how to do this."

He considers for a moment, eyes skeptical, but he knows that unless he wants to tell every other Human here that they'll never see their homes, their families, again, he's going to have to teach someone.

"I've flown smaller crafts before," I say. "It's been a while, but it's a start."

He nods but looks to Dr. Sullivan.

Irritation blooms hot within me as the doctor says, "You need to rest."

"I can rest in the cockpit."

Chapter Twenty-One
Novay

Rone

Lying in bed, I sift through bits of information, searching for Olivia. But after days of looking, I still find nothing. Her Link was there, visible from our network, until she was taken onto that ship.

And still, there's nothing.

My heart falls. Hope shrinks within me, and tears prick at the corners of my eyes. My breath catches.

"No," I say under my breath.

I try to rally my spirits, knowing that this can't be.

They wouldn't kill her.

They wouldn't.

I grit my teeth.

They'd learn nothing from her if she was dead. They'd be ruining their own experiment.

I cringe at the thought of them experimenting on her, but for now, it gives me hope. Fury spirals through me, but I can use it.

They wouldn't kill her. So, what did *they do?*

I resume my search, but it's short-lived.

"Rone!" Curata shouts.

My eyes snap open, and I turn the lights on in my room with a thought. I spring to my feet and slide the wall open. With my heart in my throat, I listen to the soft buzzing of her wings as she soars through the hall toward me. She barrels through the door, alighting on bare feet.

Her eyes twinkle as she says, "I found her!"

My knees give way, and I crumple to the floor. Tears pour over my cheeks as Curata explains a sedated quarantine to observe the progression of Atlantis without risking her presence spreading it further.

I chuckle at their assumption, likening such a sophisticated program to a simple Human virus, but it doesn't matter.

"She's alive…" I breathe, choking on the words. Relief floods me, and I smile through tears. "She's alive."

I look to Curata, vision blurred by the tears shimmering in my eyes. I blink them away, only to see a few scattered on her pearlescent cheeks.

She nods, "She's okay. Tenna and Krona are there, too. Just in case they're carrying it." She rolls her eyes, laughing derisively.

I rub my hand over my face, shaking my head. "I have to tell Reginald."

"I'm already on it," Curata says with a smile.

Her hands move, and the alonarium beneath me ripples. A stairwell appears, and I jump to my feet.

Throwing my arms around her, ever mindful of her wings, I crush her to me in a massive hug. "Thank you!" I whisper.

She laughs, sputtering through tears as her arms wrap around my waist. She nods, head moving against my shoulder.

We pull apart, and she nudges me.

"I'll send a message to Ricardo. Go, tell Reginald, now."

Nodding, still crying, I take the stairs three at a time. I sprint the length of the hallway, mirth bubbling out of me.

She's alive.

She's alive!

They're all safe.

The tunnel blurs as more tears come, and I run faster. The stairs at the end come into view, and I leap up them.

"Reginald!" I say, bursting into his room, trusting Curata to have shielded us.

He jumps from his bed to stand before me, sheets falling to the floor. Panic shines in his eyes.

"She's alive!" I choke out.

He swallows, eyes filling with tears. One shaky hand rises to cover his mouth. "She's okay?"

"She's okay." I rush forward, wrapping him in my arms. "She's okay," I whisper.

He sobs against my chest, hands grasping the fabric of my shirt. "She's alive...." he says, words mangled by a harsh cry.

All the other things I need to tell him tumble into my mind, but not yet. I can tell him about the quarantine in a minute. I can tell him later that she's unconscious, that we'll have to set off Atlantis somewhere else so they wake her up just in case she hasn't finished her new program, that they'll start their tests as soon as she's awake.

But for now, he needs this.

I need this.

I tighten my arms around him, slipping a hand to the back of his head and cradling him against me.

Chapter Twenty-Two

Novay

Reginald

My fingers trace the delicate skin of
Rone's side, and I send a private message to
Curata, thanking her for the little tunnel that
connected us tonight. A shiver moves Rone's lithe
frame against mine, and I prop myself up to kiss
her neck.

I pull back with a smile on my face, staring
into eyes that glitter in the dim light. Lying back
down, I pull her tighter against me. She nestles in
close, lips soft on mine. The warmth of half sleep
flows through me, and my eyelids threaten to
close.

But I don't want to waste the little time we
have together by sleeping.

Too soon, she'll slip from my bed, put on
her clothes, and return to her complex. Too soon,
I'll be back to wondering when I'll see her again,
and there are already too many things I don't
know.

My heart twists in my chest as Krona's and Tenna's heroic attempt to save Olivia flashes through my mind once more. I take a deep breath, trying to shove the video from my mind.

Thinking about it won't do any good.

I can't save her.

I can't even talk to her.

"What is it?" Rone asks, voice gentle. She touches the space between my eyebrows with one finger.

Breathing deeply, I unfurrow my brows, easing the lines from my face. "Just… thinking of Olivia," I say, but my voice barely moves above a whisper.

Rone nods. Sliding one arm beneath my head, she pulls me toward her, and I wrap around her, head resting on her arm and one hand on her waist.

"Want to talk about it?" she asks.

Will it do any good?

I take a deep breath and give it a shot, knowing my brain won't move on either way.

"When are they waking her up?" I ask.

Rone sighs, then says, "Not for another week, at least." She shakes her head. "They won't lift the quarantine until they know she isn't the carrier for Atlantis, which… she is. Just not in the way they think. It won't just spread because she's here."

My heart splinters at the thought of Olivia, unconscious on some alien ship, cut off from everything, from everyone. I shudder, trying not to imagine what they might be doing to her. Rage curls my hand into a fist on Rone's waist.

She takes my balled hand in hers, unfurling my fingers, and raises it to her lips. "I know," she whispers.

And she just might.

Through all their communications, through all the videos she saw of Olivia before, with everything she knows about her… Rone has come to love Olivia. I just don't know if she's realized it yet.

"They won't proceed with the experiment until they're sure *tampering with her* won't unleash Atlantis on Novay, so at least there's that," Rone says.

I close my eyes as a sick sort of relief floods me.

Rone's thumb glides over the back of my hand as she says, "I just wish we knew if she was finished with the program they really need to worry about. And I wish we didn't have to force them to wake her up sooner. I…"

Her voice catches, but she tries again. "I don't want them to start their experiments on her. It'll just be a bunch of baseline tests for now, but… that doesn't mean it'll be pleasant. Blood and marrow samples, rigorous mental testing…"

Desperate for a different topic, I ask, "But why are Krona and Tenna still unconscious?"

"In case Atlantis *infected* them. The have Links. They could be carriers, too."

I laugh, but I shouldn't. I know the specifics of Atlantis, know how it actually works, know the level of programming it took to make it.

They don't, too afraid of spreading it to have delved into it. To them, it's just another volatile product of humanity, another thing that went awry.

And they have so much to lose, so much information gathered over millennia. Having chunks ripped out and scrambled and turned into wandering patches of static seems pretty terrible.

But they have no idea what they're in for when Olivia wakes.

Chapter Twenty-Three

Regonia

Ricardo

Dr. Sullivan fusses with my IV, and I try to check my temper. I know he means well, but the cockpit is too small for all of us. Hugo leans forward, peering around the IV pole and the smallest cart Dr. Sullivan could fit all his tools on.

"Did you see what I did there?" Hugo asks.

With a groan, I shake my head. I grit my teeth and take a deep breath.

My punctured lung protests, sending a lance of pain through me and reminding me that Dr. Sullivan needs to be here. He's already making concessions allowing me to be here instead of in the medbay.

But impatience wages war against my better judgment.

I need to get to her.

"I'll be out of your way soon," Dr. Sullivan says, deep voice vibrating in my chest. But the smooth calm normally found within his words is tinged with irritation. "It'll go faster if you just let me do this." He tosses one of his tools back onto the cart with a great deal less care than usual.

I blink in surprise.

I didn't think I was being that *difficult. I'm not... Am I?*

He's always so easygoing.

My ears burn, and I drop my gaze to the instrument panel before me. "Sorry," I say. "I know you're helping me. I don't mean to make this harder."

Dr. Sullivan sighs deeply, and I turn to look at him. He shakes his head, then rubs his hands over his dark face. "You're fine. I'm just..." Another sigh. "I'm worried. We should've had a message from someone by now."

He stares out the window, eyes locked on the sky, and my stomach drops into my boots. I try to hide from his words, but I know he's right. Olivia would've sent a message if she could. And we would have received it by now, even routed through other transmitters on Regonia. A message from Rone certainly should've reached us, if she had any clue what was going on.

But even knowing all of that… I still held out hope. I still had some stupid little crumb of hope in the back of my mind that maybe she was okay, maybe she was alive, just… I don't know, busy?

But hearing it from Dr. Sullivan makes my heart fracture. My breath hitches, sending pain rocketing through my chest. I grip the armrests of the pilot's seat, the seat where Olivia should be sitting. Fear slithers through my veins, icy and jagged.

Did they kill her?

The thought is small, quiet, but somehow, it echoes through every corner of me, tearing at every fiber of my being. My vision blurs with tears, and the mountains beyond the window shimmer and shift. The waving grasses join into one fluid mass.

A sob shakes me, and my lungs spasm with pain. I fall forward, head dropping into my hands. My elbows dig into my knees, and tears roll down my wrists. Guilt slides through me in cold waves. I choke on the sobs that shake my shoulders, and agony spears my chest, my lung, every time.

But a hand comes to rest on my back.

"We'll find her," Dr. Sullivan says, voice low and comforting. A fierce undercurrent of determination moves through his words as he adds, "We'll get them back."

He rubs my back, but to no avail.

"What if…" My voice falters, terrified that if I speak the words, they'll come true.

But I need to hear them, need to hear how absurd they sound.

Need someone to tell me I'm wrong.

"What if they killed her?" My words are small, stifled by the emotions they can't contain.

Dr. Sullivan's hand stills on my back.

My sobs echo off the walls of the cockpit. Fear rattles within me, sharp edges cutting me at every impact.

Olivia…

Our baby…

The treasonous thought doesn't seem smaller now that it's outside of me though, now that silence is my answer.

They can't be gone.

I imagine her, imagine Tenna and Krona, lost to some stupid asshole aliens, dead on some fucking ship in space or on a foreign planet.

And my world shatters.

Darkness looms, reaching toward me, pulling me in. A hollow pit opens within me, threatening to swallow me and turn me inside out.

"They wouldn't kill them," Hugo says beside me, voice too certain.

I shake my head, but I want him to be right, *need* him to be right. "How can you know that?" I croak, begging him for hope.

Already, my heart grasps his words, holding on for dear life.

"They're too practical for that. They want her for a reason. They may not have intended to take Tenna and Krona, but they apparently do all sorts of experiments. I'm sure they exhausted all the experiments they can do on dead bodies a long time ago." Anger creeps into his words. "They can only learn so much from the dead. The living are always changing, always developing. They won't kill them."

Tears of relief pour out, no matter how horrific the thought of her being experimented on may be. My lungs beg me to relent as a sob turns to a hiccup.

"I hope you're right," I whisper, sitting up.

I fall back in the pilot's chair with tears still cascading over my cheeks.

"I usually am," Hugo says.

His smile lights up my periphery, and a bark of laughter bursts from me. I shake my head, staring out at the rolling plains, the river, the mountains of Regonia.

She loved this view.

I just have to make sure she sees it again.

Wars have been waged over love as long as Humans have existed. Now, it's my turn to lead the charge.

I pull in a shaky breath, wincing as my lungs protest. Swiping at my tears, I steady myself.

"Sorry…" I whisper.

I try not to meet Hugo's or Dr. Sullivan's eyes.

"No need for that," Dr. Sullivan answers, voice thick with emotion.

I turn to face him then, and the tear tracks glistening on his dark skin shock me. A glance at Hugo finds tears shimmering in his eyes, too.

Nodding, I look out at the rays of sunlight peering around a solitary cloud.

"Dr. Sullivan?" I begin, suddenly curious. I could ask my Link, but I want to speak, want to stay out of my mind for a moment. "What's your first name?"

"Doctor," he says. "My parents had my career picked out from the start."

"That's…." I falter, unable to find the word for such a power move over an unsuspecting infant.

Deep, smooth laughter rumbles behind me, and I turn in my seat. Dr. Sullivan's eyes twinkle, and his face scrunches up with his mirth.

"My name is James," he says between gasps of laughter. "My parents wouldn't have done that to me. They were wonderful people."

I stare at him, this man who never jokes, and the corners of my lips turn up in a smile. In moments, I'm laughing right along with him, as is Hugo. My chest burns with the effort of it, but we revel in the joyous freedom of such absurdity for a few minutes longer.

Shaking my head, I press a hand to my chest and say, "God damn it."

Hugo and Dr. Sullivan, *James*, laugh harder, and my face folds itself back into the shape of a laugh, pulling me back in with them. Eventually, I calm myself, holding my face steady lest it crinkle again.

A deep breath sends a jolt of pain through me, but a soft chuckle follows in its wake regardless.

I steady myself once more. "When we get them back," I say, attempting courage and confidence, refusing to say *if we get them back*, "I think I might talk to Olivia about naming the baby after you. If it's a boy, that is."

"But James is such a lovely name for a girl," Hugo says.

And suddenly, my face is crinkling up again, all of its own accord. The relief of having an explanation to hold onto, a real hope of finding her alive, has me giddy.

But I know what name I think I'd like if the baby is a girl.

Cait.

***

I startle awake with a sharp, painful breath as three short beeps ring in my ear. My heart falters. A message from Rone waits on my Link, ready to destroy me or renew my purpose.

I rub a hand over my face, trying to steady myself, but my fingers tremble all the while. I sit up, palms sweating and stomach roiling.

I project the message onto a screen beside my bed in the medbay but don't play it. Not yet.

Curata's face stares at me from the screen, teary-eyed, but maybe smiling.

But is it a conciliatory smile? Or maybe pity?

Or is it good news?

I can't read her, haven't seen enough of her. It's always been Rone that contacted us.

Did something happen?

Why isn't it Rone?

This small woman with pale blue hair and fairy wings is a mystery, basically a stranger.

My lungs protest as I try to pull in a fortifying breath. Swallowing harshly, I grit my teeth and let the message play.

"We found them!" Curata says, right off the bat, and my eyes fill with tears. She covers her mouth, choking out a small sob. Tears shine on her sparkling skin, and she says, "They're alive! We found them!"

My insides collapse, and my head drops into my hands. My shoulders shake. Agony tears through me anew as sobs batter my still-healing lung, but still I cry.

Thank god...

Curata continues speaking on the screen, but I don't hear a word of it, don't care right now. All that matters is that they're alive. Olivia and our baby and Krona and Tenna are alive. Waves of relief pulse through me, and I shudder with the cries that rattle my ribs, the cries that shatter my lung.

She's alive.

A gentle hand on my shoulder pulls my attention outward, and I jerk up to find Dr. Sullivan, *James, call him James*, staring at me with concern.

"Is everything okay?"

I nod, unable to speak through a throat tight with emotion. Endeavoring to pay attention this time, I start the message over.

Her initial words catch my breath in my chest, tighten my throat. But this time, it doesn't reduce me to sobs.

She swipes at the tears on her face and says, "They're being quarantined on a ship, cut off from our network just in case they're carrying Atlantis like a plague."

A giggle escapes Curata, and a sharp breath bursts from me.

"They think it's a plague," I whisper, shaking my head. Because Olivia's plan worked.

"We don't know if Olivia finished her new program though," Curata continues, bright eyes tense. "If she did, then we can let them keep her unconscious for now. They won't experiment on her for the time being. If she didn't, we need your help to get them to wake her."

Curata sighs, eyes falling to her lap. She shakes her head.

"I hate the thought of dumping her into an experiment, but we need…" Her voice falters, cuts out. More tears fall over her iridescent cheeks. "She copied Atlantis to your Link, I believe. I hope she showed you what to do with it, just in case, and I hope she told you whether or not she was done with Alexandria."

A deep sigh lifts Curata's petite shoulders, and finally she looks up. I swallow nervously, racking my brain, trying to remember if Olivia was done.

"If she still had work to do, then you need to get them to wake her up."

My stomach drops. Eyes fluttering as horror dawns, I shake my head. "I don't… I can't."

My mouth goes dry.

If I get them to wake her, they'll just start the experiment. I can't… I can't be the one to…

The world blurs around me, and my poor, battered lungs work overtime, hitching and seizing, sending sharp jabs of pain through my body. My gaze falls, staring at Curata's fidgeting hands in her lap.

I open my mouth to speak, but nothing comes out.

Dr. Sullivan, *James*, puts a hand on my back. "Was she done with it?"

I shake my head, shoulders rising in a helpless shrug. "I… I don't know."

"I can do it," he says. "If you transfer Atlantis to me, if you show me how, I'll… I think I can manage it."

But I know I can't put that burden on him.

The weight of leading everyone in Krona and Tenna's absence falls squarely on my shoulders, and I sag beneath it. I never wanted to lead, never wanted this much responsibility or any of the attention these acts will undoubtedly cast upon me.

But I haven't had much choice lately.

I can't let innocent people suffer if I can do something about it. I can't stand by and watch the Drennar attack, over and over. I can't let them keep coming back, knowing Olivia has the means to stop them.

And I can't push a task onto Dr. Sullivan that I'm not strong enough to do myself.

I close my eyes, chest heaving with a deep breath. I rub my hands over my face, fingers tapping lightly over my skin as they tremble.

"No," I whisper. "I'll take care of it."

I listen to Curata's goodbyes, then replace her image with a map of Regonia. Then, I pull up images of the other two planets, Regonia 2 and 3, placing them alongside the first.

I set to work, isolating the best places to initiate Atlantis on those planets, ready to let it spread across those worlds just as quickly as it spreads over Regonia 1 right now.

Then, recalling the instructions Olivia walked me through, I set up the transmission and send it.

Chapter Twenty-Four
The Realm of Stars

Krona

A cold, grey ceiling looms overhead as my eyes flutter open. My head swirls, and I rub my hands over my face. Slowly, the battle filters back in. I grind my teeth, pull in a sharp breath.

Sitting up quickly, I take in the blank walls that surround me, the smooth floor and ceiling, the sleek box of a table near this weird bed. Everything, everywhere, the same blue-grey color.

And no one in sight.

Tenna.

Olivia.

Did our battered Warriors survive?

Ice water rushes through my veins, but my fingers curl inward, digging my nails into my palms. I get to my feet, moving two steps to the wall across from me. Desperate, I run my hands over the smooth, sleek walls.

No window. No door.

No way in or out.

What is this?

My heart pounds. I turn in place, surveying the dull sameness, so much worse than even the Human stations. My breath hitches as panic builds within me.

"Tenna?" I call out, but my voice only echoes back at me, ricocheting off the walls of this tiny room. I pace its length, turning on my heel every four steps. The walls seem to close in on me, but I count my steps every time.

Four steps.

The room isn't shrinking.

But my world is.

I swore I'd never be a prisoner again, swore I'd never be separated from Tenna and thrown in a damn cell ever again, but here I am. I scream at the futility of it all.

Fury roils within me, and it's so much worse now. This time, I know the monsters that have Tenna. I know the lengths they'll go to, know that they've just harvested every pregnant woman the Human race has to offer, stealing an entire generation of babies from a species still recovering from near-extinction.

From the reports we've garnered from Rone, I know they'll stoop to anything. Unleashing a maniac on a peaceful village on a far-off planet, psychological torment, pointing Olivia's mother in our direction just to see what she'd do... Nothing is too terrible for them.

What are they going to do to Tenna? To Olivia?

To me?

And we were finally about to bring them down. All our plans lie in a crumpled heap at my feet, and I can't stand to think of it.

"Tenna! Olivia!" I shout, spinning in slow circles.

I strain my ears, desperate to pick out anything, even a whimper.

But I hear nothing.

I swallow, trying to keep myself under control, but my muscles tense, aching to break something, to break *someone*. I grit my teeth and close my eyes, trembling with rage.

Letting out a slow breath, I move forward. My shoulders hike up, reaching for my ears as tension twists me. I shake my head, flex my fingers.

I've been here before.

I've been a captive.

A muscle in my jaw ticks at the word, but I can't deny my situation. Dropping on my bed, I stare at the pale grey wall before me, eyes unfocused.

I've been here before.

Maybe I don't have Ricardo to get me out, but I do have Rone.

Sprawling my hands on my knees, I unclench my jaw and remind myself that I just have to send her a message. I string together my best approximation of a calm message, but my Link only says, "No connection found."

My entire body tenses. I'm gripped with the urge to rip the damned thing from my arm and smash it to pieces, a desire I well remember from my first time as a prisoner. I pull a long, slow breath through my teeth, then release it in a hiss.

They'll look for me. They'll look for us.

Ricardo won't let this drop, and neither will our people or Rone or Reginald.

Focusing on my breathing, I hold tight to my sanity while I wait.

Chapter Twenty-Five
The Realm of Stars

Tenna

My eyes burst open, and panic spirals through me. I sit bolt upright, gaze darting around, searching for Krona, for Olivia, for the warrior with the missing arm.

But I find only grey walls.

I send messages to Krona and Olivia, to Rone and Reginald. But nothing goes through. My Link flashes error codes, and my stomach drops.

My heart hammers against my ribs, and my breath comes in short gasps. I spring to my feet, turning in a circle, as if somehow I could have missed something.

Where are they?

Soft grey sheets lay crumpled on the bed, hanging half on the floor. A sleek table waits beside it, but its alien nature balls my hands into fists.

"WHERE ARE THEY?" I scream, gathering the sheet into my hands.

I try to rip it, but the strange fabric is too strong, even for me. Rage burns me, scorching my veins. My hands shake, and wordless screams erupt from me. Whipping the sheet back down, I slam a foot into the stupid little table, fully expecting it to break, *needing* it to break.

But it doesn't budge, doesn't even bend.

Rushing forward, I slam my balled-up hands against the wall, shouting all the while, "What is this? Where are they?"

My face contorts, scrunching into a primal mask of fury as I scream, "What have you done? You monsters!"

Reason deserts me, and tears stream down my face as lava courses through my veins. I drive my fist into the wall, over and again, breaking the skin of my knuckles. Tiny sparks of pain filter through the haze, but they don't clear my head.

Every hit leaves a smear of blood on the wall. Every impact opens my knuckles a little bit more.

And still, it doesn't give.

My mind fills with thoughts of Krona, locked away from me yet again. I wonder how he could have withstood this torment, the not knowing, without destroying himself and everyone around him.

Because all I want is to destroy this entire world.

I want to burn it, send so much electricity through it that they all fry.

They will regret the day they came for us.

My lips curl into a snarl, and I slam my fist home once more. A jolt of pain races up my arm, and I stop, fearing for my bones if I continue.

The wall still stands, unbroken, undented.

I shove my hands into my hair and scream, calling out our battle cry, but Krona doesn't answer. Wherever he is, he can't hear me.

If they hurt him, I will tear this place to pieces with my bare hands.

I slam my fists against the wall again.

If they hurt Olivia, I'll rip them apart.

My fist hits the wall again, but this time, it moves. My blood smears slide outward, moving with the entire wall.

I step back, disoriented, as the wall disappears within itself, revealing a long gray hall and two Drennar. They stand, staring at me with emotionless eyes. Blue lines and circles move within their green irises, and it sends a shudder down my spine.

I grit my teeth, dig my nails into my palms.

These monsters have too many arms, have scaly patches on their necks. Horns protrude from their skulls, just this side of the clear plates that make up the backs of their heads. My eyes dart over them, searching for weaknesses.

And then, I launch myself at them.

I knock one back, rushing into the hall. The other charges me, just as I'd hoped. I reach up, taking its horns into my hands, pulling them down, and using its momentum to drive them into the other Drennar's chest.

Blood seeps out around them, but I don't give them the chance to move. I jump into the air, driving my elbow down into the back of the bent Drennar's neck, eliciting a satisfying snap and forcing its horns to tear through its fellow as it buckles.

They crumple, and adrenaline courses through me. I smile at the carnage I've wrought, then turn to move down the hall.

I don't know if there's a network, if we're connected at all, if there's any easy way to do this.

But I'm going to find them.

The wall at the end of the hall slides open, and two more Drennar step through. These two have no mouths, no noses. Strange mesh things occupy their faces instead, and horror slithers through me.

What abomination is this?

I grit my teeth.

It doesn't matter. I'll take them out two at a time if I have to.

The wall closes behind them, and a tiny hole opens in the ceiling. Air hisses through, too sweet, too familiar.

Bellona.

These damned cowards.

My hands tremble with rage, and I rush them, determined to take at least one of them down before the Bellona puts me under. I drive my shoulder into the chest of the one on the left, but all four of his arms wrap around me. The other one moves behind me, wrapping arms around its companion and sandwiching me in.

They squeeze until the air rushes out of me, then release just a bit, just enough for my body to betray me and gulp in a huge breath of Bellona. I drive my elbows into a stomach, slam my forehead into the spot where a nose should be.

But they squeeze me tight again, forcing me to exhale. Every last bit of air whooshes out of me. Another involuntary breath pulls in Bellona, and darkness closes in.

My head swims, lolling forward.

My eyelids fall shut.

Chapter Twenty-Six

Regonia

Ricardo

I lie atop the roof of a small cottage, staring at the sky. A massive blue moon looms above, framed by stars.

But it isn't a moon, not really.

It's Novay.

And somewhere in its orbit, Olivia waits for me.

Have they woken her up yet?

I breathe deeply, tinged by a mild ache in my chest, and reach my hand up toward her. Stars shine between my fingers, and I feel like I can almost reach them.

And that feeling isn't wrong.

I'm so close. My training with Hugo has been going well. We're almost ready to try taking off.

"I'll be there soon," I whisper, willing my words to carry to her, to resonate within her heart.

A few tears fall, rolling down over my temples to pool in my ears. I shake them away so I can hear the world around me, the world Olivia fell in love with so quickly.

She said she felt more like she was part of the stars here than in the cockpit of Sparrow.

And with the stars sparkling just beyond my fingertips, with no glass or metal between me and them, I get it.

"I'll bring you back here," I whisper. "I'll bring you and Krona and Tenna and everyone else back."

A thought strikes me, and I chuckle, wondering how much chaos Krona and Tenna are sowing, even now. They must have figured out that we're all more valuable to the Drennar alive than dead.

And the thought of their vengeance spilling blood on that ship makes me smile.

To them, I say, "I'll bring you your Warriors, your Soldiers. We'll finish this together."

Quiet determination blossoms in my chest, and I watch the stars for a few more quiet moments before climbing down from the roof to turn in for the night. I'll be awake early in the morning, back in the cockpit with Hugo.

I meander through swaying grasses, running my hands over their velvety blades. Moonlight sparkles on the distant river, shines on the planes of the crystalline mountain peaks. This place has a pulse, a rhythm, like no ship could ever have, like Termana could never have, and my heart beats in time with it.

I approach the ship, a lone sentinel in a serene field. Its panels gleam in the moonlight, making even this massive metal beast seem a part of this place.

I look to the stars again, and say, "Goodnight, Olivia. I'll see you soon."

Chapter Twenty-Seven

Novay

Rone

"Can we do anything?" I ask, trying to keep a plaintive tone from seeping into my voice.

Curata leans forward, elbows on knees and chin resting in cupped hands. "I'm trying to set up a private network," she says. "But I'll have to make sure they don't know it even exists." Her brows furrow, and her face contorts as she chews at the inside of her cheek.

"Maybe something like Atlantis?" I suggest.

"I haven't tried to deconstruct it yet," Curata says. "I didn't want to try, just in case they override our new privacy settings. They know things aren't as they seem on Termana, but they still don't know what's going on down on Regonia. I don't want to risk handing them a way to break Olivia's program."

Sighing, she says, "Let me take a look at it."

I wait with drumming fingers, listening to the tapping of Lustran's toes. My nerves wind tight, and a sick weight drops into my stomach.

"It's pretty sophisticated," Curata says. "It'd probably take me a day or two to crack it..."

Her eyebrows raise, and a short breath rushes past her lips. "Maybe a week."

My chest swells with pride.

Good going, Olivia.

"How long did it take her to make this?" Curata asks, awe clear in her tone.

"I'd have to figure it up," I say. "She didn't put every second of every day into it like one of us would have."

Humans have jobs, lives. They have to stop frequently to eat, and they sleep far longer than we do. And they have emotions that demand the company of others. Once assigned, a Drennar puts every second into their project with the exception of our recharge time, which is brief.

Curata nods, knowing all of this without me saying. I half wonder if she's calculating Olivia's time invested, but I don't ask.

"Whatever she's making for us, given how much time she had to work on it during their trip to Regonia..." Curata blows out a breath. "It's gonna be one hell of a program."

I smile at her choice of words, so Human of her. Tears prick the corners of my eyes, and I marvel at what Olivia has accomplished. My throat tightens, and I swallow hard.

After everything she's been through...

She's amazing.

I take a deep breath and wipe away a stray tear.

She's a force to be reckoned with.

And she'll be awake soon.

Chapter Twenty-Eight
The Realm of Stars

Olivia

My eyes flutter open to a diffuse light. Slate grey surrounds me, closes me in. No windows. No door. Every surface, even the bed I lie on, is the same faded denim color, all-encompassing and unyielding.

What the…

It all comes back, slamming into me like a ton of bricks. The muffled sounds of battle seeping in through the stone walls of the armory. The crash of a Drennar hurtling through the wall. The screams of the other women sequestered with me.

Ricardo's screams, the sight of him falling, bloody and broken.

The terror of being snatched up and the wind whipping my hair against my face as I fought against the Drennar's hold, his blood seeping onto me from around my knife.

My heart leaps into my throat as I recall the impact when Tenna and Krona grabbed his legs, how we dipped in the air.

But we're not on Regonia anymore.

Flashes of blood and a blue-gray dome closing over us, slicing through the flesh of the bodies around us, living or dead, fill my mind. My stomach turns as I remember holding pressure on the fallen warrior's stump of an arm, and bile rises in my throat.

And then…

My head jerks around, searching for the monsters that looked in at us, the creatures that put me to sleep. But I find no mask faces.

Or anyone, for that matter.

Panic builds within me, and my heart races.

I'm alone.

My hand goes to my belly, and suddenly, I wish I were further along, far enough to feel the baby move, to know it's in there.

They wouldn't take it… Would they?

Terror washes through me, cold and slimy. My vision narrows to a tunnel, and my shoulders shake with harsh breaths.

I try to send a message to Ricardo, to Tenna or Krona. To Rone.

Nothing.

My mouth goes dry.

I've never been cut off before. I've always had access to a network, had some way to reach out to others. Even if I didn't necessarily want to, the option was there.

But now, I have nothing.

I'm on an alien planet, a hostile *alien planet, and they're going to experiment on me and the baby, and all I can do is sit here in this tiny bed and wait for it to happen.*

They're going to come for me, and they're going to hurt me.

And I'll never see Ricardo again.

They don't have enough pilots to get here, to get home.

And then, another fear grips me.

What if Ricardo didn't make it?

Everything in me screeches to a halt, and my breathing grows ragged. I gasp for air as panic overwhelms me. My hands thread into my hair, and I hunch forward, drawing my knees up to cradle my head. Tears roll over my cheeks as horrors spiral in my mind, a revolving carousel of agony.

What are they going to do to me?

All Rone could come up with was what she called baseline measurements, the least of which is the collection of tissue samples and rigorous mental testing. But it ranged to strenuous physical testing.

My heart stutters at the thought of being pushed to run to my limit, just to see how far I can go. My lungs falter at the thought of the invasive bodily exams she mentioned.

I can't do this.

I can't do this. I can't.

I slide from my bed, but where can I go? I pace the length of my little cage in just a few steps. I barely have room to step around the little table beside my bed, not that I even need a table.

Why do I have a table?

I fixate on that, desperate for anything to focus on, anything to take my mind off the looming indecencies and hardships. Stooping, I run a hand over the surface of it, trying to see only it, only the smooth gray material.

I jump when a section slides away, and two small orbs rise from its depths on a plate of slate gray. They shine, clear and pure, in the light that comes from everywhere and nowhere.

My mind latches onto the distraction, and I let it run away with curiosity. Reaching out, I pick one up, holding it, testing its weight. The slick ball slips from my grasp, splashing water on my foot when it hits the floor.

But it's so alien that it threatens to push me over the edge again.

I rub a hand over my face, closing my eyes. Taking a deep breath, I sit back down on my bed.

My stomach churns uneasily, and anger heats my blood. But resolution builds within me, and my hand comes to rest on my stomach.

I will make them pay for this.

I'll take them down, one way or another.

***

I lay in bed, eyes closed but mind working away. The dismal grey room disappears as I put the finishing touches on my little gift for these assholes. I let the rage simmer in my gut, right beside the baby I'll never let them take from me.

My hand moves to my stomach for what feels like the millionth time since I woke up here, a protective gesture I hadn't indulged in before. Back when I felt safe. Back when I had people around to help protect this child.

Now, it all falls on me, and I'll be damned if I turn out like my selfish, negligent mother.

But can I do it?

Can I keep this baby safe all by myself?

A message comes through, pinging softly within my mind, but my Link doesn't light up, doesn't make a sound. My heart leaps into my throat. I don't dare to hope, but my breath catches.

I just forgot to turn off an alarm or something.

That's all it is.

But I know better. My alarms don't sound like that. They're louder, more insistent, to make sure I don't drink through them.

I take a deep breath, then check. A message waits for me. From Rone. My mouth goes dry, and a tiny bit of hope seeps back in. I check and find a private network, heavily encrypted, but very present.

I'm not completely cut off.

I'm not alone.

Tears prick at the corners of my eyes, and I jam my palms into them. A sob bubbles up, ripping me wide open. I shake with the effort of holding it in, and another sob rushes out. I gasp, stomach clenching as all my bravado fades.

Because I know taking on the entirety of the Drennar race by myself would have been foolish, impossible. I knew I had to try, knew I couldn't just hand the baby over, hand myself over, without a fight.

But the doubts, the terror, never disappeared.

Gritting my teeth, balling my hands in my hair, I force myself to breathe. A million questions buzz through my head, clamoring to find their way into a message for Rone, but I force myself to be calm.

In the message, Rone explains how Curata set up the network, how she hid it. Then, she lays out a plan to use my presence here to our advantage and says, "Tenna's already taken care of part of it."

I watch as a smile spreads over her features, painted so crisply on the backs of my eyelids. Her eyes sparkle and the electric blue striations within them shift.

"And then, there's Ricardo," she says, voice warm.

My heart freezes. My mind fills with his screams as the Drennar carried me away, the screams that stopped not long after.

I take a steadying breath, trying to prepare myself for whatever happened to him, but my lungs stutter, hitching and heaving. My hands tremble, and I knot them together on my stomach.

Please, let him be okay.

"He sustained a few injuries, a broken rib, a punctured lung," Rone says, and I gasp. "They found him quickly though. He's healing nicely."

Air rushes out of me, and tears spring forth once more.

He's okay.

My heart soars, and I choke back a sob.

Will I ever see him again?

On the backs of my eyelids, Rone's smile widens. "And he just so happens to be learning how to fly your ship. Want to see?"

She pauses, and I nod, stupidly. Because of course, she can't see me.

"I'm kidding," she says, and for a moment, I hate that I got my hopes up, hate that I thought she was going to show me Ricardo. But she continues, "I know you can't answer me. I'll just show you anyway."

And suddenly, I see him, pulling an IV from his arm and storming out of the medbay. My hand comes to rest on my open mouth, and shock spreads through me as I watch him demand to be taught to fly, assuring Dr. Sullivan gruffly that he can rest in the cockpit.

My heart skips a few beats, and laughter escapes me on a breath. Tears flow freely.

I'll see him again.

We can raise the baby together, like we planned.

Determination steals over me, cementing my resolve. There's a lot I have to do before he gets here.

But knowing he's coming makes it so much easier.

249

Chapter Twenty-Nine
The Realm of Stars

Krona

Rone's words repeat in the back of my mind. I close my eyes, working through what I need to accomplish. Careful to keep my smile contained, I rise from my bed.

My heart thuds in my chest, overjoyed to finally know that Tenna and Olivia are okay, that they're safe, that Ricardo is healing.

And now, I have a job to do, a purpose.

Pacing, I flex my hands at my sides and mutter under my breath. No words, only nonsense, gibberish. Recalling my time in captivity on Ulysses Station, I long to flood my room with angry music, to sink into it, to really confuse the Drennar.

But the speakers of my Link will have to suffice.

"Lose Yourself by Our Last Night. 2021." Plays. It's a favorite of Olivia's, a holdover from the angry days of her youth. It fills the room, and my heart speeds along, keeping pace with its beat. I let its tension build within me, let the frenetic energy, the heaviness of it, carry me along.

My mind fills with the day the Drennar brought us here, the blood spilled, the people lost, the homes destroyed. My fingers curl into claws, and I ache for a Drennar to appear before me so that I might bring them low.

My footsteps grow heavier, bordering on stomps, and I turn the music up. The walls of this narrow room seem to close in, a far cry from the open fields I want to roam through, *should* be roaming through.

Tension pulls my muscles into knots, winds my nerves tight.

And now, it's time to give them a show.

Rage burns through me, and instead of controlling it, instead of letting it fester until I can face them, I smash the bed before me, dropping fists down upon it. It creaks, one side caving beneath the force of my attack.

Grabbing the edge, I harness every bit of strength I possess, putting my legs into it. I scream with the effort, throat burning and face contorting.

But it moves.

I push up harder, ripping the metal bed from its wall, tipping the mattress and blankets to the floor. Fury burns through my lungs, up my throat. I drive the jagged metal into the wall, throwing my weight into it. A dent appears but quickly smooths over.

Fury scorches my veins.

Slamming the crumpled metal bed to the floor, I wrench the table free of the wall, leaving a jagged tear in its place. It begins to smooth over, but I reach in, grabbing the edges and tearing them back. A strange buzzing moves over my skin, small and unpleasant.

But I let it fuel the fires raging within me.

With one last burst of will and strength, I rend the space open, just far enough to crawl through. My breaths come fast as I rise to my full height on the other side of the wall.

No Drennar wait to greet me.

But I'll find them.

I quell my music and stare into the grey abyss of a hallway. A dark smile turns the corners of my lips upward, and silent footsteps carry me forward, slinking, listening.

No voices reach through walls or around corners.

No one approaches.

With the map Rone provided, I don't need them to. It would've been easier to face them apart, to split them up, but it isn't necessary. Even now, I can see them upon the map, six pale blue dots. I turn down one hall, then another, weaving toward the outer edge of the ship where one is alone.

These monsters kidnapped us.

They took Olivia's dad.

They took so many people.

Chills run over my spine at the thought of what they might do to Olivia if we fail, what they might do to Daen Tribe in the future.

What they might do to Tenna.

I close the distance quickly, fighting to keep myself from sprinting. I check the time, wondering why they haven't come for me yet.

Are they afraid?

Do they even understand fear?

Have they any idea what they've done?

I breathe deeply, taking the last few steps toward the solitary Drennar's compartment. A message from Tenna pings in my ear, and I smile.

She's ready.

A message from Olivia comes through, and my heart quickens.

It's time.

The wall slides open at Rone's command.

I step through, jaw falling as I gape at the monstrosity before me. A Drennar sits, wires and hoses extending from its body and disappearing within the walls and panels of the ship. Every line pulses with soft blue light.

When its eyes land on me, a quick burst of pulses pour out of it, descending into the ship floor, resonating outward in ripples. A message of some sort, but Rone warned us of this.

I move forward with a smile on my face. With practiced ease, I snap its neck in one swift motion, pulling cables and cords tight.

The pulsing blue lights stop, and darkness falls.

Chapter Thirty
The Realm of Stars

Tenna

The wall slides open before me, and I step through, eyes passing the inert form of the Drennar easily, skipping to Krona. He steps away from his kill, eyes landing on me, and my heart flutters.

I dart around the dead alien, our dead ancestor, and wrap my arms around him, one hand tangling in his dark hair and the other clutching at his back. He pulls me tighter against his chest, pressing his lips to mine.

The days apart, locked in separate cages on this ship with no way to know if he was alive, wore heavily on me. Now, his mouth moves feverishly, mirroring my own desperation.

My breath catches, and I pull back, hands moving to cup his face. My eyes roam over him, assessing, assuring myself that he isn't harmed. All of Rone's assurances fall to the wayside, good intentioned as they may have been. I need to see him, need to feel him and know that he's safe. By the way his eyes dart over me, he must feel the same way.

Our gazes meet, frantic and searching. Our chests rise and fall quickly, moving in time as we each gasp our relief.

He's here.

He's safe.

I lean my forehead against his, moving one hand to his neck and letting the other slide to his chest. Gently clasping my neck, he lets out a long, slow breath.

I draw on his strength, letting him lean into mine, and for a long moment, we simply support each other. We breathe together, bodies attuning to one another again.

"Hoo kai voo mai," I whisper.

"Hoo kai voo mai," he answers, and I drink in the husky rasp his low voice holds.

But we haven't time for what that tone implies.

He meets my gaze and nods once.

Drawing in a deep breath, I pull back, slipping my hand into his. Without another look at the Drennar hardwired into the ship, we move through halls sneaking toward our remaining jailers.

My heart races, exhilarated by the promise of doing something, of finally moving forward after days locked up. I take a deep breath, filling my lungs near to bursting.

Krona squeezes my hand as we approach the room they wait in, and then we separate, pressing ourselves to the wall. A ping marks the time Rone designated, and she slides the section of wall between us open.

We wait.

A few heartbeats pass, and I listen, straining my ears for any change within the room. I listen for breathing, for words.

For footsteps.

A body moves closer, stepping lightly, precisely, across the floor. Another follows, this one larger. Another. And Another. They pause just inside the door, too smart to step into our trap.

A smile lifts my lips as the alonarium at my feet shifts, forming a dagger for me at Curata's or Rone's will. Four solid thuds resound from the room beyond as she ripples the floor beneath them, then slides them out to us, one by one.

A body slips free of the room, thrust out a little faster than I expected, and I drive my dagger down into its waiting neck. The alonarium bucks beneath it, tossing it down the hall the moment my blade comes free. Blood spatters over the walls, drips onto the floor, lending color to the otherwise blank space.

She slides the next one out, and Krona dispatches the creature quickly. My breath catches at the sight of its face, eyes perched above a strange mesh in place of nose and mouth.

But Curata sends it flying down the hall with a carefully controlled jolt through the floor, stealing it from my sight. She sends the third out to meet us, a petite thing similar to the one who attempted to calm me without Bellona, the ones I already killed.

My blade sinks into her neck with ease, and blood gushes beneath it. I jerk my arm free, and Curata clears her away.

Krona dispatches the final monstrosity, and we peek inside the room. Four pedestals stand, smooth and unadorned. Nothing else. No personal items, no sentimental objects.

These creatures care naught for their own lives, for anything beyond the next haul of information.

My stomach sours at the thought.

Catching Krona's gaze, I say, "Ready?"

He nods, and we turn away, meandering through pools of blood and stepping over bodies. Curata will take care of them.

We have a friend to greet.

Chapter Thirty-One
The Realm of Stars

Olivia

I lean against Tenna, relaxing into the arm she drapes over my shoulder. But the body before me waits.

I swallow, and though I drop my gaze, my stomach roils. I close my eyes when the baby threatens to send the tiny morsels I've eaten here back up for a second appearance.

"I have to interface… with a dead body?" I whisper.

"Think of him as a computer," Rone says, video call shining from the wall. "They did. He did. He was modified to keep everyone connected and informed throughout the ship as a sort of… analog computer."

"Won't he start to decay? I don't think I'll be able to keep from puking if it starts to smell."

Already, I can't bear to look at him, to see the way the hoses disappear beneath his skin, to trace the paths of wires winding through his body, just beneath the skin. My stomach revolts at the thought of what might ooze from him in the coming days.

I look to the screen, hoping to see some sort of solution on Rone's face.

But Curata leans in behind Rone on the screen, saying, "I'll take care of that." In an instant, an alonarium box forms around him. "Does that help?"

I nod.

I'll just have to pretend he isn't in there.

I'll pretend he's just a big computer.

I swallow roughly.

Tenna asks, "Will this work once he starts to decay?"

"We only need him for a day or so, just long enough to get everything back online," Rone answers.

I step around the box, ignoring the multitude of cables that snake out of it, seamlessly blended into it, into the floor. I watch as the wall reforms. A control panel takes shape, bending free of the wall, morphing to include buttons and switches. I stare at it in awe, thrilled at the prospect of using it.

But confusion settles over me.

Glancing up at the screen before me, I ask, "Will we actually need this?" I'd been operating under the assumption that I'd just interface with everything through my Link.

"It isn't necessary," Rone says. She smiles and adds, "But I thought you might like it. I'll have to teach you how to fly this thing. I could do it remotely, but even with such short delays in transmissions as we have from here to orbit, if anything goes wrong, it won't be fixed as quickly as if you fly it."

"I want to learn," I rush to say.

"I thought you would," Rone says, and warmth glitters in her eyes, something akin to… pride?

I falter before it.

She wants to teach me, likes that I want to learn, and she's…

Is she proud of me?

The soft tilt of her lips, the light in her eyes… It looks almost like the proud moms in all the old movies I used to watch. But no one's looked at me like that in years. More than a decade.

I take a deep breath, forcing a smile through the tears that prick at the corners of my eyes.

A seat materializes before the controls, carefully positioned with the back facing the box and the dead Drennar it contains. I settle into it, letting my hands trail over the control panel before me.

Joy bubbles up within me at the thought of piloting a ship like this. It's so much more advanced than anything we have, anything we could produce in the next millennia.

Holy shit, I get to fly this thing.

Drawing strength from a long, deep breath, I glance up at the screen before me. "Ready for me to sync?"

Rone nods, and I access the modified version of Atlantis stored on my Link, carefully stripped of the section of code that sends out a scrambled version of all surveillance footage. It retains only the protection hidden behind that smokescreen.

Unleashing it upon the ship, I wait only a few seconds for it to take hold, smiling all the while. A sigh of relief escapes me with that extra level of protection. The Drennar here weren't meant to report in for another few weeks, but this way, we can do what we need to without fear.

Chapter Thirty-Two
Regonia

Ricardo

"Ready?" Hugo asks, voice carefully modulated to hide the nerves that must coil tightly in his stomach, just as they do in mine.

I swallow hard, hoping I've had enough practice. Closing my eyes, I take a deep breath. Whether I've had enough practice or not, we can't wait any longer.

I've flown before.

I've taken off from Termana, from stations.

But my attempts to comfort myself fall short of the mark. It's been a long time since I've flown anything, and even then, it was a smaller craft. Not to mention the lack of an atmosphere to deal with.

A quick spark of pain riots through me as I fill my lungs, and I try not to think of how many lives are on this ship. I run through the mental checklist, over and again, taking no solace from the manuals downloaded to my Link or the hours and hours of instructional videos I've watched.

"Ready?" Hugo asks again, voice slightly less even.

My mouth goes dry, but I nod. I'm not. I may never be ready for this. But I say, "Let's get this done."

Hugo makes the announcements over the intercom, warning everyone of the forces the launch will have on our bodies. He sits in the pilot's seat, Olivia's seat, hands moving without hesitation over the controls.

And I play my part.

My head fills with every scrap of knowledge I've absorbed since vowing to learn to fly this damn thing, and my hands spring to action, pressing buttons, sliding levers.

Hugo signals me when he's ready for more power to the thrusters, and I oblige, easing into it, responding to his commands.

He adjusts the stabilizers as we lift a few meters off the ground, and my heart lodges itself in my throat. I try to swallow it down, try to push air past it. Olivia finds her way into my head, and I find myself wishing she were here, wishing our plans hadn't been forced to change.

"Ricardo?" Hugo asks, his tone making it evident that he's issued this particular command more than once.

Focus.

"I need more power to the thrusters."

I oblige, and we rise higher. The plains beyond the window fall away with dizzying speed.

Eyes on the panels.

Don't look out there.

Hugo is steering. He won't let us hit the mountain. Just watch the altitude, watch the life support systems, watch the maintenance monitoring systems.

I stare down at the controls, at my hands moving over them. I take in the gauges, the meters measuring nearly every atom on this ship.

My heart beats a frantic pace, but we lift higher into the sky, sending the numbers before me skyrocketing. Slowly, gently, Hugo tips us up, adjusting the direction of the thrusters as he does so.

Regonia disappears, and the sky opens to swallow us, enveloping everything. The ship creaks, but no alarms sound. All gauges appear within normal limits.

Hugo counts down, and my nerves wind tighter.

"Three, Two, One."

He works his side of the controls, doing God knows what, and I push the thrusters to full. I slam back into my seat, body protesting against the force of take-off. The ship shudders, and I fight to keep from closing my eyes.

I ignore the haze of the atmosphere on our window, eyes glued to the control panel. I check the shields, the life support, the safety harnesses of all our passengers.

All good.

All engaged.

I swallow hard, shaking in my seat.

But we burst through the atmosphere and the shuddering stops. Stars sparkle around us, and Novay looms large on the horizon. My vision closes into a tunnel, fixing on a single point on Novay, and darkness consumes everything else.

My heart beats a frantic pace, battering my poor lungs. My breaths come in sharp gasps. All sound disappears, blocked by the roar of my own blood.

Hugo's hand finds mine, pulling it back, easing up on the thrusters. "It's okay, now," he says. "The hard part is done."

I nod, but my vision doesn't clear, my heart doesn't slow. My lungs struggle to find air, and I barely notice the movement of my hand, slowing us down at Hugo's command. Numb, I blink over and over, staring at numbers that suddenly don't make sense anymore.

"Ricardo," Hugo says, words breaking through the fog in my mind. "I can take it from here. Take a walk, come back in a few hours. James is on the way to come check on you. He'll find you."

"James?" I whisper.

"Dr. Sullivan."

A shuddering breath rocks through me, and I shake my head. "A walk," I say. "Okay."

Unbuckling my harness with trembling hands, I try to blink my vision clear. I rub a hand over my face, mind filling with Olivia's excited chatter about getting to take off from a planet.

She's crazy.

But a smile spreads over my face.

Somehow, she would've loved that.

***

I return to the cockpit with a level head, settling in beside Hugo. He turns to me with a sympathetic smile.

"I was pretty nervous when we left Termana," he offers. "I'd never flown with so many lives in my hands before. It's..." He takes a deep breath, returning his attention to the stars beyond the window, to Novay looming large ahead. "It's terrifying."

I laugh, shocked. "You were so calm."

"On the outside," he says with a self-deprecating laugh. "On the inside, I was on the verge of shitting myself."

I shake my head, chuckling.

"You did well," Hugo says. "She'd be impressed."

My heart swells, and the corners of my eyes prick. A lump forms in my throat.

Sitting back in the co-pilot seat, I stare into the abyss, recalling Olivia's words about feeling small in the best possible way, like our problems aren't quite so daunting as we thought. But our problems keep getting bigger, spreading to more and more planets, stealing that illusion from me.

Silence descends on Hugo and me, letting me consider the planet hanging above us. The lights of the cockpit compete with the view beyond, and I find myself wishing for the darkness Olivia prefers to fly with. My lungs fill with a deep breath.

"Want to take over for a little while? Get some practice in?" Hugo asks.

My nerves coil into knots, but I nod. The smaller crafts of my youth were always easier to control in space than they were during docking or launching. Not to mention the decided lack of things to run into.

This should be easier than take off, at least.

"If you can handle a launch, you can handle this," Hugo says, affirming my suspicions.

Sitting forward, I let myself fall into the ship and its inner workings, its magic. Handing control over in phases, Hugo eases me in, but suddenly, my heart soars at the thought of this strange communion with Olivia.

"Mind if I shut the lights off?"

Rather than answer, Hugo switches them off for me, and instantly, I breathe easier.

The grey and blue striations of Novay seem brighter without the lights here competing for my attention. The electric blue glows faintly, vivid and breathtaking.

If only it weren't home to monsters.

I tip my head to the side, considering it as I maintain the controls at my fingertips. Olivia's words drift out of my memory, long forgotten and hidden away in a dark corner.

"I don't have much faith in humanity, but our ability to destroy things is undeniable," she had whispered. "We can break the Drennar. We just don't know how, yet. Or how many lives it'll cost us."

A remnant of her days before her suicide attempt, they ring with hopelessness that smacks me across the face. But now isn't the time to struggle with guilt over not seeing it in time to spare her.

Because she was right.

We'll break them, somehow. We'll figure it out. And now, it's time for me to do my part.

Turning to Hugo, I say, "I have to record a message real quick."

The camera monitoring our cockpit blinks, focusing on me at a command from my Link, and I begin.

"Steel yourself. School your features so my words to you do not give us away," I begin, rather unceremoniously. But it's necessary. "We're coming, but we need your help."

"We need you to help distract the Drennar. Their first reaction when confronted with something they don't understand is to observe. If every Human they've captured becomes docile, it'll stand out. They'll observe you, hopefully instead of observing the skies."

My face falls at the prospect of some of the experiments that Olivia's father has been through, and I shudder at the implications it may hold for these poor people. "I know this will be harder for some of you to do. I don't know the full breadth of the experiments they've been conducting on you all, but… We need help to bring you home. For a short time, be compliant, be numb, be ambivalent. As close to catatonic as you can get."

I lift my gaze to the camera. "Then, the next time you see me, when you hear the music, fight them with everything you have. They won't kill you. We're more valuable to them alive. They might incapacitate you, but they won't outright kill you if given any choice."

"We have a plan," I say, hoping there won't be too many wrenches thrown into the gears in the coming days. "I hope we can bring you all home soon."

I start to end the recording, but I hesitate. Knowing that this message will go to *every* Human on or near Novay, I look back to the camera.

"Olivia… I'm coming for you." Tears form in my eyes, and I swallow. "I love you."

I end the recording and send it to Rone for distribution with a program to show it only when the person in question is alone, trusting her to get it to Olivia as well. Beside me, Hugo wipes a tear away. In my periphery, I watch the highlights of his shadowed form, see him nod slowly.

Chapter Thirty-Three
Novay

Reginald

In the center of my room, I stand with my arms out and my head tipped back. With eyes closed, I turn in small circles, listening to "Poster Boy by Unlike Pluto. 2021."

I revel in the knowledge that Olivia will be here soon, that she's safe now. Tears roll over my cheeks, and a weight falls from my shoulders.

This is such a dangerous place for her to venture into, but she's been through so much, *handled* so much. And she's a far better person than I ever could've imagined.

And she didn't need me for a damn bit of it.

Olivia didn't need me. She didn't need her mother either, for that matter.

A sigh pulls my shoulders down, but I know it's true. And it's time I accept it. I turn the music up louder, trying to drown out the world.

All this time, I've been beating myself up for not doing better for her, for not doing better for everyone...

But what good could I have done?

I stop turning in place, arms falling to my sides.

I'm not as important as I like to think.

I pull in a deep breath, then let it go. Settling on the floor, I crumple beneath the weight of realization.

"I've done nothing..." I whisper.

Olivia, Rone, Ricardo, Krona, Tenna... They've all gone to bat for this. They've gone to war.

And I've done... this.

I look around my room. The walls that never truly change. even when a Drennar slides a panel away. The sleek table that offers water globes at my command. The bed that swallows me up every night.

And everywhere, grey. Dull and uninteresting. Plain and unimportant.

Just like me.

Again, I sigh. Again, I contribute nothing to the effort to save Humanity, to save the Regonians.

Falling back, I sprawl and stare at the ceiling. My eyes come unfocused, and the world blurs around me, turning to a grey smudge. I turn the music up louder, aching to push the thoughts from my head, to cloud everything and forget how insignificant I am.

Time stretches on, and I pay it no mind, listening to the song without hearing it. The sounds crash around me, vibrate the floor beneath me. But it's just sound, just noise.

I close my eyes, and all the worlds fade away. Darkness replaces the cold grey room, and I take solace in it. My arms reach over my head, stretching out, but the oversized room holds the walls too far from my fingertips.

But after years of this room, it doesn't unsettle me.

It's just one more sign of my insignificance, one more sign of how little I matter in the grand scheme of things.

The floor ripples beneath me, a strange sensation that makes little sense, unaccounted for by the music. But my mind doesn't hold it, doesn't bother to find a reason. I fade into nothingness again, falling into the obscurity I should've known was my true place all along.

A hand touches my shoulder, pulling me back into the real world. I blink my eyes open to find Rone lying on the floor beside me.

She smiles, so easy, so sweet.

But a haze shrouds my heart. I paint a half smile over my features, knowing I should.

I should be happy to see her.

I'm always happy to see her.

"Talk to me," she says.

"About what?"

Silently, I rebuke myself for my words, for my flat affect. I should have more to say. I should be bursting at the seams to talk to her, to check in, to figure out what's going on.

But there's nothing I can do, nothing I can help with.

I'm just here.

She eyes me curiously. Settling in, she scoots closer, sliding her hand onto my chest. "Well, what are you doing? Why are you down here?"

I lay a hand on hers, but my fingers don't have the energy to curl around hers. For a long time, I don't speak. I stare up at the pale, grey ceiling, barely even bothering to breathe.

I should probably breathe.

I focus on my lungs, timing every inhale, every exhale. The momentary fear that I'll die if I don't regulate them grips me.

Would it matter?

Finally, I remember Rone's question and say, "Because I'm small."

"You're down here because you're... small?" she asks, brows furrowing. Nestling in closer, she asks, "What does that mean?"

"That I'm nothing. I've *done* nothing. The universe is so big, so important. And I... am small." I close my eyes, focusing on the way the light shines through my eyelids, red and black and orange.

"You're not nothing," Rone whispers.

I'd scoff, but somehow, it feels like too much effort.

"Just because you aren't taking over an enemy ship or writing programs doesn't mean you're nothing. It doesn't mean you've done nothing," she says.

I lazily shake my head, pursing my lips.

"Reginald, look at me," Rone says, pulling my face toward hers.

I oblige, opening my eyes. Vivid green eyes peer into mine, strained with sincerity and maybe concern. The electric blue circuits in her irises shift slowly.

"You're a catalyst," she finally says.

It catches me off guard, and I scrunch my brows together.

"We're taking all these steps, making all of this progress, because you started it. You set all of this in motion."

I start to turn toward the ceiling again, unable to believe her words. But she holds my face, hand soft and firm at the same time.

"If you hadn't come here in place of Olivia, she wouldn't have been there to come up with Atlantis, to save Tenna or Krona or any of the others. She wouldn't be reprogramming that ship. She may never have realized how talented she is with programming."

"She would have," I argue. "The Drennar would have found a way to bring it out of her."

"Maybe. Maybe not. That isn't what they're testing with the group she would've been placed with."

I sigh, but I don't argue anymore.

Taking my silence as an invitation to continue, Rone says, "If you hadn't done that, Daen Tribe would still be suffering."

"If I hadn't come here, Eva wouldn't have taken Daen Tribe to begin with."

"Yes, she would have. She would've done it for Olivia," Rone says. "You don't think she would've fought? You don't think she would've broken down and pushed you away like she did to Olivia? She would've taken them, one way or another, after our people turned the telescopes on Termana toward Regonia. She would've done the same terrible things. She wasn't strong enough to hold onto her morals under duress. Eva wasn't as strong as you are."

I turn to face Rone, startled out of my foggy mind.

"I'm not strong," I whisper, voice breaking in evidence of my statement.

"One of these days, you'll realize that you are." Rone plants a tender kiss on my lips. Her eyes soften, and she touches my cheek. "If you hadn't come here, I wouldn't be who I am. Seeing you care so much about Olivia, seeing you feel so deeply… It made me want to understand you. It made me want to know what emotion was like."

I swallow a lump in my throat.

"If it wasn't you, if it was Croon..." Rone shakes her head. "I don't think I would've gotten that modification. I wouldn't have been compelled to help. I would've just gone on, blank and oblivious to an entire world of experiences, oblivious to the better version of myself that I could be, that I am now."

She searches my gaze. I open my mouth to speak, but nothing comes out.

"If it wasn't for you, for the way you made me feel, none of the other Drennar would've gotten the modifications either."

My mouth goes dry, gumming up any words I might speak. My chest grows tight as my heart strains to beat faster and faster.

"You're not small. You're not nothing," Rone says. "You're the spark that starts a wildfire."

Tears prick at the corners of my eyes, and I wrap my arms around her, pulling her close. She nestles against me, nuzzling her face into my neck as wretched sobs burst through me.

Chapter Thirty-Four
The Realm of Stars

Krona

Olivia's face lights up as she plays with the alonarium, shaping it to her will. Face scrunching in concentration, she forms it into a small bird perched upon a thin branch protruding from the wall.

The edges of the little creature ripple, and the branch sways.

But it's there.

She's getting the hang of this.

I look to Tenna and find awe dancing in her eyes. She meets my gaze with a smile.

"Do you want to try again?" I ask her.

She shakes her head and nods at Olivia. "This is all I want to see."

I sit on the small alonarium bench Curata crafted for us, slipping an arm around Tenna's shoulder when she settles in beside me. We lean against each other, watching Olivia smooth out the edges of her bird. The alonarium moves according to her will, signaled by her Link, and I spare a glance for the device in my own wrist. The thing I once hated so much now astounds me.

Curata's shining face appears on the wall before us, and she smiles at Olivia's alonarium manipulations. I look around at the walls, wondering if every surface could be a screen.

"I can hand the ship off to you now," Curata says. Her soft, blue hair floats around her face, too light to be real. "Are you ready?"

Olivia nods excitedly, letting the little bird and its perch flow back into the wall. She moves quickly toward the cockpit, and we follow along in her wake. A smile plays over my features at the prospect of going back, of seeing Ricardo, of making sure he's safe and healing.

Smooth, grey walls pass by in a blur with my thoughts occupied by the troops that will fall under our command once we reach our own ship, barely stopping to register my possessive thoughts over that other ship. Again, I marvel at the transformation within my own mind.

Where a box once contained a dead Drennar turned computer, now only a raised platform waits. He still rests within, but all cables and hoses have been retracted within, no longer needed.

Three seats sit upon the platform in a neat triangle. The smallest sits at the front, waiting for Olivia. She slides into it easily, and Tenna and I take our places behind her.

I don't even flinch when Curata or Olivia, it's hard to say which, slides harnesses free of the alonarium to secure us into our seats.

Tenna takes my hand, lacing our fingers together, and my heart skips a beat. I smile at her, squeezing her hand, and whisper, "Let's go get our people."

She nods, and Olivia begins the countdown to takeoff.

Chapter Thirty-Five
The Realm of Stars

Olivia

The stars whiz past on the screen before me, and though I hate the layer of alonarium between me and those bright lights, it comforts me at these speeds. Somehow, the thought of having mere glass between me and space, moving this quickly, just doesn't seem like enough.

And maybe it wouldn't be.

I don't ask my Link to do the calculations, because I don't want to know the answer. Instead, I focus on the task at hand, piloting us as safely as I can toward our ship. Toward Ricardo.

All Rone's assurances as to his safety, his healthy recovery, have done nothing to loosen the knots in my shoulders or the nerves coiled tightly in my stomach. I need to see him, need to speak with him.

Secondhand information isn't cutting it.

And though he seemed to speak well enough in the message he had Rone and Curata send to all the Humans on Novay, the message they passed along to me too, I need to hear his voice in person. I need to run my hands over him, trace every inch and make sure there are no new wounds that haven't been tended to.

My heart races, and for a second, I wonder if it's trying to keep pace with the ship. My chest grows tight, and I force myself to think of something else, anything else, lest I have a heart attack.

But only after reassuring myself for the millionth time that he's okay.

***

The day passes with my hands gripping the controls, relenting only when Curata accesses the ship remotely to allow me rest. She pilots it while I toss and turn, mind unoccupied and wishing Ricardo were next to me.

Eventually, exhaustion claims me, pulling me into a darkness every bit as absolute as the vacuum of space. When I rise, I take my post, eager to have the ship under my control again, eager to fly, to feel the movement of the universe.

To do something to bring me closer to Ricardo and further from the Drennar.

A hint of guilt gnaws at me, knowing that I've left my father there, but we're going back.

And I won't leave him there again.

The day passes uneventfully, broken up by jokes shared with Tenna and Krona, by messages from Rone and Curata going over the plans for our assault.

Another night creeps in, and tension builds within me. I pace my room, hand on my stomach, muscles aching to move, to get to him already.

Eventually, I shower and lie down, but my mind races. With my new program done, with nothing to do and no one to talk to, my brain calls out for the bottle, just to have a break.

I grit my teeth, setting my resolve.

Pulling the blankets up higher, I put a gentle hand over my stomach and the bump just starting to form. I fill my lungs near to bursting.

I won't be that kind of mother.

I won't drink while pregnant.

Exhaling, I remind myself that I don't intend to drink *after* giving birth either, reaffirming my decision to stay sober.

I'll have to take up a hobby to keep myself occupied.

Granted, figuring out how to raise a child on an alien planet may occupy my time quite enough.

My mind wanders, exploring all the possibilities of living on Regonia. Ricardo and our child. A garden for food. A home to maintain. A Tribe that calls me family. Maybe a Malakar to ride into the skies eventually. The peace of that life budding on the horizon lulls me to sleep.

***

Waking with a smile, I spring from bed and dress quickly.

Today's the day.

I race down the halls to the cockpit, skidding to a stop when I reach it.

Stars twinkle on the screen ahead of me, dwarfed by the one at the center of the Regonian system. Halos of light peek around the silhouetted planets, marvelous and beautiful.

But something else, something closer, draws my attention.

In the distance, a dark shape forms. Light reaches past it, highlighting the planes of the ship I know so well. The metal gleams as it speeds steadily toward us.

My heart leaps into my throat.

He's so close.

I step closer to the screen, sliding into the pilot's seat. Curata says farewell for now, returning control of the ship to me, and I stare up at the majesty of space.

I send a quick message to Tenna and Krona. "Almost there. Get ready to disembark."

With my hands on the controls, I close the distance, hailing them as soon as we're in range. I brace myself for Hugo's voice, all the while hoping it'll be Ricardo who answers.

The connection goes through, and I rush to say, "This is Olivia Dobovich, aboard a ship with a stupidly long string of numbers and letters for a name. Requesting permission to dock."

Deep laughter answers me, coming straight from my memories. "Permission granted," Ricardo finally says. "I can't wait to see you."

My heart leaps into my throat, nearly choking me. "I can't wait to see you," I answer.

"Hurry up then," he says, and I can almost see his teasing smile. "It's taken you long enough to get here."

"Hey, I flew most of the distance. You didn't even meet me halfway."

The smile never leaves my face, but I push the little craft harder, thankful it can take it.

"I'm not sure you can hold that against me," he says, voice thick with emotion. "You do have a much fancier ship right now."

I chuckle, and tears of relief spill over my cheeks. The massive ship comes into full view, and I force myself to slow down so I don't accidentally punch straight through and kill us all.

Maneuvering carefully, I steer us upward, sidling up next to a maintenance airlock and settling in with a gentle thud.

"Coming aboard," I whisper.

Within the cockpit, I hear shuffling, followed by Hugo's voice.

"Welcome back, Olivia. I'm not sure we need you to fly this thing anymore though. Ricardo's pretty good."

I laugh, but my chest swells with pride. My hands whir over controls, and I issue commands with my Link to speed up the process, foregoing the wondrous connection that buttons and panels bring.

"He's kidding," Ricardo says. "You're much better."

More shuffling, then Ricardo says, "I'm coming to meet you. See you soon."

The hope in his voice makes my breath catch. "See you soon."

I power the ship down, suddenly hating all the steps involved. Tenna and Krona enter the cockpit, settling into their seats behind me to wait.

With everything done, we move to the back of the ship. I send out a few commands with my Link, directing the alonarium reserves onboard to reach out and form a hall for us to pass through. I redirect the life support systems to this new section of the ship, then slide the wall free.

The outer wall of the Human ship shines in the light of this Drennar craft, sparkling beneath our feet as we step out onto it. The alonarium hall extends a few feet, reaching out to overlap the maintenance airlock.

Kneeling before the hatch, I let my Link issue the appropriate commands, and it swings open before us. Tenna and Krona approach behind me, footsteps echoing on the metal.

Peering in, I take a deep breath. Then, I swing myself into the hatch, descending the ladder as quickly as I can.

My feet hit the floor, and I turn, searching for the door and hoping this one has a window. But it doesn't. Only cold metal awaits me.

Tenna and Krona climb down. I close the hatch behind them, eliminating any chance of a breach if my control of the alonarium falters.

The airlock door opens, and amber eyes stare in at me. For a moment, I stand paralyzed, heart skipping so many beats I fear it may give out altogether. Swallowing, I take a step, eyes roving over Ricardo's frame, searching for injuries, for anything new.

He rushes forward, dark hair flying about his shoulders. He scoops me up in his arms, lifting me, kissing my neck. I throw my arms around him, wrapping one hand in his hair. Heat blossoms within me, and tears stream over my cheeks.

Our lips meet, and fire burns everywhere we touch. His hand finds the back of my neck, pulling me closer, holding me tighter. Our mouths move together, tasting, reacquainting.

My nerves finally release, but another tension builds, deep within. My breathing grows shallow, but he sets me down, pulling back. His hands find the sides of my face, and his eyes search mine.

"Are you okay?" he asks, voice frantic. "Is the baby okay?"

Nodding fervently, I stare into those beautiful, golden eyes. "Are *you* okay? How's your lung? Your ribs?"

He chuckles, pulling me against him once more. "I'm fine." He shakes his head, then nuzzles into my hair. "God, I'm glad you're back."

A soft sound draws us from our trance, and we turn to Tenna and Krona. They rush forward, wrapping us in a tight embrace, and finally, our little family is whole again.

Chapter Thirty-Six
Novay

Rone

Lustran sits with an arm around Curata's shoulders, careful not to pinch her wings. She smiles wide, planning out the coming assault, but my stomach turns at the disconnection she's proposed. I swallow, nodding along because I know there are no other options.

We know almost nothing of Olivia's new program, keeping it within her mind and Link, possibly on Ricardo's Link as a backup, to keep the other Drennar from getting their hands on it prematurely.

But that means that we don't know if it could jump to us through the network we all use so frequently.

Curata works through the timing, piecing together every step we need to take. She calculates down to the second, ironing out contingencies that I never would have considered.

"I'll take care of the facility manager," she says aloud.

That's one of the problems that had somehow eluded me. The facility manager, the only Expressionless Drennar here who outranks Curata in authority and intelligence, could have thrown our entire plan out the window, but she already has a plan, no doubt tailoring her distraction specifically to him.

My head spins. I go over what I know of the plan to reassure myself.

It's simple.

We attack with Curata leading the distraction.

A small part of me longs to see what she has in store for the alonarium manipulations, but I'll be elsewhere.

Olivia will secure her connection. Reginald and I will gather the Humans from their facilities. When Olivia's ready, we'll make our case and await their decision.

For now, we just have to wait while the Humans' ship lugs them through space.

I take a deep breath.

It's simple.

It's all been planned out, by Curata, no less.

We'll be fine.

But a deep uneasiness floods me. I can only hope it isn't the Humans' intuition or the Regonians' sense of what is.

***

Lying in Reginald's arms, illuminated by the light of the tunnel Curata opened for me, I whisper my concerns. "There's so much that can go wrong… What if we haven't thought of something? What if something happens?"

"If something goes wrong, we'll improvise. We'll make it work, one way or another," he says. He kisses the top of my head, in much better spirits today than he was last time. With a chuckle, he adds, "I know that's exactly what you wanted to hear."

"Not quite."

Because how can I improvise while disconnected?

"What has you worried the most?" Reginald asks. His hazel eyes search mine in the low light, and his hand smooths a tendril of hair back behind my ear.

"I've never been fully disconnected before. The most I've done is pause my data streams. I've always had all the information I needed to make a decision. What if I choose wrong? What if someone gets hurt *because* I chose wrong?"

"Then… We take care of that person or we mourn. And we try to do better in the future."

My heart drops, and I frown. "How is that good enough?"

"Sometimes it isn't. But it's the best we can do." He rests his forehead to mine.

"But how can I be sure? I really can't be sure before doing something? There's no trick? No ancient wisdom from your ancestors?"

Chuckling, Reginald shakes his head. "Welcome to Humanity, my dear. We do the best we can with what we have. If we fail, all we can do is try to do better next time."

A chasm opens within me, and my jaw falls open. "That's terrifying."

"That it is," he says. "And now, you truly understand us."

Chapter Thirty-Seven
The Realm of Stars

Tenna

My footsteps ring out on the metal catwalk of the cargo bay, but their echoes get lost in the commotion below me. Our Warriors spar with Human Soldiers and Taron Warriors alike, running drills in preparation for the coming assault.

I lift my chin, heart swelling with pride. So many rallied to come with, to aid our Human allies and see to the safety of our children and grandchildren.

Bodies bend and sway, stretching, fighting. Humans jump back, dodging blows from practice axes and swords. Our Warriors dance around them, nimbly avoiding the inert lightning rods, things the Humans call tasers, rendered ineffectual by the removal of something called batteries.

Armor clangs and rustles. Voices rise and fall with the flow of the fights.

Leaning onto the rail, I watch, cataloging my notes on the techniques of various fighters. My Link prepares the messages, set to send them as soon as the fighters in question finish sparring.

I lift my gaze from the maelstrom below, finding Krona similarly engaged on the catwalk at the other end of the cargo bay. His hands grip the rails, and his eyes roam over the crowd beneath him. His dark leather armor shines in the lights of the ship.

He leans forward, assessing a particular pair of fighters, and my heart skips a beat, wondering what he may have seen, what insights he might provide them.

Breathing deeply, I return my gaze to the fighters before me. I pace back and forth, sweeping every pair, taking notes on the form of every fighter.

And so, the day passes, rotating groups for training.

As evening rolls in, Krona saunters around the catwalk, moving toward me. His gaze moves over my figure, sending shock waves through me.

The smile on his face makes my skin warm. A single strand of hair hangs in his face, black ink over pale grey, loose from the tie that holds the rest of his hair back. I take a deep breath, relishing the feel of those beautiful eyes on me.

He steps close, arms sliding around my waist. His lips meet mine, but only briefly, leaving me wanting.

"Want to spar?" he whispers, voice deep and husky.

I nod, readily assenting to the promise of truly stretching out, of moving with him.

He pulls away, hand sliding into mine.

We take the stairs, footsteps too loud on the metal. My heart races as we move through the crowd. On all sides, fighters switch off, watching another pair as they rest between bouts. But their eyes find us, gazes curious and excited.

They part to let us pass.

An opening forms around us, and we stretch, preparing our bodies for the trial we'll put them through. A nearby pair offers us their practice weapons. The wood is heavier than the bone of our real weapons and not nearly as sturdy.

But it's close enough.

Testing the weight of my newly acquired axe, I fall into my preferred stance. Krona spins the sword he's been offered, and though I know he prefers the axe as I do, he knows his way around a sword.

His eyes trace my form, and heat builds within me. My breaths come faster, and my lips lift into a smile.

He bends his knees, angles his body, stepping back on one leg. I watch the shift of his posture, the change in his eyes as he raises his sword, up and out, tip pointing toward me.

Our chests rise and fall, almost in time.

On the catwalk above, Ricardo calls, "On my mark."

Krona and I nod, and the cargo bay falls silent.

Ricardo counts to some arbitrary number Humans seem to prefer, then calls out, "Sve!"

We move, but not quickly, not yet. We circle each other, waiting, picking our moment.

I watch Krona's gait, watch the way he moves. One step falls just short of his normal stride, and I know he plans to move.

He bursts forward, sword rising in an arc. I duck, swinging my axe for his legs. Leaping over me, he hits the hard metal with a roll, coming up as I spin to face him.

But I don't give him time to recover, time to turn. Rushing toward him, I ready myself to swing again. He brings his sword up to block, knowing me too well. Our weapons collide.

My blood sings in my veins, and I know his must too.

He heaves upward, throwing the strength of his legs into the act and rising beneath our locked weapons. The force sends me skipping backward, easily avoiding a slash from his sword as he spins to face me with a devilish glint in his eyes.

We fall into the fight, dancing, moving together. Our weapons clash, and our bodies warm to the exertion. We explore each other, trusting, knowing.

And every time our eyes meet, the heat within builds.

The worlds around us fall away, and it's just us, just the stretch and pull of our muscles, the strength and agility we've built together for years.

For a moment, I wonder how those Human scientists could have taken this from me so easily. But that only sweetens the reality of having it back.

I spin around him, dodging a blow that could have ended our spar had it landed, and pride dances in his eyes.

My heart races, blood roaring in my ears, and I throw myself forward, bringing the axe down toward his shoulder, ready to cleave through to his chest. His sword comes up, driving toward my abdomen.

Neither of us block.

But we stop ourselves just shy of hitting.

His eyes peer into mine, crisp mint shining with exhilaration. His chest rises and falls just as quickly as my own.

Smiling wide, I let the axe fall, placing my hands on his neck. He grips the back of my neck, pulling me in for a kiss that could shatter stars.

I slip my hands into his hair, relishing the sweat of our exertions. Casting his sword aside, he wraps his arm around my waist, sending shivers over my spine.

On all sides, our people whoop and cheer.

We pull apart, though the pool of heat in my belly begs me to do anything but. We dismiss everyone for the day, chuckling at the awestruck expressions on Olivia's and Ricardo's faces.

Krona slips his hand into mine and pulls me through one corridor after another. We step around a corner, and he presses me against the wall, hands in my hair and body hot against mine. Our lips crush together, and I pull him tight against me.

But only for an instant.

I push off the wall, lips still moving hungrily over his, and I back down the hall.

We break apart only to run, sprinting through the ship for our quarters. Bursting through the door, we barely give it time to slide shut before I push him onto the bed.

We pull at our armor, and my insides burn at the delay. I kiss his neck as he works at the buckles on my chest piece. My hands busy themselves with his armor, and a groan of relief tears through me as he casts mine aside.

His leathers fall away, and I feast upon him. Desperate and hungry, we collide, moving together in a frenzy. Moans fill the air, and sweat rolls down my back as I move over him.

He flips me to my back, pulling a fevered moan from me, and then we're together again, pushing, rushing. His hands grasp my hip, my hair. I dig my nails into his back, twining my legs with his and pulling him deeper.

He moves faster, nipping at my bottom lip. I arch my back, inviting, begging. And he obliges, lips moving to my neck. He moves lower, teeth grazing my shoulders.

Shivers work through me, and I call out his name. His teeth clamp down on my shoulder, biting down, breaking skin, and I scream out, nails carving into his back.

He drives home, and I fall to pieces, relishing the feel of him, the force of his muscles, the strength of his soul.

One final push sends him crumbling after me, gasping against my skin.

Our lips meet, suddenly tender, and I tangle my hands in his hair. Staring up into those wondrous eyes, I marvel at their tenacity, staying with me even when all else was lost.

Chapter Thirty-Eight

Novay

Reginald

The wall before me transforms, illuminating the room and the Drennar posted in the corners. My jaw drops at the forces gathered in a field on Regonia, all swathed in dark leathers and ready for a fight.

They tried to protect her.

And though thanks to Rone I know the outcome, know that they took Olivia, Tenna, and Krona, know that they're already safely away from here, my blood turns to ice.

I don't want to watch this, don't want to see them take her.

But I school my features.

The Drennar don't know that I know those things. I can't even remember if they know I know she wasn't on Termana when they went for her.

I rack my brain, searching through all the horrors they've made me bear witness to over the years.

The travesties that Eva subjected so many people to. The neglect Olivia suffered at her mother's hands.

The experiments on Daen Tribe. The battle to save them. The Awakening.

Olivia's suicide attempt.

I nearly double over at the thought, and I give up on remembering what they've shown me, on trying to separate those things from the horrors my mind subjects me to in sleep.

Sitting forward, I let my gaze roam over the screen, taking in the slant of the sunlight and the shadows it casts among the ranks of warriors and soldiers. I stare in wonder at the mountains, the river in the distance, the strange creatures at the front of the line.

Only then do I remember that all the cameras on Regonia should be blocked. Panic spikes through me.

Did they crack Atlantis?

How much did they learn?

But a massive, winged Drennar drops into view, and my breath catches.

This must be the view from the ships they took.

Horror and revulsion war within me. My palms sweat, and my face scrunches into a frown.

How many did they kill?

How many died to protect Olivia?

And though it warms my heart to know they'd try, I know they failed.

More and more Drennar fall from the ship, wings unfurling as they take to the air. The battle commences, and beasts descend from the mountains, launching themselves upon the airborne Drennar.

I shake my head, slow, disbelieving.

Swallowing, I try to prepare myself for the bloodshed, but it's so much worse than I expected. My stomach turns as gore rains from the sky and chaos erupts below. Screams and feathers fill the air. Blood coats the ground.

And in the end, they find her anyway.

My heart leaps into my throat as one of them soars through the air, carrying her along in its arms. The fate I tried so hard to prevent all those years ago is right there, staring at me from the screen.

But Krona and Tenna leap to save her, grabbing at him. They pull him to the ground, and Regonians descend upon the beast who would have taken my daughter.

I pull in a deep, hitching breath, somehow relieved despite knowing that they took her to a ship one way or another. Drennar come down, descending in a horde, and shape an alonarium sphere around them, slicing through flesh and bones and earth as they imprison Olivia and the Regonian royals.

Leaning forward in my seat, I cover my face with my hands. Tears spill out.

They really took her.

Somehow, it hadn't hit me, hadn't fully sunk in. But seeing it…

I really, truly failed her.

The room goes dark as the screen shuts off, and I thank whatever god may have spared me the sight of them taking her, putting her under, monitoring her.

But my heart crumbles, regardless.

My breath grows shallow, catching in my throat.

I tried so hard to make sure she had a good life.

I tried.

Light fills the room, and the floor shifts before me, transforming and raising a desk from the alonarium. The surface shines with a multitude of equations.

A morbid chuckle escapes me.

"I'm supposed to do some fucking math problems now?" I stare at the Drennar nearest me. "You're kidding, right?"

But they don't joke, don't know the meaning of it.

These Expressionless bastards pride themselves on knowledge, on understanding, but they don't understand anything.

I shake my head, inhaling until my lungs feel like they may burst. I set to work, recalling Ricardo's message, recalling the plan. We still have so much to do, and it isn't time to cause a scene just yet.

I grit my teeth, working through the equations with ease.

I have to lay low for a little while. I have to cooperate.

I take another deep breath.

I have to cooperate for Olivia. Because I can still help her. I haven't failed her yet.

I have to cooperate for Daen Tribe. For all the Humans being held on Novay. For Rone and everyone working with her, everyone risking so much to help us, to save us.

Rone's words from a few nights ago come back to me, circling in my head as they have so many times since.

You're not small. You're not nothing. You're the spark that starts a wildfire.

I close my eyes, breathing deeply.

Though I still don't feel like a spark that could start anything, it helps just to know she thinks so highly of me.

With a slow nod, I run through the rest of the equations without a broken breath, without a lump in my throat.

Olivia is safe on our ship with Ricardo, Krona, and Tenna.

Everything is in progress.

I just have to get through another week like this.

Chapter Thirty-Nine
Novay

Rone

My hand shakes as I bring it to my chest, resting my palm over my heart. Incoming data streams stop. I close my eyes as the world goes quiet.

I begin my count, measuring it down to the nanoseconds, but panic builds within me. 3.452 seconds in, I pull my hand away from my chest.

Data streams back in, filling my mind in an instant, and relief floods through my veins. I take a deep breath, trying to center, to calibrate.

Opening my eyes, I look around at the others gathered around me. Lustran seems similarly stricken, as do Raktorn and a few others.

But Curata and Sentrah stand with eyes closed, hands still resting over their hearts. Peace and wonder rule their features, and I gawk at them.

How are they not terrified?

Haven't they considered the possible implications, the possible failures?

But even if Sentrah hasn't, I know Curata has. Yet, her lips are parted, and her brows are lifted in awe. There seems to be an extra glow beneath her already shining skin.

I glance at Lustran, contrasting his stricken eyes with his companion's even countenance. It brings a smile to my face.

But Curata and Sentrah give me the courage to try again.

Taking a deep breath, I raise my trembling hand once more. Biting at the inside of my cheek, I place my palm over my heart, stilling as the world goes silent once more.

All data streams cut out entirely.

It's okay.

I'm not making any decisions right now. I don't need those data streams to stand in place.

This is just practice.

And I've paused them before. This is just a pause. A... more complete pause.

But the nanoseconds tick by, and tension builds, twisting my gut into knots, winding my nerves tight. Every muscle grows tense, itching to move, to pull my hand from my chest.

But I hold.

9.845 seconds.

Almost a third of the way through.

I monitor my lungs, cataloging the volume of each breath, the length of time for each completed inhale and exhale. But it isn't enough to occupy my mind, isn't even close.

The clock running in the background, timing my disconnection sequence, seems to scream at me, counting off every single millisecond.

21.627 seconds.

I measure my heartbeats, forcing myself to find something, anything, to focus on aside from this.

How did Reginald live with a countdown over his head the whole time leading up to the breach of the space stations?

How did he stand it?

27.914 seconds.

Full disconnection looms, just a couple seconds ahead. My mouth goes dry.

I pull my hand from my chest.

Information pours in, giving me access to the knowledge of our entire race, everything we've gathered, everything we're still gathering, and my knees go weak. Dragging air into my lungs with great heaving breaths, I shake my head.

I can't do this.

I can't.

Not yet.

I settle on the floor, weakened by my own limitations. My brows reach for each other, seeking comfort.

How do Humans live like this?

How do Regonians *live like this? Their brains are closer to ours than those of the Humans. They must need more stimulation. They have to.*

How can they stand this?

My hands shake in my lap. I ball them into fists to try and stop them, to no avail. Swallowing, I wonder if maybe, in all our modifications and enhancements, we lost something fundamental.

And yet, we always thought ourselves so superior.

Tiny feet appear before me, drawing my attention upward. Curata smiles down at me, eyes twinkling and wings completely still behind her. She settles before me, taking my hands in hers.

"Don't worry so much. This is just practice," she says with a gentle smile. "You'll be an expert by the time you actually have to do this. I trust you to do what's right when the time comes."

I look down at our joined hands, wondering why I'm even surprised that she knew what the real problem is. "But… Can I…" I swallow, then try again, "I don't know if I trust myself. I've never had to before. I've always had all the data necessary to make a decision."

"You have the information you need, even when you're disconnected," Curata says. She releases my hand and taps one finger over my heart. "We're just replacing one data stream with another."

Mouth agape, I stare at her. Tears prick at the corners of my eyes, though I don't know why.

And then, I realize that I don't need to know why the tears are there. They feel right.

They *feel* right.

Nodding, I see the truth in her words. I still have a guide, even disconnected. The same guide that led me to Reginald. The same guide that led me to Olivia, Tenna, and Krona.

"I think I want to try again," I say, voice shaky but resolute.

Chapter Forty
The Realm of Stars

Ricardo

Days pass aboard the ship, and tension builds within us all. The oncoming invasion looms, heavy and foreboding. I try not to count the casualties we can expect, try not to imagine the bodies we'll bring back with us.

If we come back at all.

My nerves wind tighter with every passing second, but I have a plan, if only for a brief distraction to keep our minds from spiraling during our off hours. A plan inspired by Olivia and her love of learning.

I roll to find her finally sleeping peacefully. Heartburn kept her awake long after her shift in the cockpit ended at midnight.

Swallowing, I rise from our bed, dropping a gentle kiss on Olivia's brow before I dress. I move quietly, trying not to wake her now that the pregnancy symptoms have decided to let her rest.

But she stirs.

"Hmm?" she mutters, eyes fluttering open. "Where are you going?"

She lifts her arm, rubbing at her eyes, and the sheet slips away, revealing the shadows at the hollow of her collarbone and the gentle curve of her breast.

"What time is it?" she asks.

"It's early still. Get some more sleep. I'm going for more training in the cargo bay."

Her chest rises with a deep breath, and warmth moves through me. I reach out, cupping her cheek and smiling down at her.

"Come see me before your next shift?" I ask. "I might have something to show you by then."

She furrows her brows, but sleep still tugs at her eyelids, begging them to close. A yawn bursts over her, and she nods, lazily covering her mouth with her hand.

Chuckling, I kiss her forehead once more. "I love you."

She touches my neck and whispers, "I love you too."

I lean in for a kiss, tender and sweet, then let her drift back off to sleep. She tugs the sheet back up, nestling into the covers.

When I leave our room, I cast one last glance at her. My heart softens at the waves of long black hair spread over the pillow, at the peaceful set of her features, her perfectly warm skin. A smile lifts the corners of my lips.

***

The sounds of practice swords and axes, cheers and constructive criticism, buzz from the cargo bay long before I reach it. The halls vibrate with the echoes, and I double check the time, wondering if somehow I was mistaken.

When I find that it isn't even 6:00, I marvel at the dedication of the Regonian Warriors. Krona and Tenna stand close to the entrance, watching their people run drills with the Warriors of Taron Tribe.

Coming up beside them, I say, "I have an idea."

***

I hold a wooden sword, standing in one of the basic stances I've practiced for the better part of two hours. Krona analyzes the position of my feet, the bend of my knees. He takes in my hands on the hilt, assessing my frame and God knows what else. My heart races, waiting for a correction.

But none come.

After circling me a few times, he nods, and I don't bother to suppress my smile.

Taking his cue, I switch to a different stance, the one he used to start his spar with Tenna a few days ago. I step back with one foot, lifting the sword, hilt even with my face, and angling the point toward him.

He circles again, looking over my form, taking everything in. With a nod, he signals me to switch once more.

We move through every stance he's shown me, and each time, the giddiness of this whole thing multiplies.

I brought this idea forth as a practical matter, meaning to make sure I would know what to do in case I had no other weapon nearby, meaning to make sure all our soldiers would know what to do if left no other choice.

I even proposed teaching the Regonians how to use our weapons for the same reason.

But now, with the sword in my hand, I can't help but feel like I've stepped into an old movie, like I'm about to face a dragon. It's oddly exhilarating.

When I move into the final stance and Krona finds no major faults, he says, "You learn quickly."

My heart swells with pride.

I glance around at the Soldiers taking instruction from Regonian Warriors throughout the cargo bay, and my smile grows.

Chapter Forty-One
The Realm of Stars

Krona

Goosebumps rise on my arms as I lift the thing the Humans call a taser. I swallow, breathing hard as I stare at the sleek, black thing.

Gripping the hilt, I keep my finger off the trigger. But I don't know where to put it. My hands are too large for this thing. My trigger finger reaches almost to the end, the part where the lightning erupts from the infernal device. I settle on wrapping my finger around the hilt, tucking it alongside the rest.

Turning to Ricardo, I ask, "You're sure this won't hurt me?"

"I'm sure." He offers up an encouraging smile. "It's designed to keep the person using it safe."

Somehow, that doesn't comfort me. All my fears of technology, of star-sickness, come flooding back in. Those early days in my cell, fearing the very thing implanted in my wrist, the new voice of the translator ringing in my head, it all rushes through my mind.

Taking a deep breath, I step forward, footsteps ringing out in the silent cargo bay. Tenna steps up beside me.

My heart races. My chest heaves.

I swallow again.

Casting a glance over my shoulder, I check the doorway. Empty. Our people are still asleep or eating their first meal or enjoying each other's company.

I take a deep breath, raising my arm, bearing death itself in my grip.

Better to do this before they get here, to be able to tell them with confidence that they can safely fire these things.

Tenna raises her arm as well, aiming her taser at the little practice dummy standing a few meters away.

But it doesn't seem far enough.

The lightning will be too close.

"It won't…" Tenna clears her throat. "Lightning sometimes jumps from one person to another on Regonia. Especially if we're this close. It won't do that… will it?"

"It won't. This isn't as powerful as lightning," Ricardo says.

And though I know his words must be true, having felt the bite of a taser once before and survived, I can't conceive something stronger. Something worse.

My breath echoes in my mind, too loud. I look to Tenna.

"The one they used on you on Odyssey didn't send lightning leaping from you to anyone else," Ricardo reminds me. "And nothing happened to any of your people on Termana when we used them against the Drennar."

I nod, letting his words flow through me, trying to let them fill me with peace. Turning, I ask Tenna, "Ready?" And though I know I've spoken, the words are barely audible over my heart, my lungs.

She meets my gaze and nods, chest rising with a full breath.

Ricardo counts us down, and on his signal, we pull the triggers. Little prongs fly across the open space, hooking onto the dummy.

Bits of smoke rise from it, but it doesn't convulse, has no muscles to do so. The thought of a person flailing in the throes of this torture makes me sick, reminds me of the Lost Ones of The Awakening.

But they died in beds crafted for their execution. Gutless and heartless, Eva Dobovich killed them without mercy.

This is different.

This is for justice. This is for the Humans taken by the Drennar and for the Regonians they could take in the future.

This is for Tenna and Olivia, for myself, for the woman who bled out from her missing arm in that alonarium dome.

I stare at the dummy, at the black marks surrounding the prongs we fired at it. And though I know it may come to this, though I know I might have to use one of these things to save my people, horror slithers through me.

"After you fire the prongs," Ricardo says, "the next attack would have to be closer."

He steps up to the dummy, brandishing his own taser. "Or you can do this first. But you only have one set of prongs to fire. After they're gone, you have to press the end directly against the body. Just make sure you're not touching them when you pull it. Only the taser touches them."

He does so, pressing the taser against the dummy before pulling the trigger. Wisps of smoke rise, and black mars the surface near his taser.

I reach out for Tenna, taking her hand. We approach together, and she squeezes my hand every bit as hard as I squeeze hers. We press our tasers to the dummy, and I fight the urge to close my eyes.

We pull our triggers.

Smoke and darkness, a horrid smell. I swallow.

"Okay," Ricardo says. "They're pretty simple. Now, remember to click the safety switch before putting it back in the holster."

He gestures to the one on his taser, and we follow suit. I don't bother with the holster, leading Tenna to a table set up near the door.

Depositing the thing there, I step back, staring at it. My nerves calm when Tenna does the same.

Ricardo smiles at us, amber eyes alight. "That went far better than I expected. I thought it might freak you guys out more than that."

Swallowing, I turn to face him, careful not to turn my back on the table full of lightning.

"I know it's best to understand all the weapons at our disposal," Tenna begins, "but I hope I never have to use one of those again."

I nod my agreement, and Ricardo chuckles softly.

"I can't say I blame you," he says. His eyes grow serious. "I just want to make sure that, if this is all that's left for you to use," he gestures to the tasers, "you can use them safely."

Footsteps sound in the hall, drawing our attention. I find Tenna's gaze, and we rest our foreheads together, drawing strength from each other.

Three Warriors step through the door, eyes glued to the table full of lightning weapons. We pull apart, preparing ourselves to explain the inner workings of these strange things, as far as we can.

Knowing makes them less scary, and we need every bit of help we can get.

Chapter Forty-Two
The Realm of Stars

Olivia

Novay looms over us, consuming the horizon, swallowing the sky. The slate-grey beast stares in through the window of the cockpit, wearing crisscrossing rings of vivid blue.

I itch to move us along faster, to just get there already, but Curata has a very specific timeline for us. I won't be the one to mess that up.

The speakers within the cockpit reverberate, filling my ears with "Stabbing in the Dark by Ice Nine Kills. 2018." I lean back in my seat, tracing the strange blue lines that encircle the planet, cutting it into too many sections to count.

My head tips to the side, and I purse my lips. My eyes leap from one blue line to the next, and I wonder if it matters which one I hook into.

Curata said they're all linked under the surface…

Any should do.

With a thought, I have my Link place a little spot of light on the window, marking my dad's location, then another for Rone's location. At this distance, they align into one dot.

But as we move in, as we drop into the atmosphere, they'll separate. My heart drops at the two kilometer distance between them, at the fifty kilometers the other Humans are sprawled across, knowing that all our allies have to cross that distance in tunnels and secrecy.

Is it safe?

Did they get enough of the filters done last night or the night before?

Sighing, I try to focus on something else, anything else. But with only Novay to stare at, my mind runs in circles.

Unlocking the private channel Curata set up, I prepare to send a message to my dad. I sit up straighter. I smooth my hair. My fingers tap restlessly at the arms of my seat, and I stare blankly at the panel before me for a long moment, eyes unfocused.

Eventually, I signal the ship to start recording and offer up a smile that I hope doesn't look too nervous.

"We're almost there," I whisper. "I can't believe I'm going to actually get to see you again."

Pulling my eyes up from the control panel, I stare forward at the little white light on the window, the point where the ship records me from.

"For years, I thought…"

I trail off, nearly choking on the words.

"I thought you were dead."

I run a hand over the bottom of my face, shaking my head.

"I…" My chest rises with a deep breath. "I don't know if I ever told you… but thank you. For everything you did for me. I love you, Dad. I can't wait to see you again."

My heart twists in my chest, and tears prick at the corners of my eyes. I end the recording with another smile.

Slouching back into my seat, I stare once more at Novay. The beast stares back, as impassive as most of the Drennar that walk upon its face.

Placing a gentle hand on my stomach, I whisper to the baby, "Almost time to get your grandpa and your new grandma. She isn't the woman I thought would help me welcome a baby into the universe, but…"

I take a deep breath.

"She's better."

Chapter Forty-Three
Novay

Rone

Curata moves silently ahead of me, fluttering through our winding tunnel. My heart pounds, despite having done this before.

Every step threatens to call the Expressionless down upon us. Every breath, every blink, every fire of every synapse.

Anything could alert them.

Behind me, the rest of our allies follow in a single file line, orderly as ever. But their hands fidget. Their eyes dart upward.

If only the tunnels were wide enough for me to fly.

But my wings lie against my back, restless and fluttery. My footsteps ring out, hollow thuds echoing in the tunnel.

But we're almost there.

The end of the tunnel comes into view, and I know that when we reach it, Curata will shift the alonarium, opening new branches for us to venture into.

Just as she did last night, and the night before.

I try not to count my heartbeats to calm myself, try not to take refuge in the smooth predictability of the chemical makeup of each breath I take.

Instead, I draw my focus to the people I'll operate on this evening. I've been assigned fifty people, and my heart skips a beat just thinking of the number.

It's too many.

I swallow, throat growing tight, but I go over my plan for the task. I review the map of their compound, the groupings they reside in. I think back on the surgeries I've done in nights past, figuring my efficiency and applying that to the task ahead.

I should have an hour left before we have to turn back.

Should.

Just in case, I review Curata's progress over the past couple of nights. She'll be in the compound next to me, working with forty-two people.

She'll be done long before me.

If I fall behind…

I shudder at the thought of failing everyone so badly.

I won't fail them. I'll get everyone through their surgeries safely and with time to spare.

I nod, sealing my resolution just as we reach the end of the tunnel. The blue-grey walls undulate softly, pulsing the alonarium back toward our compound for storage, at least for the time being.

And for all that, Curata only has to move her hands a few times.

I marvel at her as additional tunnels open up, branching out beneath the compounds that hold our Human allies. I tap my pocket, ensuring that the tiny alonarium filters are still present, and then set off down the tunnel toward the compound I'm assigned to this evening.

The stairwell carries me up into their common room, and I find them all waiting for me. They stare uneasily. A few of them flinch, gazes darting from me to their neighbor and back again.

I smile, hoping to warm them up to me.

"Hi," I say. "I'm Rone."

Off to my right, a tall man with a shaved head says, "I'm Jasper." He steps forward, extending a hand.

I take his hand, completing the Human gesture with a grip gentle enough not to break his fingers.

"You really are different from the rest of them, aren't you?"

I chuckle. "I certainly hope so."

Shocked glances pass through the crowd, and furtive smiles sneak onto their faces.

"Are they… Are our people really coming for us?" Jasper dares to ask.

"They are," I say, nodding. "It took some doing. A bit of a revolution, really. A couple of your Ministers kidnapped a group of Regonians, that's a race of people from a different planet, and started experimenting on them."

Gasps echo through the room, and jaws fall all around me.

"But there were good people back on a couple of your stations and on Termana, and they put a stop to it," I say. "They're working with the Regonians now and bringing them with. But I can explain all that later. We have a lot to do tonight."

Someone hidden in a far corner asks, "Why do we need these things, anyway? If you're going to make tunnels for us, why cut us open?"

I turn, trying to find the speaker. A small woman with bright eyes stares at me from behind two tall men, barely visible through the gap between them.

"Just in case something goes wrong," I say. "If the Expressionless find out, if they find us… If they breach the tunnels… These filters will protect your lungs."

Beside me, Jasper nods, dark eyes distant as he considers my words. His gaze focuses on me, and he says, "I'll go first."

358

Chapter Forty-Four

Novay

Reginald

No timer hangs above my head tonight, but it pulses in my heart as I wait for word of Rone's safe return to her compound.

I lie awake, tossing and turning, staring at the barren, grey ceiling above me just as I have done for the past two nights, and I know I'll fall asleep in my testing again today.

But it doesn't matter.

For the first time in the twelve years I've been here, I've realized that I don't have to perform to my best abilities in my testing. Anything I do, any reaction I give them, is something for them to study.

And that's all they want.

That's their only purpose.

I shiver at the thought of such an empty life. Sickness roils within me at the thought of the horrors they've inflicted on others in pursuit of their one great purpose.

Even in all the time I spent studying during my schooling and all the time I spent in the labs back on Termana, I had a life. I had love and a family.

Something more to live for. Something to stop me from going off the deep end.

Like them.

Like Eva.

Sighing, I close my eyes and try to sleep. It'll be a few hours before I hear from Rone, after all.

Unless something goes wrong.

My heart lurches, and my eyes snap open again. My fingers tap at my sides, and I draw my hands up, knotting them together on my stomach just to still them.

I have to relax.

If not for their testing tomorrow, then for my sanity.

But a soft ping in my ear alerts me to a message, sent through the private channels, and my blood runs cold.

No.

She has to be okay.

Please, please, let her be okay.

I hesitate, afraid to let the message play, afraid to witness whatever terrible fate may have befallen her if she was discovered, afraid to learn what will happen to the people she was meant to help.

I grind my teeth, jaw popping as I clamp it tighter.

Nothing will change. Not watching, not listening... It won't change what happened.

I take a deep breath and let the message play.

Relief pours through me when Olivia's smiling face appears on the back of my eyelids. She whispers, "We're almost there," and my heart swells.

"I can't believe I'm going to actually get to see you again." She finally looks up, eyes focusing on the camera, and I choke out a sob.

I can't believe it either.

My shoulders shake, and I jam my palms into my eyes. The message pauses as red sparks move over my vision. Pulling my hands away, I let the message resume.

"For years, I thought..." she trails off, words catching in her throat. "I thought you were dead."

Tears stream freely, running over my temples and cascading into my ears. I cringe at the pain on her face, in her voice.

She smudges a hand over her face, shaking her head.

"I… I don't know if I ever told you," she begins, "but thank you. For everything you did for me. I love you, Dad. I can't wait to see you again."

Her message ends, and my body shakes with the ferocity of my sobs. My mind whirls, struggling to process everything, but my heart swells. A deep breath fills my lungs, shuddering and hitching.

She'll be here so soon, and now that I know there won't be hatred or blame lurking in her eyes, I'm not scared to see her.

I hate the danger she'll face when she gets here, but my arms ache to fold around her, to pull my little girl into a hug for the first time in far too long.

***

The message comes in from Ricardo, and I know the Humans spread throughout our facility will descend into chaos when they get it.

And for once, I have a part to play.

The Drennar posted in the corners of my testing room will get a show today. They'll have plenty to study.

I rise from my chair, letting the impotent rage that's simmered in my gut for over a decade come to the surface. It boils in my veins, never far from reach.

And today, it isn't useless.

I turn to the nearest Drennar and scream. The Expressionless creature stares on, impassive. Every fiber in my being wants to let this all out, to drive a fist into the beast's face.

But I've learned the limits over the years. I know the outbursts they'll tolerate without incapacitating me.

So, I stomp to the wall, pound my fists against the alonarium.

Blue fans of light sweep over me.

The floor vibrates beneath me with the fury of every Human on this God-forsaken planet, and I know they're heeding Ricardo's message, know they're unleashing their fury for the sake of our distraction.

I let out a scream, wondering if I'll break my voice in the coming days, but it doesn't matter. A sense of community washes over me, and though it's a violent, furious community at the moment, I'll take it.

Chapter Forty-Five
The Realm of Stars

Tenna

Two more days aboard the ship pass by, and Novay consumes every forward-facing window. It blocks out the stars, the worlds beyond.

Perched in a hall above the cockpit, I stare at it, and I shudder at the sight of this frigid, barren place. No grasses or trees grow. No mountains rise. No rivers flow.

No animals live.

No creatures exist but the Drennar.

They created this entire planet, forsaking nature, forsaking life, in the name of greed. They lust after knowledge, tearing through lives and love.

Tension builds within me, but I'll have my release soon.

Only one more day. We'll bring them to their knees.

My fingers curl into claws. I narrow my eyes, staring at the home of these vile creatures.

Taking a deep breath, I pull myself away from the window, pushing myself toward the cargo bay for some final drills.

A message from Rone stops me in my tracks. Krona's eyes tighten as he looks to me, and I see his Link flashes with the same message.

We work with our Links, transforming the window before us to show the message. Rone's wings flutter behind her, and her hands fidget in her lap.

"I… I found out. Well, Curata found out what your experiment was, why the Drennar were monitoring you." She swallows.

And so do I.

Krona takes my hand, lacing our fingers together.

"You're… like us. A *version* of us." Rone shakes her head, drops her gaze.

"What does that mean?" Krona asks, but I have no answer.

My mind grasps at the words, trying to piece them together in a way that makes sense, but finally, I resolve to wait out Rone's explanation.

"You… Your ancestors were put on Regonia to see other paths our evolution could take. An entire generation of Drennar were split over three planets, divided up. A group on one planet was told everything, given access to all the same information. They were the control group."

Rone sucks in a breath, then raises her eyes to stare straight at the camera, straight at us.

"Other groups were settled across the planets, split across continents, and told different things. They just…" A breath of morbid laughter bursts from her. "They just wanted to see what would happen, how you would evolve, but…"

Her face falls, eyes tightening. "They were taking samples, every now and then. Taking people. Any time a group's evolution converged with another, they took one group and studied them."

So, they really would've come for us eventually.

My mouth goes dry, but my resolve for this war grows stronger.

"Or in your case… When your evolution converged with that of another cluster, they showed the humans that you existed to see what they would do."

My stomach drops, and my teeth grind together.

***

My heart pounds as I lie awake. Every muscle tensed with anticipation, despite the sleep I know I need.

Krona rolls toward me, arm slipping over my waist. His breath rushes across my skin as he moves closer.

Lifting his head from the pillow, he peers down at me for a moment, squinting through the haze of sleep. "Are you still awake?"

"Unfortunately," I whisper.

Krona leans down, pressing his lips to my neck. "What's wrong?" he asks, breath hot on my skin.

Strands of dark hair brush over my collarbone before he pulls away. Propping himself up on his elbow, he peers into my eyes, pale green vivid against the darkness that surrounds us.

For half a breath, I consider what it must be like to be a Human, to see no more than shades of grey and black in the night. But Krona's brows reach for each other, prompting me to answer him.

"Nothing," I say. "Just ready to move, to finish this."

He chuckles, and his thumb moves back and forth, trailing waves of fire across my stomach. Heat pools in my center.

I breathe deeply, relishing his touch as the tension within me transforms. He knows me so well, knows the way my body builds too much energy before a battle, the way I need a release.

Staring up into those crisp green eyes, I touch his face, unsurprised that even with everything else taken from me, I never forgot those eyes.

I slide my hand to the back of his neck, pulling him toward me. Our lips meet, and he dips his hand to my hip. I moan as he grips my buttock, sigh as he positions himself between my legs. The worlds crash down around us as I grip his back, pulling him into me.

My lips part with a gasp, and he ravages my neck. My hands roam over his back, sliding to caress his abdomen, his chest. I slip my hands into his hair, tangling my fingers in the silken strands.

He slides an arm beneath me, cradling the back of my neck and tipping my head back. Nipping at my nape, he teases.

I move my hips in time with his, arching against him, rising to meet him. We move faster, pushing ourselves toward a breaking point.

Sweet, delicious agony burns within me, begging for more. His name bursts from my lips, and I wrap my leg around his, driving him deeper.

Our eyes meet, and the universe cracks open within me. I shatter, crying out and tensing around him.

He moves faster, biting my neck, cupping my breast. His thumb moves in slow circles, and he pushes me to another peak.

He slides deeper, pushes harder, and his release comes over him with a shudder. Breathlessly, he gasps, "Tenna…"

I stare up at him, breathing hard and trembling with our union. He smiles, leaning his forehead against mine.

"Hoo kai voo mai," I whisper.

"Hoo kai voo mai." His lips brush over mine as he answers, and my heart skips a couple beats.

My body melts, and we roll to our sides, staring into each other's eyes. He touches my face, hands soft despite the strength I know they hold.

I slide a hand over his chest, tracing scars, recalling the memories associated with each one, and I make a silent vow. Whether at the hands of the Humans or the Drennar, no one will suffer an experiment as we did. I won't let anyone lose the ones they love to the tampering of another. I won't let these spineless Drennar take anyone else.

Certainty sweeps over me, and I nestle into Krona's embrace, sated and relaxed. We twine our limbs together, and I breathe deeply of him.

Tomorrow, this whole mess comes to an end.

Chapter Forty-Six

Novay

Rone

Curata stands before me, sending out a final message to the Humans here on Novay. I know what it says, having seen Ricardo's message before she did.

Be calm now. Be catatonic if you can.

Wait.

We're coming.

She smiles when the message goes through, nodding and sending the ambient light shimmering over her iridescent skin. Vaguely, I wonder if she's already looping their catatonic footage to cover the escape or if she'll wait. Beside her, Lustran raises one hand to his chest, and she follows suit.

I hold my hand over my heart, feeling every beat beneath my palm. The constant streams of information stop, and that old familiar trill of fear skips through me.

But only briefly.

I focus on the so-called data stream that pulses within my chest. I zero in on the emotions it beats in time with, not even bothering to argue with myself over the location of the synapses that actually control emotion.

Because my brain isn't where I feel them.

It's something I never understood before, something I never thought possible. A whole sense we never credited.

Because we don't know as much as we thought.

And this madness has to end.

My timer goes off, a soft beep in the back of my mind, and I marvel at how much easier it was this time.

Whether it was the practice, the necessity of it now that the day is here, or that I concentrated on my new guide, I can't say. But suddenly, fully disconnected from Drennar society, I feel free.

Free to do what I feel is right, to be who I need to be.

And right now, I need to be someone who ends this.

I step up to Curata, ready to test my proximity transfer abilities. With our networks, we haven't needed them in centuries, but we might need them in the coming hours.

Before I can lean down, Curata flutters her wings, hovering at my height. We lean our foreheads together, clasping one hand on the side of each other's neck.

She sends a burst of data, the layout of the tunnels she's already hollowed out for us. I focus, propelling a simple acknowledgment across the channel between us.

She nods, dropping her hand. As she pulls away, she smiles, and the light that always radiates from her seems warmer, softer somehow.

I step away, ready to distribute the map and help others test their proximity transfers, as well. With everyone off the network and all our plans safe from the prying eyes of the Expressionless, we distribute everything we have.

I spread final plans for the assault, the location where we'll go topside to load everyone safely into the ship, the exact route we'll travel through the tunnels to free the Humans.

And the list of those going above to aid in the attack.

More above than below, but I'll be down here with Reginald. When I see Curata's plans for her distraction, I almost wish I could see it in action. But these grey tunnels and the Humans they'll lead me to will be my work for the day.

And I can't wait to see the faces of these people when we take them to their ship.

Armed with all the information I can gather, guided by the heart I neglected for far too long, I descend into the tunnel. My chest feels too tight, too small, to contain the heart that hammers away within.

Because I'll see Reginald soon, and then, we'll work together to fix this.

He should wake soon.

And Curata's distraction will pull his guards away first. The people need to see him, the spark that started their wildfire.

We pass through the tunnel quickly. Sentrah smiles, skull plate shining in the soft light, when I turn to look back at her. Serenity hovers within her gaze, just as it did in Curata's, and I wonder if my own eyes look the same or if the steely determination that straightens my spine has hardened my gaze.

We reach the stairs that lead to Reginald's room, and I stare up at the thin sheet of alonarium that covers us. I check the time, but I needn't bother. Right on schedule, the floor slides away, and Reginald descends.

A smile perches on his lips, but his eyes are resolute. The flecks of green and blue amid the hazel dance with relief and sheer force of will, and I decide that this must be the mirror of my own expression.

Pulling in a deep breath, I take his hand, and we set off deeper into the tunnels for the rest of the Human race.

Chapter Forty-Seven
The Realm of Stars

Krona

In our room, I step into my suit, something the Humans back on Termana "printed" for me. I'm not sure what that means, likely some technological thing they have on hand, but it doesn't matter. They said it will stave off the electrical impulses of the coming attack, and that's reason enough to wear it.

But as I pull it on, it clings to me like a second skin, and I hate it instantly.

Tenna makes a face as she pulls hers up, and I suppress a laugh. My eyes sweep over her, relishing the way the suit hugs her powerful thighs and buttocks, her strong arms, the curves of her breasts.

Maybe the suit isn't so bad after all.

She catches my gaze, and I smile. Her chest rises with a full, deep breath as she looks me over, and I wonder how much my own suit shows her.

"Later," I whisper.

She nods, raising one eyebrow. "We have a war to fight first," she says, eyes darkening. Her shoulders go back, and she raises her chin.

My heart gallops, and I set to work pulling my armor on over the insulated suit. Tenna does the same, and we step out into the metal tube that leads to the cargo bay, ready to meet our people and end a war.

Chapter Forty-Eight
The Realm of Stars

Ricardo

I stand behind Olivia's seat as she and Hugo ready us for descent. Her hands move over the controls with ease, and I marvel at her. Flying this beast gave me perspective and a fierce appreciation for how smoothly and effortlessly she works with it.

The grey monstrosity of Novay lurks, but thanks to her, thanks to Rone and Curata, the Drennar don't see us, don't expect us. My lips curl into a smile.

"We'll be going down soon," Olivia says, turning in her seat. She looks up at me, eyes wide. "You should probably strap in. They don't have an atmosphere since everything's just closed in, so the landing won't be as shaky as on Regonia, but…"

She doesn't have to speak the rest.

But they might find us. They might attack before we land. They might blow us right out of the not-quite-sky.

I nod slowly, and she rises. With careful, measured steps, she walks with me into the hall outside the cockpit. I stop before we move too far, knowing she needs to stick close, and turn to face her.

The stark lights glitter on the beads of sweat on her face. She stands before me in full armor, just like my own. The dark suit shines, as does the thick, glossy braid of hair that drapes over her shoulder.

I take her in, desperate to remember everything. My eyes linger over the curve of her neck, the sweep of her cheekbones, the flecks of gold and blue and green in her beautiful hazel eyes.

Because this might be it.

This might be the last time I see her.

Her eyes dart between mine before dropping to her hands. They worry at each other, twisting and wringing.

I take them in mine, lacing our fingers together.

"If this…" she begins. Her voice cracks, and she clears her throat, trying again. "If this doesn't work, if something happens…" She meets my gaze. "I love you."

Despite everything that could go wrong in the coming hours, I smile. Stepping forward, I slide one arm around her waist and use the other hand to cup her cheek.

"I love you too," I say.

My lips whisper over hers, but it isn't enough. Last night wasn't enough. Every night we've had wasn't enough.

But this might be all we get.

So, I press myself to her, pulling her close and begging the universe to be kind as she throws her arms around me. Our mouths move together, just as desperate to remember as we are.

The taste of her, the feel of her, the scent, I commit it all to memory, hoping this isn't the last time.

My Link emits a soft beep, alerting me to the time, and I clutch her tighter.

I can't let go yet.

She kisses me harder, as if we can keep the coming battle at bay if we never pull apart.

But there are people counting on us.

My next alarm goes off, and this one, we can't ignore. We have three minutes to buckle in and initiate our descent, and god knows what else Olivia has to do in the cockpit to make that happen.

I pull away, grinding my teeth together. I lean my forehead against hers for a second, drawing from her strength and offering her my own, just as Tenna and Krona do for each other.

I step back through the dismal grey hall, never turning my back, not letting go of her hand until we're so far apart that our hands slip apart.

She touches her stomach, swallowing so hard I see the movement in her throat.

We have to be okay.

I'll make sure she's okay, make sure the baby is okay.

No matter what.

Only when she slumps into her pilot's seat do I turn and buckle myself into a seat in a hall that branches off this one, sticking close to her, serving as her personal guard throughout what she has to do.

A few Specialists line the wall, already buckled in. They glance at me as I fasten the last buckle on my harness, but I can't look at them, not with so many tears in my eyes. I can't speak to them with the emotions so thick in my throat.

Chapter Forty-Nine
The Realm of Stars

Olivia

My hands tremble as we descend, and I worry that I may hit a wrong button, move a lever just a bit too far.

Will they see us?

All I can do is trust in Curata and her promises that the sudden change in every Human on Novay will warrant distant analysis and full attention. I can do nothing but hope they don't step foot into a single room, don't look into the footage she's manufactured for them to watch.

So much rides on this, on her being right.

But she knows them better than we do.

I stare at the planet ahead, growing larger by the second. Individual facilities burst into view, grey grids outlined by strips of vivid blue.

No one walks between them, safely concealed within their alonarium walls. There's no one outside to look up. At least, not that I can see.

Do they see us through cameras?

Would they ever think us capable of coming here?

The shape of the whole planet bulges outward at Curata's command, making room for us to land, and I gasp. Though I knew this was coming, I never expected the whole planet to shift. I stare on, hands moving of their own accord.

How much can she do?

The ship bucks as my hand slips, but I quickly regain control. Hugo and I settle us easily upon the surface of Novay, but I feel none of the wonder that filled me when we landed on Regonia.

My heart races, not with awe, but with fear. My nerves wind tight in my gut. For a moment, I wonder if the fear will transfer to the baby, if it'll be more anxious when it's born because of the circumstances surrounding the pregnancy.

But this baby has my genes.

It'll be anxious no matter what.

Focus!

The baby has to be born first. Which means we have to get through this.

We sit on the surface, waiting, but Curata doesn't leave us hanging for long. Within seconds, the planet shifts again, reaching up to enclose our cargo doors and build an airlock.

The sensors at the doors signal me when the air content outside them reaches an acceptable level. Hugo speaks to the Soldiers and Warriors in the cargo bay, voice booming across the speakers throughout the ship.

My personal guard unbuckles in the hall, and we start the process of unleashing our Warriors and Soldiers upon this unsuspecting planet.

Chapter Fifty
Novay

Tenna

The cargo bay door lowers, right on time, unleashing us upon the Drennar world, showing us the world we could've shaped. But chaos already rules.

Strange music pulses through the air, something electronic, something that sounds like menace and broken things. A glance at my Link reveals it to be "Oxbow B by Lorn. 2014."

It stands the hairs up on the back of my neck. It shakes the little alonarium building we pour into, rattles the floor beneath us.

But then, the alonarium ceiling rises, pushing outward, meeting with those of other buildings, absorbing them. A dull grey hall opens before us at Curata's command, ushering us forward into the facility that once housed the Humans.

Ahead, Drennar stand motionless, exposed in the newly open field of their facility now that walls melt into the floor. I peer past them, eyes locking on a large cluster of these foul creatures.

The roof continues to rise, granting us far more space than we could ever need, but I see the reason soon enough.

Curata.

She saunters out of a tunnel, wearing some strange thing over her face. The mask blocks the shining hues of her skin, covers her pretty blue hair.

She squeezes the hand of another Drennar, a man named Lustran. Nodding once, she steps away from him. The rest of the newly emotional step back, and a light flashes on her strange mask.

She rises on a wave of alonarium, rippling the floor beneath her. All around, Expressionless stare on, fans of light sweeping over her.

With a twitch of one hand, her wave surges forward, carrying her along. Shapes take form at the front, galloping ahead, and I gasp when I realize she's made Vyrtons. Pale-grey Vyrtons. She pushes forward, funneled by the strange blue strips that circle the planet as more and more walls melt into her wave, revealing more Drennar.

Dumbfounded, I glance at Krona, but my gaze snaps forward when I hear a scream.

Blood gushes over the floor in her wake, pouring from one of the Expressionless, impaled upon a pike of alonarium. Another snaps from their analytic catatonia, rushing up the wave of alonarium. He grapples for control, stuffing some of the strange material down.

But she wrests it from his control quickly, sending a spike through his gut with the flick of a finger.

My jaw falls open, and I wonder who we've allied ourselves with.

"Ready?" Krona asks, voice low and made unsteady by this display.

The newly emotional Drennar charge, taking their cue from some internal timer Rone mentioned. Mouth suddenly dry, gaze fixed on the unmoving Drennar staring up at Curata from the blue channels, I nod.

But a twinge of guilt creeps through me.

I've never killed anywhere but a battlefield or a hunt, never slain a foe that wasn't fighting.

I think of the people we lost on the field on Regonia when they came for Olivia. I fill my mind with the Humans who've suffered at their hands, the Humans Rone and Reginald lead through tunnels toward us even now.

The Humans we're helping to save.

I think of our future generations, wonder when the Drennar will come for us, trying to assuage the strange guilt within me.

But the Drennar do it for me.

As Curata nears the center of their facility, they snap out of their stupors. Some sprint for her. Some fly.

Some turn to face us, rushing forward to meet us, and the battlefield turns familiar.

For a second, I wish Kala were here to run to battle with us, or perhaps Efsi. My heart twists, and my lips form his sound, the soft, trilling coo. Then, I make the sound of the Awakening, screaming the desperate fury of such a loss, a loss that never would've come to be if they hadn't informed the Humans of our existence. The sound burns my throat, then rumbles through our ranks.

Axe drawn, I rush to meet our enemy and launch myself upon the first Drennar I reach. Its cold eyes peer into me, merciless, and I dodge its first swing.

But its second punch hits me square in the stomach. I duck when it tries to grab me with its second pair of arms and drive my axe into its chest. Blood pours out, and I kick it back, pulling my axe free.

Then, I move to the next.

Chapter Fifty-One
Novay

Ricardo

The cargo bay door lies open before us. Hugo and a few Specialists stare out, watching the chaos of the battlefield. I peer past them, taking in the rippling alonarium.

The grey metal bends and sways impossibly, shaping itself to Curata's will in the cavernous space she's made for us. My jaw falls open, and I marvel at what she's done.

For a brief moment, I wonder how long the Drennar have known of us, if maybe they visited Earth in the distant past, if maybe they were the gods the old religions built themselves upon.

Shaking my head, I focus on the matter at hand, doing my best to ignore the miraculous control she exhibits and the vast depths of her mind. I watch as she sweeps Drennar up in the wave she rides upon, barreling over them and cocooning them in alonarium.

And they just stand there.

They watch her, just as I do. They stare at the Regonian Warriors, the Human Soldiers. Odd blue sheets of light flit out from their eyes, sweeping over everything, but they don't move. Briefly, I wonder if they're trying to use the alonarium against her, relying on it as heavily as ever.

But it won't do their bidding now.

Either way, they analyze, just as Curata said they would when faced with something new.

I swallow, unsure of the conclusion they'll come to. My nerves wind tight, and I pull out my taser. My heart jumps into my throat, beating my windpipe to a pulp as I wait.

Curata pushes forward, apparently crossing some invisible line they've drawn, and those nearest her begin to move. I don't see what they do, but her response is clear enough.

A spike of alonarium sends blood gushing from a body, a shock of color in a grey world. Then another. And another.

The rest spring to life, most launching themselves at Curata. But a few hundred turn this way, sprinting headlong for the warriors who've already exited our ship.

I tighten my grip on my taser, hoping none of them make it past our ranks to us. They move closer, coming into view, showing me the details of their modified bodies. Some have too many arms. Some have extra legs. Some are enormous, while others are closer to our height.

They meet our ranks, and the Humans and Regonians in the front lines slit open gills, tear strange mechanical bits from flesh. Crimson pours over dull grey, painting this barren place the color of death.

I track Krona and Tenna, watch their graceful forms push the Drennar back. They lead Warriors and Soldiers, sweeping the floor of enemies, corralling them toward the wall that encapsulates this strange place.

Keeping them away from us.

Hugo takes the first steps down the ramp. Four Specialists descend with him. Knees bent, they creep forward, tasers out and at the ready.

I raise mine, pointing it up, finger carefully outside the trigger. I stalk down the ramp, sticking close to Olivia. She holds her own taser, but my breath catches at the thought of her needing it.

We reach the alonarium landing, and the rear guard descends. Making slow progress, we step over strewn body parts and puddles of blood.

The noise of the battle and the music Curata blares conspire together to disguise our footsteps, and we push forward into the heart of this facility. Krona and Tenna command our forces, spreading blood near the wall. On our other side, Curata shapes the planet to her will, wrapping enemies in a rippling, blue-grey blanket of death.

Pedestals stick up from the floor, arranged in a circle with empty aisles radiating outward, and we weave through them. Foreign symbols flash on their tops, but I pay them no mind, unable to read this language.

Some bear images, video feeds from other places, but they show exactly what Curata wants them to. Humans standing and sitting in their rooms, unmoving, unblinking. The footage she used to distract the Drennar continues, assuring them that they have nothing to lose in focusing on us.

Dragging my attention away, I scan the area around us.

Still clear.

At the center, we find a master pedestal, larger and more complex than the others. Miniscule screens decorate its top, showcasing imagery, graphs, data streams, and countless other things I could never hope to make sense of.

But Olivia moves to it, taking the controls in hand with ease, and we arrange ourselves around her. My chest swells with pride that she might be able to make heads or tails of the mess on those screens, but my stomach drops.

Because if even a few Drennar slip away from Krona and Tenna, from Curata… I could lose her.

No.

Trust them. They know how to handle this.

Chapter Fifty-Two
Novay

Reginald

I fight the urge to hug every single Human present, knowing we don't have the time. But I haven't been this close to another Human in twelve years, and the impulse keeps popping up, trying to take control of my arms.

Swallowing, I try to force my heart out of my throat and back down into my chest where it belongs.

Rone squeezes my hand, face vibrant and eyes alight. I return the gesture, overcome with the urge to kiss her, to thank her, to assure her that I know the weight of what she's done and will never forget it.

But we have so many people left to free.

With a silent wave, we usher the group of two hundred down into the tunnels to join the rest. Trekking forward, we meet up with the group we left in another tunnel, adding them to our ranks before continuing onward.

Thousands of footsteps echo in the tunnel, but the noise above drowns it out. The ceiling ripples, but never comes within a meter of our heads. Screams ring out and thuds reverberate. Music blares from speakers buried in alonarium, likely made of alonarium.

And we move, undetected, toward the last group of people. Four hundred Humans wait in the largest experiment room yet, and we close in on the cold grey stairs that will lead us to them.

Climbing up, I'm greeted by a dark-skinned man with a shaved head. He beams at me, rushing forward to crush me to him. His hands clap my back, and he squeezes tighter, chuckling all the while.

"I can't believe it's really happening," he says, voice low and still a bit hoarse from the screaming he must've done in our days of fury. "It is really happening, right?"

He pulls back to stare into my face, still smiling.

I laugh. My voice cracks as I say, "It is. Can't you hear that outside?"

He nods, and excited whispers roll through the massive crowd behind him. They cling to each other, holding hands, embracing. Every face glows.

Disentangling myself from the man before me, I turn to Rone. "Ready?"

She nods, taking my hand once more, and we lead the last Humans into the tunnels.

Chapter Fifty-Three
Novay

Krona

The Drennar fall back, fighting vigorously, but we outnumber the ones here. We swarm, sweeping them into a group, pushing them against Curata's wall.

She pulls mounts from the floor for us, offering us Vyrtons made of alonarium. I swing up onto the nearest one, holding tight as it gallops forward. Peering out between its massive antlers, I survey what's left of our foe.

Half the ranks of the Drennar have been dismantled. I let out a joyous shout, relishing the echoes that sweep through my people.

The metal Vyrto's head bows as we breach the line of retreating Drennar, and I think it a sign for my coming dismount. But it scoops its head down low, exposing me to the enemy for a moment.

Sharp antlers puncture two Drennar, and my unliving mount jerks its head back up, flinging them upward. Their bodies soar over our ranks, raining blood over Warriors and Soldiers alike.

On all sides, tasers bite into flesh and blades slice straight through strange clear plates and skulls. Cries ring out above the pounding music Curata fills this cavernous space with.

A group of Drennar stands ahead, clustered around two of our Warriors. I glance at Tenna and direct her gaze.

She nods, and we rise to our feet, standing upon our mounts' backs. Careful to balance on the jolting, jerking beast, I run up its neck in two strides, pushing off on the last.

I fly through the air, crashing into one of the Drennar outnumbering our unfortunate Warriors. My axe sinks into its face, spraying blood over me, but the Drennar cushions my fall.

Tenna looks up from her prey after landing beside me, smiling with blood spattered on her face, dripping down her neck. My heart flutters, and I return her smile.

We rise, joining our warriors and dispatching the remaining Drennar from this little cluster. Crimson spills over the floor, growing slick beneath our feet, but we have far to go still.

Our enemy retreats, drawing us further. The bright blue channel that runs through this space hums as we near. My heart pounds, and blood roars in my ears.

A Human beside me fires his taser, sending the barbs flying at a Drennar. Its limbs jerk and jolt, and it falls over. Panic beats within me for just a second as I'm overcome with the need to turn and run, to hide from the lightning.

But it doesn't arc, doesn't leap to me.

Swallowing, I raise my axe and plunge into battle. A Drennar with a scaled body sprints toward me with arms raised. Massive spikes stick out from elongated forearms.

It barrels forward, and my jaw drops when its spikes shift, turning to point toward me. Eyes blank, face slack, it watches me, analyzes every move I make.

But this thing doesn't know me, even if it thinks it does, even if it's been watching me my whole life.

At the last second, I drop low, rolling and slamming my axe into its leg. Blood pours over me as it tumbles, headlong. A spike digs into the alonarium, and the Drennar flips.

I turn in time to see Tenna drive her axe into its neck, sharpened bone gliding through the Drennar's scales easily.

And it never flinches, never bats an eye. Never makes a sound as the blood leaks from it.

What are these things?

How could Rone ever have been like this?

I shudder, deciding that I don't actually want to know. I'll keep her in my mind as she is.

I fall into sync with Tenna once more, moving quickly to take down the next nightmare to turn on us. The four-armed giant lumbers forward, footsteps shuddering through the floor.

We split up, each taking a side.

I stare up at it, unaccustomed to doing so. It turns to face Tenna, and my jaw drops when I find another face on the back of its head.

Two arms bend toward me, thick, meaty fingers grasping for my head. The clear plates on its forearms catch the light, blinding me, but I duck out of its grasp.

It reaches again, and I roll to the side, bringing my axe up. It connects, sending fingers flying through the air.

No scream crosses its lips. No lines appear between its brows.

I pause, startled yet again by how barren these creatures are.

Tenna covers my lapse, slashing with her axes and taking a leg out from under the beast. I leap, sinking my blade into its neck and bringing it down with a thunderous crash.

The alonarium ripples beneath me when I land, and for a moment, I think it from the weight of the beast. But long after this creature settles, the floor still shakes.

The music stops, replaced by a shrill scream, and I spin on my heel. Curata's wave of alonarium trembles erratically. She seizes, limbs twitching and head jerking from side to side.

"No!" I scream, voice blending with Lustran's.

But Curata goes still, tiny body frail and limp. Her waves and Vyrtons fall, liquefying and settling back into the floor.

My heart stops.

Bits and pieces of the floor shudder open, revealing the Humans we aimed to save, vulnerable in the tunnels Curata made for them.

My blood runs cold as Lustran launches himself forward, wings beating furiously, propelling him at the Drennar who brought his love down.

But this man, the only Drennar present stronger than Curata, sends a spike of alonarium up to meet him.

It cuts into flesh, piercing Lustran's chest and coming out his back. Blood pours down the length of the spike, and he goes limp, arms and legs dangling, head slumped forward. His wings hang uselessly over him.

The floor comes up around us, wrapping itself around our feet, our legs. I fight against it, thrashing and screaming with rage, but it pins me in place.

Horror slides through me, and I try to turn, try to see the heart of the facility, try to see Olivia.

Chapter Fifty-Four

Novay

Rone

Reginald and I sprint through the tunnels, buoyed by adrenaline. Excitement buzzes through my veins.

Thousands of footsteps pound the floor behind us, and I take heart that Curata has thought this all through so clearly, that she has music and battles to cover the sounds of our escape. The world above us rattles with the noise she rallied, just for this.

We round a corner, and the final staircase comes into view, waiting to lead us onto the ship. My heart hammers away in my chest, and a smile spreads itself over my face.

Gripping Reginald's hand, I push harder, closing the distance. He cries out beside me, triumphant, and the voices of the Humans behind us rise to echo him.

But the alonarium shudders and ripples and bucks.

I glance at the ceiling as it seizes. It twists and contorts in ways that Curata would never sanction, surely not. A jagged corner plunges down, nearly knocking me down, before it's ripped back up.

"Watch your heads!" I scream over my shoulder.

They must be fighting her, trying to take the alonarium from her.

And if they're coming this close, it means the facility manager has come.

I swallow, trying to hold waves of icy fear at bay. There was only a small chance that he'd come out this early, and now that he has…

My mind races, but my heart freezes in place. The time we have to escape just got cut in half.

"We have to move!" I scream.

The ceiling above us dips, flexing and sweeping over us, just barely missing our heads. I crouch, running as fast as I can. Reginald pants beside me, barely keeping up.

Feathers tickle my skin as I fold my wings against my back, desperate not to have them broken by the chaos above.

But we're almost there.

"Just hold him at bay a little longer," I beg silently, knowing Curata can't hear me, knowing she'll do whatever she can.

Despite the frenzy within the alonarium, our exit begins to open over the stairs. Relief washes through me, warm and giddy, but it's short-lived.

The alonarium goes still.

Our ceiling, our stairwell, our exit… All movement stops. Less than a meter open, we'll have to file through the gap at the top of the stairs far too slowly.

The music overhead stops.

Silence falls everywhere but in the tunnel. Footsteps ring loud and thunderous, but we have to move, have to get out. This many people would crush us if we tried to stop.

I try not to think about what this silence means for Curata, focusing on the Humans instead.

I have to get that stairwell open.

But reconnecting isn't an option. It'll take too long, and it could give us away.

Pulling in a deep breath, I turn to Reginald and say, "Slow them down. I have to get it open further."

He nods, hazel eyes wild, and releases my hand.

Chest heaving, I hope that this won't be our last touch. I push myself faster, leaving him and the Humans behind, hoping to open it before they even reach it.

I launch myself forward, wishing to use my wings, wishing the tunnel were even just a bit wider.

But Curata has given us so much already. How could I dare ask more?

My heart twists in my chest, knowing that if that exit isn't opening further, she's likely beyond help now. Tears prick at the corners of my eyes, and I realize with stunning clarity that…

I'm going to miss her.

A sob racks my chest, but I push onward, sprinting up the stairs with blurred vision. At the top, I peek out, grateful that no one stands close by.

Ducking back in, I stand beneath the plate of alonarium that blocks our way. Inching up the stairs, I crouch beneath it, then dig in my heels. My thighs tense, and my entire body strains.

I push upward, hating the way it creaks and moans noisily before it gives way. But it gives.

Slowly, painfully, it rises.

The gap widens.

And then, it opens completely, commanded by someone. All the force I was exerting sends me upward, throwing me off balance. I right myself but find no glee at the missing barrier.

The Humans in the tunnel stare upward, faced with crowds of Drennar approaching slowly. The Expressionless stare down at them, at me.

Blue fans of light burst from their eyes to sweep over the bedraggled, exhausted Humans. Alonarium slips upward, coiling around our ankles to hold us in place, and dread seeps into me.

Chapter Fifty-Five

Novay

Olivia

Everything stops, and I look up from the control panel. Alexandria waits on my Link, ready to go.

I only needed a few more seconds.

My face falls as I look at the battlefield.

Curata's wave of alonarium has collapsed, and she lies limp upon its remains. Lustran hangs on a pike.

My heart drops, and a thick lump forms in my throat.

They're… gone.

A message from Curata waits for me on my Link, beeping softly, but Expressionless Drennar close in. The alonarium wraps around the feet of my guards, twines around my ankles, but fear grips me tighter than it ever could.

A Drennar with the body of a lizard slinks forward. Its face looks so much like Lustran's that it startles me, makes me turn to stare at him. Pale and lifeless in death, his face resembles this new Drennar's face even more.

Hugo raises his taser and takes aim. The beast falls in a mass of jerking limbs.

Three more come our way, pulling alonarium up and shaping it into weapons I can't even name. Projectiles fly from their ends, soaring toward us.

The tiny grey things hit three Specialists, spreading and wrapping around them on impact. The alonarium presses their arms to their bodies, clamps their knees together. They drop to the ground, and the floor comes up like a blanket, tucking them in.

But this isn't how it was supposed to go!

I try desperately to refocus my attention on the control panel, but one of their projectiles hits Ricardo. He deflects it with his taser, but the weapon flies from his hand.

The Drennar pulls back an arm, summoning a spear of alonarium and sending it flying. It lands true, sinking into Ricardo's shoulder.

My heart stops, and I scream.

A sleek Drennar soars toward us, borne by dull grey wings. Its eyes sweep vivid blue light over us, and it stares down at me as it scoops the floor up to wrap around Ricardo.

And I can see it now.

He'll tuck Ricardo into the floor, stealing him away for some experiment. And then, it'll be my turn.

Everything will be lost.

They'll keep taking people, keep hurting them.

When the facility manager reaches for the spear in Ricardo's chest, I break.

"Wait!" I scream.

The one who speared Ricardo grabs the weapon, ripping it free of his body. Blood pours from the wound, and Ricardo sags in his bonds.

My heart lurches, and tears pour over my cheeks. His face seems sallow, his golden eyes dull. I try to step forward, but the alonarium wrapped around my ankles holds me in place, pins my feet to the floor.

"Speak," the facility manager says.

I tear my eyes from Ricardo, and my hand presses to my stomach. I force myself to speak, but my voice cracks immediately.

Taking a deep breath, I try again. But my hopelessness comes out in my words.

"You've studied us. You know enough of Human history to know how this will go. Even if you drive us out today, even if you kidnap us all or… kill us…"

Fear tries to still my tongue, but I push forward.

"Even if you kill every Human here, we'll keep coming. Over and over again. That's what we do."

My spine straightens, and I try to take heart in the things I say.

"When we Humans know we're right, hell, even sometimes when we know we're wrong, we keep fighting. We destroy everything in our way, and we fight until we either succeed... or die."

The facility manager blinks, infuriatingly calm.

My eyes drift to Ricardo instead, and everything in me fractures.

I whisper, "In this case, we know we're right. Being the underdog doesn't scare us."

My chest heaves, and yet the Drennar stare on, impassive.

I shift my gaze to the facility manager, eyes hard. "You know I'm right. And you know, either way, you lose a lot of data."

I tip my head, and venom seeps into my voice. "Whether that's because we win and fry everything you have or we die out. Can you stomach that loss?"

With a silent thank you to Curata, I use our private channel to access the controls. They stare down at me, considering, calculating, while

Ricardo bleeds, while Lustran hangs dead, while Curata lies limp and broken, her shimmering wings now motionless and dull.

But I set up Alexandria, ready to burn their libraries down.

"If another Human or Regonian suffers by your hands," I say, voice pure malice, "you'll lose everything."

I stare at them, and finally, maybe, just a little bit, I understand my mother's need to end their hold on us, to destroy the things they hold dear. Her drive to end this, even at great cost.

But unlike her, I intend to make sure they pay the price, not us.

The facility manager steps forward, green eyes bright with electric blue streaks. It pulls alonarium from the floor and presses it to Ricrado's chest.

"What are you doing?" I scream. "Leave him alone! Didn't you just hear me? You'll lose everything."

But I don't care what they lose. The truth of my misery pours from my lips. "Please," I beg. "Please, don't hurt him."

Panic overwhelms me as Alexandria doesn't kick in, doesn't destroy them.

Is the trigger for the program not working?

The facility manager doesn't even glance at me. "I am repairing him."

Stunned, I fall silent, watching as Ricardo's eyes flutter, impossible as it may be.

"I ran the calculations," the facility manager says. "Your lives are worth more to us than your deaths."

I stutter, but I say, "You can't keep experimenting on us. You can't keep using us."

Tears pour over my cheeks, but I say, "The Survival Coalition will be in touch to work out details, but you can only watch from afar. We're so much more than you realize. And that goes for the others you experiment on, too. You can't keep doing this."

The facility manager stills again, blue striations in its eyes moving and shifting with some new calculation. "What have you put into our system?"

"Alexandria," I say. "If you hurt any more people, if it detects any harmful experiments, any non-consensual experiments, it'll burn everything you have. If you tamper with it, if you so much as look at the coding for it, everything is toast."

"We will contact your Survival Coalition," the facility manager says.

My shoulders droop with relief.

Ricardo's eyes open, and he searches for me. Panic shines in his gaze until I smile. Tears blur my vision, and the second my alonarium shackles slip away, I sprint for him.

His bindings fall away. He rights himself, suddenly whole, bracing himself just in time to catch me as I throw myself upon him. Our lips meet, and our tears mingle as I kiss him. My hands tangle in his hair, and he holds on tight, as if clinging for dear life.

The world beyond my closed eyes flickers blue, and I pull away to find those strange lights sweeping over us.

I shudder, hating that they've ruined this moment for us, hating that I didn't think to cut off their stupid blue fans with a warning or a secondary trigger to burn some of their data each time they do it.

But we're alive.

And they agreed to my terms.

The Coalition will have a slew of addendums and clauses as they form a treaty full of everything they can think of to keep us safe from these monsters, and I don't envy them the task.

But Alexandria will be here, ready to unleash herself upon the Drennar if they break that treaty or try to tamper with Atlantis or Alexandria.

I turn back to Ricardo, smiling despite their strange analyses. Over his shoulder, I see Tenna and Krona bounding our way, see the Warriors and Soldiers rejoicing behind them, free of their bonds.

And Humans.

Humans everywhere, overflowing from trenches to join us, to thank us.

The Drennar stand by, unmoving, sweeping us with blue light.

Tenna and Krona reach us, folding us against them in hugs just shy of bone-crushing. "They showed us," Tenna says. "They showed us what you said, what he said back. You were amazing!"

"You two have the makings of true Inerans," Krona says, and my chest swells with pride.

Beside me, Ricardo stands taller, beaming up at our friends. They wrap us in their arms once more, but Tenna pulls away, jerking her head to the side to draw my attention that direction.

I turn, and everything stops. My jaw drops as I take in the hazel eyes that so closely match my own that it's like looking into a mirror. Wrinkles line his face, aging him far more than the twelve years apart should have, but I know him.

"Dad…" I breathe, stepping forward.

His jaw falls open, and he stares at me, shaking his head slowly, as if unable to believe that I'm here. "Olivia," he says, voice a hoarse whisper.

I run to him, closing the distance in just a few strides, and throw my arms around him. I bury my head in his chest, relishing the feel of his arms around my shoulders, his head resting on mine.

My tears overflow, soaking his shirt, and sobs rack my body. Little droplets fall from his eyes, seeping into my hair, and his body shakes. He squeezes me tight, pressing my head to his chest.

"I can't… I can't believe it," he whispers into my hair. "You're really here. Olivia, I'm so sorry… I'm so sorry for everything. But I'm so happy you're here."

A small chuckle bursts from me, and I pull back, staring up at him in disbelief. "Sorry? What could you possibly be sorry for?" Another laugh bubbles up my throat, and I fold myself into his arms once more.

He's here. He's real.

He's alive.

I'd been half convinced that I'd just imagined his messages, that he was long gone and I was just deluding myself into thinking he was okay. But he's here, arms tightening around me.

I have a dad…

I swallow, struggling to wrap my head around it.

My baby will have a grandpa.

I pull back once more. "Dad, I'm having a baby! Did Rone tell you?"

He chuckles, swiping tears away. "I know. Rone didn't tell me, though. They did." He inclines his head toward the facility manager.

My brows furrow, marveling that they might think to tell him that, but my mind switches tracks quickly.

Rone!

"Where's Rone?"

I look around, finally glancing at the people nearby, and find her quickly.

Her massive black wings flutter behind her, and her pale fingers worry at each other. She offers up a shy smile, but that isn't enough.

Rushing forward, I throw my arms around her. After a moment, she returns the hug, and I don't let go.

"Thank you," I say, voice thick with emotion. "Thank you for everything, for helping, for giving me my dad back. Thank you, thank you, thank you!"

My words run together, and she giggles softly.

I step back, and instantly, she reaches for Dad's hand. I smile, heart skipping a beat for them. Tugging Ricardo forward by his hand, I introduce him.

My nerves wind tight, hoping they'll approve, that he'll approve of them. Ricardo's shoulders go back, and he reaches out a hand to shake.

But Dad pulls him in, crushing him into a hug. He whispers into Ricardo's ear, low enough that I'm clearly not meant to hear, but his words reach me anyway. "Thank you for saving her."

My eyes fill with tears, and my throat goes tight. I take a deep breath, horrified that he knows I tried to throw away the life he gave me.

I swallow and wipe the tears away before they fall.

He knows.

And he still loves me.

***

The door closes on our room, and I sink into Ricardo's waiting arms. He holds me tight, kisses the top of my head.

I grip the back of his shirt, pulling him tighter to me. "I thought… I thought I'd lost you."

He whispers, "I did too."

And somehow, that's what does me in. I fall to pieces in his arms, hands gripping the fabric of his shirt. Relief and terror wash through me in alternating waves, and I nearly buckle beneath their weight.

He holds onto me, breathing me in, shuddering. Slowly, we ease onto the bed, lying together, hands tangled in hair.

Our clothes slowly fall away, and we ravish each other, exploring, reacquainting ourselves with each other's bodies.

Reassuring ourselves of our safety.

His kisses linger, trailing over my skin, and his touches burn like fire. He sighs beneath me, rolls me to my back, and holds my gaze.

Our worlds splinter, and our pieces fall together.

***

Lying in Ricardo's arms, I stare up at the ceiling, listening to the soft beeps of Curata's waiting message. My heart falters, aching to forget, just for a little while, that she's gone.

But I can't.

Ricardo's fingers trail up and down my arm, leaving fire in their wake, but I have to do this.

"I have a message from Curata," I say.

He stills.

"She sent it… before. *Just* before."

My throat tightens.

"Do you want me to give you some privacy?" he asks.

I shake my head, face moving against his chest. "Will you stay?"

He kisses my forehead. "Of course."

We push ourselves up to lean against the wall, and I set the little device on the nightstand to project her message onto the wall.

Her face appears before me, serene and beatific, iridescent skin glittering in some unseen light. My breath catches.

But no battlefield looms behind her.

She must have recorded this before.

The message begins, and she smiles, soft blue hair floating around her pixie face.

"Olivia… I would've liked to meet you," she says, and my tears flow.

She knew she'd die?

"There is so much for me to say, but let me start by saying that your mind and your determination are truly impressive. You and your friends and your father… You brought me true understanding."

She shakes her head, eyes falling for just a moment. "It eluded me for so long… But you handed it to us."

A deep breath fills her chest, and she looks back up to face the camera.

"I know. There is a fifty percent chance that Lustran will survive the battle. By now, you know the answer to that. But I…" She sighs. "I die."

A choked sob rattles through me, and all I can see is her lifeless form, blue hair limp on the ground. Lustran hanging on that pike.

Ricardo's arms tighten around me.

"But rest assured, I know my fate, and it is only what I deserve. Tasboor is the facility manager, the highest ranked Drennar in the facility charged with Human experiments."

She pulls in a deep breath, and I brace myself for whatever she may say next.

"But I am the assistant facility manager. I played a role in approving or denying every experiment request. I approved the experiment on your father. Lustran is the one who took him, who would have taken you if not for your father's trade."

My jaw falls open, and I shake my head as the world falls out from under me once more.

"When Rone gave us the chance to understand you better, we leapt at it, as did many others, and it showed us that we were wrong."

Tears fill her eyes and spill over, a mirror of the shining tracks glistening on my own cheeks.

"I know, if it hadn't been me, another Drennar would have held my position, would have approved or denied all the same experiments that I did based on their statistics and the amount of knowledge that could be gained from each. I know it wouldn't have been much different, maybe it wouldn't have been different at all, but…"

Her voice cracks.

"I regret my part in all of it. That's why I've done everything I can to make this work, to save your people. That's why I'll go to battle for you, die for you. I have much to atone for."

"Lustran and I know what awaits us in the battle. We know our odds. I know I won't survive. And I know you'll do what needs done to ensure your safety, the safety of your people."

She sits quietly for a moment. Her mouth opens, moving as if to form words, but she closes it without uttering a thing.

I choke back a sob, dumbfounded.

"It can't have been her…" I whisper.

"It wasn't," Ricardo says, voice thick with emotion. "She was a different person then. The Curata we knew never would've hurt any of us."

My vision blurs, and I swipe the tears away, nodding.

Finally, Curata speaks again. "I know I've done too much, hurt too many people without even realizing it," she says, tears falling down her face, "and I know I don't deserve your forgiveness, but the Human part of me still hopes that one day, eventually, you might be able to forgive me."

She sniffs, suppressing a sob. Looking away, she rubs a dainty hand over her face. When she looks back to the camera, her bright eyes shine behind a layer of tears.

"I know my fate. Tasboor won't let me live after the destruction I have planned for his facility, not with the threat I pose to the Drennar race. They can always make a new me, one without human emotion, to test and experiment on, and they likely will."

I shudder at the prospect, but she seems so calm.

"Just know that I'm sorry. I hope my actions over these past weeks and my actions tomorrow will show you that I truly mean it."

The message ends, and shock settles over me.

Ricardo's hand moves to my stomach, to the little bump. He stares at the image frozen on the wall before us, at Curata's smiling face.

"If the baby is a girl…"

I nod, not needing to hear the rest. "We'll name her Curata. Lustran if it's a boy."

Chapter Fifty-Six

Regonia

Reginald

Regonia sprawls out before me, and a few thousand people come to welcome us. They tower over me, over Olivia and Ricardo, but they welcome us into the fold as family.

My heart swells.

And yet, it also twists.

So many of my choices have brought them pain. Going in Olivia's place sent Eva down the path that spelled death for a third of their people, their families, their friends. It brought war to their planet when the Drennar came for Olivia anyway.

But they welcome me as a hero, cheering and smiling at me, the man they say helped free his people, the man whose daughter saved them from meeting a similar fate.

Guilt slithers through me because I know I'm not who they think I am. I languished in my cell on Novay, doing little more than think.

But Rone's words whisper through my mind. "You're not small. You're not nothing. You're the spark that starts a wildfire."

And really... Can they all be so wrong?

I'm no hero, but maybe I'm not as useless as I think.

My eyes drift from the crowd to the world beyond, and my mind slips away from the self-recriminations and my fledgling attempts at rewriting my thoughts.

A real planet waits, full of mountains and rivers and plains, bursting with life, with animals.

With people.

The sky above looks so open and clear. The dull grey of my room, the cold metal of Termana's shell... They're nothing compared to this.

My jaw slowly falls open as I take it in, as I breathe in the marvelously fresh air, different from the recycled air I'm used to in ways I never imagined. My chest fills with it, near to bursting, before I exhale.

Rone squeezes my hand. I turn to her with a smile on my face. Shaking my head, I mutter something, but the words come out hushed by this place.

A smile lights up her face, and she leans against me. "It's beautiful, isn't it?"

I nod, freeing my hand from hers only to wrap my arm around her waist. I gape at the world before me.

The people milling about fall silent as a sleek Drennar ship touches down beside ours, a black pall on such a marvelous day. But Krona and Tenna step forward, falling seamlessly into their role as leaders.

They tell their people the turns the battle took, tell them of the deal Olivia struck with the Drennar on behalf of us all. She tells them that details are forthcoming, but that we're all safe from Drennar attacks and abductions.

The back of the Drennar ship slides open to reveal hundreds of Regonian warriors who chose to bunk on that ship to stay near the Humans they befriended.

And to ensure that the Drennar didn't renege on their word.

A Drennar ambassador stands aboard the ship, watching people file out, waiting for them to separate themselves out. Raktorn, the newly emotional Drennar with a third eye and a scaly centaur body, eyes the Expressionless Ambassador carefully.

Those staying here disembark, carrying crates of food that would have fed the Humans on Novay. Those returning to Termana say their goodbyes and remain aboard. Enough crates of food lie within the depths of the ship to feed all those aboard.

The Warrior Queen and Warrior King of Daen Tribe descend the ramp, leading their people into the village, into their homes.

I wait, leaning against Rone. I watch them embrace their loved ones, watch them rejoice in their victory. Olivia embraces a pregnant woman with long, dark hair, someone named Maria from Odyssey station, standing just beside the ramp of the Drennar ship. My heart soars, and a smile spreads over my face.

"Ready?" Rone says.

I swallow, nodding slowly.

We take slow, even steps down the ramp, hand in hand. My eyes dart around the magnificent planet, and my mind whirls with curiosity.

The lush grasses sweep toward us, bending with a gentle breeze. I close my eyes, drinking it in, so used to the still, stagnant air of ships and stations. My shoulders fall as I exhale, loosening up with the motion.

The teal grass reaches for me, brushes my hand, my legs. I step free of the ship, and the planet welcomes me. The soft dirt cradles my feet with every step. Long strands of aquamarine and cerulean and mint and seafoam bend, curling against me, caressing my bare forearms.

Children laugh and play in the distance. Someone begins singing in the Regonian language, the Drennar language, and I open my eyes to seek them out. But the whole Tribe joins in, voices rising and falling together.

And somehow, though the very air would kill me were it not for Rone's filter, this place feels like home.

Epilogue One
Rone

The Memory Markers depart, meandering across the bridge. Two moons shine overhead as I turn to Reginald. His sheer robe flutters in a soft breeze, and my own brushes against my legs. He smiles, and moonlight dances in his eyes, sending shadows darting into the crinkles around them.

His newest mark wraps around the base of his neck, reaches over his collar bones. The vivid blue ink seems to glow against his burnished skin.

I spare a glance for my own, reaching a finger up to touch the line that matches the length of his middle finger. The tender skin rebels against the light touch, but I love it all the same.

With our partnering ceremony complete, we spare only a cursory glance for the Memory Markers retreating into the village. I step forward, sliding my arms around his waist, and then his lips find mine.

***

Olivia and I recline against the wall surrounding her cottage, drafting messages to Sentrah, our Drennar ambassador. I smile, knowing that the emotions that guided her to help us in our battle on Novay will serve her well in drafting the treaty.

Olivia's fingers fly over the keys of her laptop. She thinks through everything, mind working effortlessly to ensure the safety of her people, whether here or back on the Human world.

Children run down a path, laughing as they greet their parents. But one of them, a boy with pale skin and short dark hair, stands off to the side.

He scuffs his boots on a rock, dark eyes downcast.

My heart twists, and my eyes dip to his hands. They bear the marks I feared I'd find.

Both parents lost to battle.

"Where does he stay?" I ask.

Olivia looks up from her beloved laptop, perched nearly on her knees thanks to her belly. "I don't know." She seeks his marks, face falling when she sees them.

Krona, Tenna, and Reginald meander toward us, hands stained with Juno sap. They laugh together, moving up the path.

"How many children are like him?" I ask them. "Does he have nowhere to stay?"

Their eyes soften as they consider the boy.

"Moora stays with a friend now. The Awakening took his parents," Tenna says. "Most lost only one parent. A few lost both parents but reside with older siblings or grandparents."

"He's one of three who have no remaining family," Krona says.

The empty bedroom in our cottage springs into my mind, and I look to Reginald. "Do you think...?" Tears prick the corners of my eyes, but I never learned how this was handled within Daen Tribe. "Could we take them in?"

He smiles. Turning to Tenna and Krona, he asks, "Would that… be okay?"

They nod, saying, "As long as they're amenable to it."

My heart leaps into my throat. Maybe it won't be the same as giving birth. And sure, I missed the earliest years of their lives.

But Reginald and I could have a family.

Epilogue Two
Krona

"If there are any battles in the foreseeable future," Tenna says, "I'd like you to go in my stead. Krona and I will see the Memory Markers and Healers soon to begin our family."

Kala's dark eyes light up, and she rushes forward, throwing her arms around us. I laugh, glad to finally see her happy again.

Without Efsi, her life was thrown into chaos in so many ways, but this news means that at least one aspect will return to normal. She'll be destined for the battlefield once more.

"Have you told Mother and Father yet?" she asks, pulling back and sweeping her black hair behind her ear.

"You know we came to you first," Tenna says with a chuckle. "You're our Ullavena."

A brief wave of sadness sweeps over the two sisters at the emptiness left in Efsi's wake, the loss that left only one Ullavena. Their voices join together in a soft, trilling coo.

His sound.

They lean their foreheads together, clasping hands on each other's necks to draw strength from each other. A sad smile lifts my lips, and I pull in a deep breath.

Tenna pulls away from her sister and slips her hand back into mine. She squeezes once.

Looking down into moss green eyes, I say, "Are you ready?"

She nods, and we wish Kala a goodnight. As we meander over stone paths to the Memory Markers, I wonder how long Kala will keep this news to herself.

Will she rush back to Melnara and tell her immediately?

Will she tell her parents?

Though I'd love to tell them myself, to spread the news far and wide, there's nowhere I'd rather be than here.

I gaze up at the moons, luxuriating in the warmth of Tenna's presence. She sighs when the soft hum of a contented Vyrto drifts over the fields.

Smoke rises from chimneys, and soft light peeks out beneath shutters drawn tight. Quiet voices reach into the night, seeping out from a few homes, but most are quiet.

The cottage we seek comes into view, as comfortably quiet as the rest. Soft laughter bubbles from open windows.

Stepping through their gate, we meander up the stone pathway that bisects the small garden chock full of healing herbs. Having gone to seed last year, leaves and flowers clamor for space, reaching over each other to seek the sun. They tickle my ankles, my calves, as we move toward the door.

I knock. The laughter quiets but doesn't stop. Footsteps cross flagstones, and then the door opens.

Sagourna smiles at us, white robes vibrant beneath her dark blue braid. Behind her, Murgasta sits at their table, hands wrapped around a steaming mug. She looks up, peering past her sister at us.

The Healer and the Memory Marker offer warm smiles. "Welcome, Inerans. What brings you to see us this fine evening?"

"We'd like to start our family," I answer.

They exchange gleeful smiles, and Murgasta jumps up from the table. She bustles about, gathering herbs and a bowl to prepare the fertility tonic. Her pale blue braid slips over her shoulder as she moves.

"Come in, come in!" Sagourna insists, bright green eyes shining. She opens the door wide, stepping aside and waving her hand to usher us inside.

We step over the threshold, smiling as the door shuts behind us.

I can already envision the lines that will move down from Tenna's breasts, over ribs and stomach, before swooping inward. I can see the crisp blue point where they'll converge beneath her belly button.

My heart leaps into my throat, and I squeeze Tenna's hand.

***

Winter reaches toward us on the breeze, but my coat holds it at bay for now.

We stand at the edge of the river, staring upstream. Our Warriors flank us with a few Human Soldiers and Specialists mixed into their ranks, and those of Taron Tribe stand beside us.

I squeeze Tenna's hand, then cast a glance at Relnoc and Dresde. Relnoc nods to me, dusky skin glowing. The early morning light dances on the scales of the Malakar behind her.

We turn our attention forward once more, and my eyes trace the approaching forms of Roon Tribe. Chief Mourgam rides upon his Vyrto at the head, his partner riding on hers behind him as his subject, not his equal.

Anger simmers within me, but it isn't just for this blatant refusal to admit his own fallibility in his rulings, his refusal to accept counsel, being flaunted in their riding positions.

The impressions of Eva's tampering lingers within me. My own mind fills with the haunting memories of betrayal, of uncertainty, in my own partnership. The cell on Ulysses Station, the desperation and the heartache, the violent fury and agony of it all comes back at the sight of him.

But the images themselves, the false memories that tried so hard to break me, are gone. All that remains are the echoes, the emotions, left in their wake. I force myself not to imagine them, not to picture Tenna crawling to him, lying beneath him.

She squeezes my hand, as if sensing the path my thoughts wander. Her thumb strokes the back of my hand, and I turn to her.

A smile dances in those moss-green eyes. Light plays beautifully on skin the shade of a predawn sky.

"Never," she mouths.

I pull in a deep breath, realizing only now how tense I am, how my body has begun to slip into a battle stance, how my blood boils at the sight of Mourgam.

Exhaling, I release the tension, raising my head, ready to at least hear him out.

The Roon Warriors stop, as does Chief Mourgam's partner. He rides forward alone.

I grind my teeth together.

He greets us but makes no move to draw his partner forward. No advisors join him, no council.

We incline our heads respectfully, but I find my eyes darting over his Warriors, ill-prepared for battle.

"Your time in The Realm of Stars seems to have brought your numbers low," Mourgam says. "It would seem that you might have difficulties fending off any advances from Vaerkin, were they to come for you."

No condolences for the people we lost.

No gentle, tactful mention of our pain.

And an insult to our strength as a Tribe.

I pull in a long, slow breath.

"But I might be amenable to an alliance. We could fight alongside you, were they to come. So long as you extend the same courtesy to us."

A vicious smile curls my lips, and I remember what Dresde told us last night. That the Vaerkin have moved north to track the Vlahkair herds. That they've been crossing the river to raid Roon farms.

That the Vaerkin found raiding to be such a profitable endeavor that they didn't even follow the herds when they moved south last spring.

Mourgam seeks no alliance. He wishes only to manipulate us into aiding him.

I laugh under my breath, eyes tracing his ash-colored form. The light of the sun shines upon his freshly shaved head, showing off the marks his scalp bears.

I raise a brow, wishing I could see the scar Tenna left on him, but his heavy coat hides the puckered skin from view. A crisp, cool breeze teases the fur that lines it as if to taunt me.

"We are better informed than you think," Tenna says. "We know their movements, know they're no threat to *us*. And even if they were, we know we could turn them away."

My chest swells with pride, because even after the losses we've faced, we could hold our own without aid.

With Taron Tribe fighting at our side?

We could destroy any force the Vaerkin might send against us.

"What else could you offer to gain such an alliance?" Tenna asks.

But I hear her tone, hear the test in her words.

Offense turns his features sour, purses his lips. He spouts off a list of crops, clearly improvising. "But surely, our willingness to stand with you against the Vaerkin, to protect your children, is more than enough without those things."

The sound of axes and swords being drawn behind me raises the hairs on the back of my neck.

"You offer trades, change the aforementioned terms of your alliance," I say, "without consulting your people? Without consulting an advisor? Even your partner?"

Relnoc and Dresde stand tall beside me, but I see the anger in their faces.

They take their advisors' words seriously, acting against them only when absolutely necessary.

And though we have no council like that of Taron Tribe, we plan things with our highest-ranking Warriors, sometimes consulting Tenna's parents, the previous monarchs. We consider our people in every decision.

And never do we make such decisions without consulting each other.

My eyes dart to the woman who partnered this man, and I wonder what compelled her to do it.

Mourgam's eyes roam over the crowd of anxious Warriors at our back, the people who fight for us because they know we take their needs into consideration, and he seems to realize his mistake. "Of course… I could always consult them later."

Murmurs slip through our ranks.

Their words filter through the breeze, and I look to Tenna. A glance over my shoulder reveals glares directed at Chief Mourgam, and I know our people stand with us on this decision.

"Never," I say.

Never could we ally ourselves, ally our people, with someone so foolish as to believe himself beyond error, so arrogant as to escape even a shred of doubt in his decisions with so many lives in the balance.

His jaw tightens, but he turns to rejoin his people. They ride away, and Tenna whispers, "Kala will be happy. She might get her battle sooner than we thought."

And though I had hoped we could avoid bloodshed for a while, we can't forsake who we are.

After all we've lost, we still have our honor.

And we will always fight for that.

Epilogue Three
Tenna

I toss a blanket onto my Vyrto's back to fend off the chill. Small bits of ice fall from the sky, bouncing as they hit us. They crunch beneath the Vyrto's massive hooves, beneath my feet, as I lead my mount in from the field.

A glance skyward reveals dull, grey clouds stretching as far as I can see, and I know this storm will last and worsen.

"I hope you got enough exercise today," I say to my Vyrto. "Looks like you'll be cooped up for a little while."

She snuffles in answer, breath clouding before her.

"I know," I say, placating. "I wish we could stay outside too."

The barn rises up before us, sturdy stone walls waiting to welcome us, to warm us. A soft glow peeks out beneath the door, and I wonder how much wood Savsta stacked within the hearth.

Hopefully enough.

New to caring for the Vyrtons, she fears building the fire too high, too hot, considering their thick coats. But the chill will only worsen today as the ice falls and piles up atop the roof. We need to keep it melted off, lest the roof buckle.

I open the door, and a wave of heat greets me. My muscles relax, and I droop with relief as the winter leaves my blood.

"Much better," I say, patting my Vyrto as I lead her to her stall.

Savsta rises from the hearth, dark eyes strained. "Is it enough?" she asks, hands clasped in front of her.

"It is," I say with a smile.

She grins, eyes lighting up. The young girl rushes forward to pull my Vyrto's blanket from her haunches then tuck her into a stall. The giant beast does her bidding without complaint, a feat owed in part to superior training and to Savsta's uncanny ability to gain these animals' trust.

It reminds me of myself at her age.

"You have visitors," she says without turning. "The bekta leaves were finally ready."

My heart leaps into my throat.

Though she doesn't look up, I see her lips turning up into a smile, hear the excitement in her voice. But she tends to her charges, drying and brushing their coats, caring deeply for the Vyrtons and their welfare.

Savsta gestures toward the larger door of the stable, and I rush toward it, toward the room which holds all our Vyrtons' food stores.

I push into the smaller barn, weaving through towering bales of lentar grass, past small buckets of Lahrike and other treats. Rounding a corner, I find Krona, Olivia, and Ricardo waiting for me. Illuminated by a lantern, they twiddle their fingers impatiently.

"They're ready?" I ask, hand going to the tiny bump of my stomach.

All three look up at me, beaming with excitement. Krona holds up the tiny silver leaf, freshly plucked from a greenhouse, and my heart skips a beat.

He rushes forward, urging me to come away to the house for the test. But I glance at Olivia, to her cheeks rosy with the chill of winter and her bulbous stomach, and give in to my own excitement.

Shaking my head, I start hefting lentar bales, arranging them as a bed. Krona moves to help while Ricardo holds Olivia's arm, helping her waddle closer.

My lips spread wide in a smile.

I jerk my coat off in a hurry, burning up with the heat of this place and the excitement of knowing. Lying down upon the bed of lentar, I pull my shirt up to expose my stomach. The little bump where the baby grows stretches the marks of the fertility ceremony. The tiny leaves hidden within the lines are almost visible. Gaps of my own dusky skin show through between little shapes of vivid blue, telling us I'm just far enough to know what we're having.

Excitement builds within me, and I can't wait to see the exact pattern the Memory Marker etched upon my skin, the delicate veins within the leaves so precise, the twining vines so crisp. I long to move through time, to let the baby reveal the hidden beauty of my marks as it grows within me.

Krona traces a finger down one mark, then up the other, and a shiver rolls through me. Olivia and Ricardo smile at us, each with a hand resting on Olivia's belly.

"What else do we need to do?" Olivia asks.

Ricardo helps her settle to the floor beside me, then eases down next to her. They stare on, eyes shining. Olivia bounces, eager to see, to learn.

"Just this," Krona says, holding up the leaf. He settles it gently upon my stomach, and we wait.

Slowly, the leaf curls upward, folding itself to oppose the curve of my stomach. Tears prick at my eyes, and I look to Krona.

His eyes shine with moisture, and he reaches out to touch my stomach. I lay my hand atop his and sit up to kiss him. Our lips meet, soft and sweet, as the leaf flutters to my lap.

When we part, Ricardo asks, "What does it mean?"

I laugh, and so does Krona. Turning to our friends, I say, "It means we're having a boy."

"What would the leaf have done if it were a girl?" Olivia asks, eyes glued to the tiny, silver leaf.

"It would have curled downward, melding itself to my stomach."

Her eyes sparkle with curiosity, and Krona begins explaining the moderately magnetic properties of the leaves, the static charges we all carry.

But I only half listen.

I stare at him, soft black hair falling to touch his coat, pale skin glowing with the light of the lantern and the joy within him. His mint, green eyes dance, and I smile, glad to have him in my life, to share this with him.

Our time together burns bright in my mind, and again, I can't believe it was ever taken from me.

Glancing at Olivia and Ricardo, my smile widens. I reach for them, wrapping my little family in an embrace that cuts off Krona's explanation and pulls giggles and chuckles from their lips.

"I'm so happy you're all here," I whisper.

And I can't wait to meet you, little Efsi.

Epilogue Four
Ricardo

James crouches at the end of Olivia's birthing table, improvising the equipment aboard the ship for the procedure. Having expected a pregnancy-free voyage, we have no baths, none of the nerve blockers specialized for labor. I stare at the kind doctor, gritting my teeth and hoping he can manage an old-fashioned birth.

Olivia squats atop the table, and I rub her back, hold her steady. Another contraction rocks her, and she cries out. My heart twists, and I wish I could take this pain from her.

She squeezes my hand, hard enough to crush bone, and for a second, I wonder if there's something in the water here that makes people stronger. I grind my teeth together, vowing to say nothing of my own pain, fully aware that it's nothing next to having your nether regions ripped open by a tiny human.

Sweat glistens on her brow, sticks her hair to her scalp. She screams out, grasping her knee with her free hand and bearing down hard.

But she isn't breathing right.

"Breathe," I whisper. "Breathe, Olivia."

She blows out a long breath, then scrunches her face and screams as she pushes again.

She sways, squatted as she is, but I steady her. The bones in my fingers protest her death grip, but I don't pull my hand from hers.

Her scream ends with a whimper, and a tiny wail pierces the air.

"I've got her," James says, catching our daughter.

For one breathtaking moment, we stare down at our baby, and my heart skips a beat. Tears prick my eyes as I count the tiny fingers on waving arms, the little toes on kicking feet.

"She's beautiful," Olivia whispers, voice hoarse.

And though our baby's little, red face is scrunched with her cries, though slick and coated in things I can't identify, she's perfect.

"Lay her back," James says, then amends, "Gently."

He looks to me, and I nod. I steady Olivia, holding her weight up while she lets her legs slide forward to dangle over the edge of the table. She winces as she settles herself down.

"Lay back," I whisper. "Don't sit."

She moves as I bid her, and I slide my arms beneath her, lifting her to move her up toward her pillow. Utterly exhausted after ten hours of worsening contractions and an hour and a half of pushing, she hangs limp in my arms.

But she's glorious.

Her eyes sparkle, and her lips turn up in a wistful smile. Her chest heaves with ragged, exhausted breaths, but she reaches up to touch my cheek.

I set her down on her bed, smoothing sweat-damp hair out of her face. My lips press to her forehead, to her lips.

Beyond the end of the table, beyond the curtain of Olivia's gown raised between her knees, James and a nurse work. The nurse takes our perfect little baby, cradling her to her chest, and James pulls a rolling tray close. The needles and scalpels glint in the light, and I offer Olivia my hand to squeeze through the stitches.

She grits her teeth, and I whisper, "Breathe."

I almost say that the worst part is over, but having no experience with this, I can't really say that for sure. So, I hold her hand. I wipe her face with a damp towel and tell her how sweet little Curata is. I tell her that the nurse is cleaning her, wrapping her up.

"Okay," James says. "We'll let that numbing stuff take effect, then I'll stitch you up. Should only need three stitches."

The nurse walks toward us, footsteps soft despite the metal she walks upon. Her dark eyes are alight as she gazes at the baby in her arms, *our* baby, wrapped in a soft olive-colored blanket.

My throat tightens.

I slide an arm under Olivia and reach to prop another pillow behind her. The nurse settles the little bundle in Olivia's arms, and I fold the flap of the blanket down, gazing into bright, golden eyes, shot through with streaks of blue, a strange and gorgeous version of hazel.

A tiny hand reaches out, pawing at Olivia's chin, and Olivia leans forward, planting a kiss on Curata's forehead. I reach out, stroking one finger over five tiny ones, and they wrap around mine, squeezing tight.

My breath catches, and my heart swells. Tears cascade over my cheeks, and I kiss Olivia's temple, staring down at our little star baby.

***

Reginald and Rone come in, eyes brimming and faces warm. Krona and Tenna follow, circling around us to gaze at Curata. They take turns holding the delicate little bundle, cradling her with great care.

I stare on in wonder, vacillating between incredulous awe and the complete and total inability to believe any of this is real. Olivia grasps her father's hand, tears spilling forth from even that simple act, something she never thought she'd be able to do.

Rone stands near me, struggling for words. "So, I never—" I start to say, but she speaks at the same time I do.

I don't catch what she meant to say, so I tell her to go first.

"You'll have to keep the baby here for a little while," she says. "But I can safely manage the filter implantation next week. Then, you can go home."

My breath catches because I know she doesn't mean Termana. She means our home, our house here on Regonia.

It brings a smile to my face.

A wave of fear whispers through me at the thought of a surgery so soon, at the thought of our baby on the operating table.

But it's Rone.

I trust her.

And she got plenty of practice on Novay.

"Thank you," I whisper, voice thick with emotion. Then, I say, "And thank you for bringing Reginald back to her." I nod at Olivia, though Rone clearly knows who I meant. "I never got a chance to say it before. Thank you, for everything."

"I only did what was right," she says.

"Don't deflect it," I say with a laugh. "You did a lot for us, and I want you to know it's appreciated."

Then, because though Rone may not know, I'm well aware of how delicate emotions can be, how easily we can talk ourselves into thinking we don't belong, I say, "And I want you to know that you're a welcome addition to our family. You'll be a wonderful grandma."

She lets out a quick laugh, tears glimmering in her eyes, then pulls me into a hug.

When she releases me, I tug her toward the bed. Having noted that she stared at Curata with longing but wouldn't quite let herself reach out, I say, "It's time you hold your granddaughter."

Olivia reaches for me as her father hands Curata off to Rone. We lean together, and I meet Krona's gaze. He nods approvingly, as does Tenna beside him.

And my heart soars.

Epilogue Five
Olivia

Minister Croon smiles on the screen, but dark circles hang beneath his eyes. The negotiations with the Drennar are going well thanks to the leverage I've made for Humanity. With the help of Sentrah, Raktorn, and the other newly emotional Drennar, the treaty is almost finalized.

But the stress of it has aged him, even if his daughter's safe return put a spark back into his eyes.

I send a reply, confirming that the program includes a fail-safe that prevents them from tampering with it. If they try to learn the secrets of Alexandria, if they try to figure out how it works, it'll be activated.

They'll lose everything.

I ask if they've found a new Minister of Defense or a Minister of Medical Research and Scientific Development, then send the message off.

Mulvaney and my mother left holes in the Survival Coalition. I can't imagine the remaining members will want to stretch themselves so thin for long.

Perhaps they'll put the Honorable Judge Supreme Martine forward as a candidate. She certainly proved herself capable in Mommy Dearest's tribunal.

I sigh, closing my eyes as I think of her. My stomach twists, but I know now what could push a person so far, got a glimpse of it on the battlefield at Novay.

My mind fills with the sight of Ricardo impaled with the spike, the thought of them taking me and experimenting on our child. My throat tightens, and I wonder how far I would go.

But some lines can't be crossed.

I wouldn't kidnap and experiment on thousands of innocent people. I wouldn't *kill* thousands of people.

I'd work myself to the bone. I'd sacrifice myself.

I'd make a program to destroy vast reserves of information that another species spent centuries, possibly millennia, hurting others to gather.

But I'm no killer.

I'm not my mother.

I pull in a deep breath, struck by the sudden realization, the sudden acceptance.

I'm not her.

My eyes open, and I stare at the screen before me. Buttons and switches and levers line the instrument panel, but I look past them, letting my Link transform the screen before me, turning it transparent once more.

Regonia spreads out before me, lush and beautiful.

I'm not her.

And that's why I'm here.

I brought them back. I helped save them.

I choke on a sob, but this time, it isn't one of sorrow. A small laugh bubbles up between the tears, and I swipe at my cheeks.

I helped put an end to all the suffering.

I got my dad back.

Breathing deeply, I rise from my chair, eyes tracing the distant mountain peaks, the river sliding through the plains. Turning, I move through cozy metal halls to our quarters with a smile on my face, even though each step is agony thanks to the stitches that aren't quite ready to come out.

Ricardo sits on our bed, gently rocking Curata, and my chest warms at the sight.

We can do this right.

We can have a happy family.

He looks up when I step through the bulkhead door, golden eyes lighting up at the sight of me. His strong, capable hands cradle our child, and I melt.

After planting a gentle kiss on his lips, I carefully settle on the bed beside him. I stare down at Curata, reaching up to stroke her chubby cheek with one finger. Dark lashes flutter, and she opens gold eyes streaked through with crisp blue.

My heart skips a beat.

"Hey there, beautiful girl," I whisper. "Ready to go home?"

She coos softly, tiny fist waving through the air, and that's answer enough for me.

Ricardo kisses the top of my head, and we rise. The ship unfolds around us, and the maintenance airlock welcomes us. Curata giggles as the doors close behind us, moving into a full-blown fit of laughter as the door to the world begins to open.

I look to Ricardo, chest swelling and eyes alight. I lean my head on his shoulder, gazing upon the tiny bundle of life in his arms.

The door lowers. Sunlight and fresh air stream in to greet us, and Curata's laughter quiets to a gentle sound.

One of awe, as if she knows the significance of this moment, as if she senses it.

And maybe she does.

***

Maria and Matteo smile in the pictures they've sent me, holding the babies I'll never meet. My heart twists at the thought.

But they're home. They're safe.

And that's all I can ask for now.

I read through their message, heart fluttering as they tell me about the commune Nico, Hans, Francis, and Giselle found on Termana. Maria goes on about the possibility of a baby with red hair and green eyes, ecstatic at the prospect, especially since they've already started their first attempts at artificial insemination.

The Human world is going on without me, but I guess it always did. It was never really my home, my place.

I smile for them, but my eyes dart to the window over my bed, to the mountains and the moons hanging above them. My gaze falls to rest on Ricardo's sleeping form, then drift to Curata in her little bed.

And I know I've finally found my true home.

***

Dresde and Relnoc soar down from the mountain on their Malakarns, beams of light reflecting off black scales. Someone clings to Dresde, and I squint against the sun, hand raised to block some of the light. My breath catches when I see pale, grey skin and a dark, blue braid.

Sevlah?

Relief washes through me.

He's okay!

It doesn't seem real that he should be okay considering how bad his legs were, how much blood he lost. But I suppose they are a warrior tribe. They've likely treated worse injuries.

Another dark shape soars through the sky, drawing my attention away from the man I wasn't sure survived. A third Malakar trails along in their wake. The sleek black feathers of its wings beat the wind into submission as it descends with the Taron leaders.

Curata watches them move through the sky, giggling and screeching happily.

They land before us on the outskirts of the village, and my heart jumps into my throat. With a smile, I hand Curata to my father. He holds her reverently, eyes glowing as she grips his finger.

Looking up at me, he says, "Be careful."

I nod, unwilling to let even my need to fly keep me from coming back to Curata. With one final glance, I move to the edge of the field.

Dresde and Relnoc wave me over, and Tenna comes loping toward us, beaming. The Taron leaders dismount, then rush to help Sevlah down, handing him a cane once his feet are under him.

They amble over, keeping Sevlah's pace, and we embrace when they reach us. But impatience buzzes through my veins.

My eyes dart to the Malakarns standing just meters away. They watch me with curiosity. Dresde and Relnoc's mounts bump each other, then settle on the ground.

But the third tips its head to the side, considering me.

With Dresde and Relnoc's approval, I approach the massive beast slowly, heart in my throat. And though I know I won't fly today, I'll only be meeting the Malakar meant to be my mount, I can't hold in the joy that rushes through my veins.

I reach out a hand, and it pushes the top of its head against my palm.

Epilogue Six
Reginald

I scoop up a dollop of moftahn paste, lathering it over my hands. The Juno sap hangs on at first, but the grit of the ground up moftahn stems wears it away quickly.

My mind fills with the chemical makeup of the plant, the way it breaks the Juno sap down, the way the Juno sap reacts with the leather of Regonian armor. I pick through everything I know about it, marveling at the change that the sap and leather work upon each other.

The wind sighs over my skin, cool and gentle. I shake my head, stunned by these people.

Eva took them as barbaric. She assumed they were simpletons because they fight with swords and axes and never left their planet.

But she was wrong.

They're a different version of the Drennar, after all. They don't have access to all the information their counterparts hold, but they're intelligent.

They've found ways to work *with* their world, not against it, to get everything they need. They've found ways to strengthen materials we might consider unsuitable back on Termana to make them stronger than anything we've come up with.

Krona sets a bucket of water before me, and I dunk my hands in. The foamy substance fizzles out, diluting in the water.

But even this won't go to waste.

I smile at the simple bucket of water, the thin layer of foam atop it. Krona's and Tenna's Vyrtons will drink this oddly nutritious mixture.

Sweet laughter bounces down the path toward us, and suddenly, the water isn't as interesting. My head jerks up as Rone and our three adopted children, Moora, Sagasten, and Trivee, sprint toward me. The sunlight plays on four different shades of grey skin, dances in four pairs of beautiful green eyes.

My heart leaps into my throat.

Sagasten reaches me first, throwing her arms around my waist. Only seven years old, her head already rests upon my chest.

Laughing, I pat wet hands on her soft blue hair. She giggles, squirming away.

I delight in the sound of her laugh, something we've heard more and more of late.

Moora and Trivee reach us, arguing playfully over who got here first. Friendship has blossomed into brotherhood between them. Trivee's bright green eyes dance in the fading sunlight, and glee shines in the dark recesses of Moora's eyes.

I wrap them in my arms, and Rone leans over them to brush a kiss on my lips.

"Ready to go?" she asks.

I nod, and we leave the tannery behind. Krona bids us a temporary farewell, assuring us that he'll meet us there with Tenna. We walk along the paths, laughing and smiling. And though I love this new life, my heart twists, just a little.

If only I'd had this with Olivia.

If only I could've been there for her.

We meander toward the river, and there she is, cradling Curata and lounging with Ricardo in the freshly shorn grass. Her face lights up as Moora, Trivee, and Sagasten bound over toward her, as Krona and Tenna saunter up.

I take Rone's hand, lacing our fingers together, and smile. As the people of Daen Tribe begin singing, celebrating the harvest of plants that went to seed last year, my heart warms.

All four moons move higher in the sky as we sing and dance. My family moves around me, and all eyes are alight with the joy of an unexpected harvest.

And I know.

Even though I didn't have the family I thought I would, even though I missed so much with Olivia…

I have a second chance.

Thank you!

For buying this book. For reading it all the way through.

If you liked it, please leave a review on Amazon, Goodreads, Barnes & Noble, your blog... Anywhere, really. Reviews are the lifeblood of authors, helping books get noticed in the almighty eyes of search engine algorithms. Even if only a few words, a review is incredibly helpful.

Eager to stay up to date on the latest dark fiction from Elexis Bell?

Sign up for her newsletter on her website.

www.elexisbell.com

Other Books by this Author

Literary Fantasy Novels

Soul Bearer

The Gem of Meruna

A Heart of Salt & Silver

Allmother Rising

The Sword and The Savage

Literary Thriller Novellas

Annabelle

Things Left Unsaid

Literary Post-Apocalyptic Novel

World for the Broken

The Regonia Chronicles

Awakening

Faltering

Ascending

About the Author

Elexis Bell is a quiet nerd with too many hobbies, including everything from gaming to shower-singing and even archery, weather permitting. She specializes in sarcasm and writing stories that make people feel. She's made a home for herself with her husband and a small army of cats.

She writes dark, gritty stories, sprinkling gut-wrenching emotions over high fantasy romance, thrillers, post-apocalyptic romance, and science fiction.

For further information, follow her on Instagram, Twitter, or Facebook, or check out her blog on her website. There, you can sign up for her newsletter to stay up to date on all future book releases, giveaways, and ongoing projects.

www.elexisbell.com